SKINNY
BITCH
GETS
HITCHED

ALSO BY KIM BARNOUIN

Skinny Bitch in Love

Skinny Bitch

Skinny Bitch in the Kitch

Skinny Bastard

Skinny Bitch: Bun in the Oven

Skinny Bitchin'

Skinny Bitch: Ultimate Everyday Cookbook

Skinny Bitch: Home, Beauty & Style

Skinny Bitch Book of Vegan Swaps

SKINNY
BITCH
GETS
HITCHED

a novel

KIM BARNOUIN

GALLERY BOOKS

new york london toronto sydney new delhi

G

Gallery Books

A Division of Simon & Schuster, Inc.

1230 Avenue of the Americas

New York, NY 10020

First Gallery Books hardcover edition May 2014

GALLERY BOOKS and colophon are registered trademarks of Simon & Schuster, Inc.

For information about special discounts for bulk purchases, please contact Simon & Schuster Special Sales at 1-866-506-1949 or business@simonandschuster.com.

The Simon & Schuster Speakers Bureau can bring authors to your live event. For more information or to book an event contact the Simon & Schuster Speakers Bureau at 1-866-248-3049 or visit our website at www.simonspeakers.com.

Interior design by Jaime Putorti

Manufactured in the United States of America

10 9 8 7 6 5 4 3 2 1

Library of Congress Cataloging-in-Publication Data

Barnouin, Kim.
  Skinny bitch gets hitched / by Kim Barnouin.—First Gallery Books hardcover edition.
      pages cm
  1. Women cooks—Fiction. 2. Vegan cooking—Fiction. 3. Restaurateurs—Fiction. 4. Weddings—Fiction. 5. Santa Monica (Calif.)—Fiction. I. Title.
  PS3602.A77714S54 2014
  813'.6—dc23   2013032577

ISBN 978-1-4767-0888-1
ISBN 978-1-4767-0893-5 (ebook)

To Kay Warren, a beautiful person who has touched my life with her friendship and wisdom

SKINNY
BITCH
GETS
HITCHED

1

How to handle a hungry crowd on a forty-minute waiting list for a table at Clementine's No Crap Café? Have Matteo, the smoking-hot Italian maître d', hand out sample plates of bruschetta brushed with rosemary-infused olive oil and topped with thinly sliced, lightly sautéed eggplant and tomato, along with shot glasses of my frozen white-grape smoothie. Hell yeah, it worked.

The kitchen was running an unusual twenty minutes behind on this busy Friday night. As owner and executive chef of the two-month-old vegan restaurant, I needed to be out there doing damage control in the lounge and among the tables, schmoozing it up, asking how the gnocchi was, if table six liked the Argentinean wine the waiter had recommended, and assuring tables three and seven that their entrées would be out in five minutes and dessert was on the house. Instead I was on sauté with my sous chef, Alanna, who wasn't bringing it tonight. Alanna was usually A-game all the time. But tonight, she was forgetting ingredients, leaving the refrigerator open, knocking baskets of garlic to the floor, and snapping at everyone.

First of all, snapping at the staff was *my* job—not that I did much of that. I ran my restaurant the way I'd always wanted a kitchen to run. On teamwork. High morale. And precision timing. If I told you what went on in some of the kitchens I'd worked in when I was coming up from trainee to salads to line cook to sauté to sous chef, you'd swear I was exaggerating. A face pushed down into a bowl of cucumber soup because it went from just-chilled to room temperature before the waiter could pick it up. Being called a string of nasty swear words for slicing a portobello mushroom a hair too thin for a burger. Forgetting to salt the water before the pasta went in to boil? You don't want to know what became of that guy. So just trust me. A few executive chefs I'd worked under would make a drill sergeant wet his tighty-whities.

"Plate that *now*, Alanna," I said, maybe a little harshly, but she was staring into a sizzling pan of fusilli with the roasted-red-pepper sauce I'd just worked on, and it was starting to singe, as were her two other pans of yellow squash, zucchini, and eggplant for the seared-vegetable napoleons.

She blinked and shot me a "Yes, chef" with the gravitas of a saluting soldier, quickly plating the fusilli and stacking the vegetables—a little sloppily, but the napoleon still looked delicious and she had to make three more. As she hastily moved one plate over to make room for the others, the plate of fusilli clattered to the floor so loudly that my typically unflappable vegetable chef, Gunnar, glanced up, and he rarely glanced up.

"Fucking fuck, Alanna. I almost sliced off my thumb," Gunnar shouted from across the room, a yellow squash in one hand and a sharp knife in the other. He ran his hand under the sink at his station and slapped on a Band-Aid.

"Sorry," Alanna called to him, then went back to staring at the sautéing vegetables.

"Focus!" I shouted to everyone. I glanced at Alanna, beside me at the next station. "You okay?" I whispered. "What's going on?"

"Fine. I'm fine. I'm plating." She blew an escaped red ringlet of hair out of her face and quickly stacked the other three napoleons along the stainless steel counter and restarted the fusilli. At this point on the wait scale, I'd have to comp table six's check. "Up!" she shouted, and a waiter appeared with a tray.

I'd been hoping to leave early tonight to get started on the hundreds of tiny, edible seashells for the wedding cake I was making as my gift for my boyfriend's half sister, who was getting married tomorrow afternoon. But no way could I leave Alanna, about to spontaneously combust, on her own right now. At thirty, Alanna was a few years older than I was, and such a trustworthy, talented, hardworking up-and-comer that

I considered myself danged lucky to have her. Right now, though? Lukewarm mess. Her chef whites were covered in splotches of mole sauce and olive oil, odd for the pristine Alanna McNeal. Her long, curly, flaming red hair, usually in a braid or chopsticked bun, was all bird's-nesty, frizzy swatches sticking out of her lopsided braid and tendrils plastered to her face. Her expression was half-pissed, half-I'm-going-out-of-my-mind, and maybe a smidgen of I-might-cry. Alanna never cried. Besides, my kitchen was a cry-free zone.

"Alanna, take a break," I told her, lowering the heat on the red-pepper sauce. "I've got you, okay?" I really had no time to back her up. My barbecue chili needed attention, and dessert orders were coming in, which meant I'd have to take Evan, on helper duty tonight, away from Gunnar, who needed support on vegetables since the napoleons and the roasted-root kebabs were a huge hit. Between backing up Alanna and handling desserts, I'd need Evan's help with warming the mini-chocolate-lava cakes—five seconds too hot and the cake would turn sludgy.

I probably needed an extra line cook, especially Thursday to Saturday nights. But I couldn't spare a thought to that right now or my head—and my red-pepper sauce—would explode. Note to self: at the wedding tomorrow, when the minister is reading all the Indian poetry that the bride told you she added to the ceremony, think about up-and-coming chefs you've heard good things about.

"I'm fine," Alanna said, stirring the fusilli with one hand and giving the vegetables a toss with the other, but when the steam from the boiling pasta hit her full in the face, she looked as if she was about to lose it.

She wasn't fine, but she wasn't talking, either, not that talking was allowed between the hours of 6:00 and 8:00 p.m., the busiest time in the kitchen, especially on a Friday night. You could curse, you could shout at one of the McMann twins, either Evan or Everett, twentysomethings fresh out of the Vegan Culinary Institute, who switched off between line cook and all-around helper, to get you more garlic from the produce bins or another block of tofu from the refrigerator. But you couldn't start talking about what you did last night or how you and your boyfriend almost broke up. Yakking it up was reserved for prep and the staff meal before the dinner rush started. In my kitchen, you focused on the food, your job, and the clock.

Because if you listened to gab, you might miss that one of your busboys, a wannabe model whose young–David Beckham face let him get away with stealing tips and leaving early at least twice a week, had to be fired. I hated firing people.

Alanna was just having a bad day. No big whoop. We all had 'em. To be honest, I didn't like nights off from the restaurant, even if it meant escaping somewhere amazing on the back of Zach's Harley. I'd live at Clementine's No Crap Café if I could. I arrived around noon and stayed till closing—eleven o'clock—spending the hours before prep in my tiny office beside the kitchen, going over the books, inventory, mail, bills, recipes that needed reworking, specials that needed revamping, and staff issues, and lately there had been issues.

"There are always going to be issues," Zach had said last night as he'd massaged my shoulders and back. "All kinds. From staff to codes to food to the receipts' not balancing. That's the restaurant biz." Had my boyfriend of seven months cared that I smelled like garlic and blackened tofu and spicy chili? No. Zach owned a restaurant too, a bloody mess of a steak house called the Silver Steer, which was even more packed every night than Clementine's No Crap Café, so he understood thieving busboys and distracted sous chefs, even if he wasn't often at the Silver Steer. As CEO of Jeffries Enterprises, which he'd started himself at the age of twenty-three, Zach balanced more plates in the air than I did. Did I always listen to his occasionally veering-on-know-it-all advice? No. But he knew his shit.

Truth: I *loved* my eleven-hour days. With my own place, my own kitchen, working so hard was pure pleasure. No, I didn't love sitting at a desk going over paperwork, but I loved when the clock struck three and the staff arrived for prep and the staff meal, in order to taste the specials and describe the dishes to the waiters. It was important for the waiters to know every ingredient in every entrée for when diners asked, and they always asked.

"So there are no eggs in the fusilli?" a woman had asked her waiter yesterday when I was out schmoozing at the next table. A smart ten-year-old who didn't work at the restaurant could likely answer that one, but despite a sidebar of the menu that stated in bright orange that the restaurant was strictly vegan and a boatload of press we'd gotten recently for being the hot, new vegan place in LA, people still asked. "I'm a vegan and want to make sure," she'd added. "If there are eggs in the pasta, I can't eat here." She'd shivered for effect.

"Eggs? *As if,*" the waiter had said. "Clementine's is vegan all the way. No eggs. No dairy. Nothing that comes from an animal."

That same woman asked for regular cream for her tea not forty minutes later.

My customers ranged from hard-core vegans in PETA T-shirts (I was wearing one today under my chef jacket), to vegetarians kicking it up a notch, to carnivores such as Zach, who always left my restaurant commenting that he felt like Popeye after downing a can of spinach. *Just keep coming back, people* was what I cared about. Clementine's No Crap Café was years in the making, and at a mere two months old, despite good reviews and packed tables every night, I had to work my butt off to keep the place a success. LA had a slew of great vegan restaurants, and new ones were opening up all the time. My mission was to keep Clementine's hot, customers happy, and food critics raving. That meant no distractions. Such as a sous chef whose red braid tip was now dipped in a hot sauté pan of olive oil as she bent over to pick up the zucchini she'd dropped.

That was it. I drew the empathy line at hair in pots. "Alanna. Go home. *Now,*" I said. I took her pan and dumped it in the trash. "Something's obviously bothering you, so go home and deal. If you need tomorrow off, call me, okay?"

She looked relieved for a split second. "But you're off tomorrow for Zach's sister's wedding," she said, twisting her braid up into a bun. She grabbed a chopstick from her apron pocket and stuck it through her thick hair. "You need all morning to work on the cake, and the wedding starts in the afternoon, right?"

Shitballs. The wedding was at three. I wouldn't get out of here till midnight. Then I'd have to wake up at 5:00 a.m. to start on the cake. "If you need tomorrow off, don't call me," I amended, shooting her a smile.

"I won't let you down, Clem. I'll be fine. I'm just . . . distracted right now. I'll be fine tomorrow. Swear."

Hey, sometimes it happened. And it never happened to Alanna, so she got a pass. "Go. If you need to talk later, call me, okay?"

She nodded and practically ran out.

"Gunnar, you're acting sous chef tonight," I told him. "Evan, take Everett's spot as line cook. Everett, you're on vegetables."

"Don't you mess up my station," Gunnar hissed at Evan. Gunnar, late twenties and stick skinny with a mop of blue-black hair and narrow, green eyes, was famous for a serious approach to vegetables and his lack of a sense of humor, but he managed to make me laugh every night. Despite being so young, he was long divorced and had a nine-year-old daughter he adored, who looked just like him, minus the constant smile. Gunnar wasn't a smiler—except when it came to his girl.

Within ten minutes, Gunnar and I made seven stir-fry specials, four orders of fusilli, and eight vegetable kebabs. I'd scalded myself with boiling water, had red-pepper sauce in my hair and wet flour under my nails, but we were only five minutes behind. Fuck yeah, we got it done.

Until a party of ten came in and we ran out of tofu for the blackened-stir-fry special. How the holy hell had I let that happen?

I took over Alanna's and my job, sent Gunnar back to vegetables, and sent Evan to Xander's—one of my favorite late-night markets—for five pounds of firm tofu pronto.

No more distractions, I ordered myself. While I'd been checking inventory earlier, even *my* normally focused mind had wandered to whether to substitute agave nectar for the sugar in Zach's sister's wedding cake. When I *should* have been thinking about how many blocks of tofu we'd gone through. *Next time one of Zach's relatives gets married, don't volunteer to make a wedding cake for two hundred and sixty guests when you have to be at the wedding on prime Saturday night during prime kitchen time,* I mentally yelled at myself as I stared into the refrigerator.

Six minutes later, Evan, whose flushed face and mussed hair indicated he'd sprinted to the market and back, returned with the wrong kind of tofu because he was in a rush and I'd freaked him out. You should have seen his exhausted, hangdog face. How could I yell at him?

I'd yell at myself. Inventory was my thing. And I'd better step it up and fast. In six weeks, a *New York Times* reporter was coming to the restaurant as part of a piece on "veganmania" across America. For the travel section in a *Sunday* edition. This was a shot at Holy Grail–level publicity. Only a few restaurants from a handful of US cities would make it into the article. Clementine's *had* to make it in. Which meant the minute the wedding was over tomorrow, I was sneaking away from the reception and Zach's zillion relatives and coming back to work. From now on, there would be no running out of firm tofu. There would be no running behind schedule. There would be no sautéing braids.

There would be *no* distractions.

2

At just before 6:00 a.m. the next morning, I started setting out the ingredients for the wedding cake on the huge center island in Zach's kitchen, and my mind went where it usually did when I had flour and sugar and vanilla extract in front of me. Desserts for the restaurant. Minicupcakes. Chocolate-hazelnut with coconut-pecan icing. Lemon-raspberry with lemon frosting. Gingerbread with caramelized mango. A mix of three per serving, I decided as I added six cups of flour and an ungodly amount of sugar to the big silver mixing bowl on the kitchen counter. This was distraction in reverse and okay by me.

I grabbed my little notebook from my bag to jot down the cupcakes, which got me thinking of slightly gooey German chocolate cake with caramel and maybe fresh-peach crostata for tomorrow night's specials. I added a note to call Alanna around ten to see if she was all right. I couldn't afford for her to be off her game on a Saturday night. I could always call my good friend Alexander, a vegan chef at Fresh, the restaurant where I used to work, to see if he could cover for her if he wasn't working tonight.

I had so much on my mind that I jotted that down too and suddenly felt eyes on me. Charlie, Zach's ancient, little beagle. Giving me that begging look. Not for a lick of the bowl, since I'd barely gotten started on the cake. Charlie wanted to go out—now. I glanced at the clock on the wall. It was 6:08.

Glancing out the dark window, I asked the dog, "Can't you hold it till Zach wakes up?" The sun wasn't even up yet. I was barely up. And Jolie's wedding started at three. I had to get cracking on the cake. Five tiers, Pacific Ocean–blue fondant, tiny seashells cascading. The venue was a three-minute drive down Ocean Avenue from Zach's house, at a boutique hotel's private stretch of beach, which was why I'd decided to use Zach's state-of-the-art kitchen, since transporting would be a breeze. And that had included myself down the stairs from his bedroom before the tush-crack of dawn.

Charlie looked at me with those huge brown eyes. No, he couldn't hold it.

"You're lucky you're so cute," I told him, leaning down to give him a scratch behind his ears.

As I looked around the kitchen for Charlie's leash, I thought of Zach, sleeping upstairs. What I wouldn't give to be back in his incredibly comfortably king-size bed, snoozing for another couple of hours myself. But Jolie and Rufus's wedding cake had to be perfect. I adored Jolie, badass daughter of Zach's father and the second of his three wives (a fourth was imminent). Jolie was only eighteen and marrying a musician she'd been dating since her sophomore year of high school, which technically wasn't that long ago. She wasn't pregnant or immature or even out of her very young mind. She was in love, and she was getting married, whether anyone liked it or not. Several family members, including Zach, *didn't* like it.

Jolie had told her father, of the *You'll get married and be an actress over my cold, dead body* pronouncements, that she'd rather give her up megatrust than not marry her baby-faced fiancé and go for her dream of becoming the next Jennifer Lawrence. Her father had finally relented. But to avoid the possibility of anyone's objecting during the ceremony, such as Zach or his father lunging from his seat and screaming, *"She's eighteen and ruining her life,"* Jolie had wisely told the minister to cut the traditional "speak now or forever hold your piece" spiel.

Hopefully she'd do away with some other traditions too, such as the mind-numbing bouquet toss. A lineup of single women vying to be "next"? *Shiver.* I'd been to three weddings in the past two months, and at last Saturday's nuptials, my high school friend Carrie's, I had to bear witness to the grinning fourteen-year-old nephew of the groom sliding the something-blue garter up the red-faced thirty-seven-year-old bouquet catcher's bare leg.

Brides of the world: Just say no!

Case in point: Three Saturdays ago, at my sister Elizabeth's wedding, a disgruntled single guest in a hot-pink sheath dress had walked up to Elizabeth as the reception wound down and asked when she was planning to do the bouquet toss. The woman added that she didn't want to miss the lineup while freshening her lipstick in the ladies' room.

My sister, the least sentimental, least nostalgic, least super-stitious person alive, had let out her trademark snort. "If I'm tossing the bouquet to anyone, it's straight at my mother-in-law, who paid over four hundred bucks for it."

"But your mother-in-law is *married*," the single guest had protested.

I'd been able to tell from Elizabeth's expression that she was dying to lecture the woman on archaic, antifeminist tradi-tions that made her blood boil. Elizabeth got seriously worked up over these things. But she held her usual let-loose tongue. "I just meant I'm not doing a bouquet toss."

The single guest walked away with an "Oh," shoulders kind of slumped, heading back to her table of singles, where she'd been seated between a ten-year-old cousin using a rubber band to slingshot crap at unsuspecting guests all night and the groom's mentally unstable bachelor uncle. Elizabeth called out the single woman's name, and when the guest turned around, my sister, who was much kinder than she let on, tossed that bouquet, albeit with a slight roll of her eyes, directly into the guest's hands.

With a surprised smile—and a silent, triumphant *I will be next!*—the single guest went back much happier to the ten-year-old, who'd barfed up his third piece of wedding cake on her chair.

"Jesus H. Christ on a Ritz cracker," my best friend, Sara, had said as we'd watched the woman's entire demeanor change from despairing to hopeful. "If I ever get like that, which I never will, please slap me really hard across the face to snap me out of it." Sara and I were both in committed relationships, but marriage—and cheesetastic wedding rituals—was the furthest thing from either of our busy minds. If anyone tried to toss a bouquet in Sara's direction, she'd instinctively drop-kick it.

"Oh, I will," I'd said. "And same here." Not that either of us would be getting married anytime soon. I'd been with Zach seven months, and Sara and Joe had been together for six. Couple newbies! But spring wedding season, with its bouquet tossing and ice sculptures and bands still playing Kool & the Gang, had taken over our lives.

Last month, Sara and I had attended our Pilates teacher's wedding, the bride and groom in lotus position in the woods. Zenia, one of the coolest women we knew, had shocked us by calling for the single women to line up for the bouquet toss. Zenia, of all people!

"A wedding itself is traditional, is it not?" Zenia had said in her usual Zen style to our "How could you!" questioning afterward.

"I'm making a statement by not lining up," Sara had whispered to me. "Can you imagine if I actually caught the bouquet? I don't want to be next! I'd run for the hills. Join a nunnery. Anything to not be next and marry *that* guy."

We'd glanced over at Sara's boyfriend, the loudest person at any social event, but especially in the calm quiet of the woods, telling another cringe-worthy story about "the loser schmuck wannabe chef" he'd humiliated as host of his own weekly TV show, *Eat Me*, on the Food Network. Sara was something of a cohost, and how she'd landed that gig was a frightening story for another time. But her boyfriend, Joe "Steak" Johansson, was the only person alive capable of embarrassing Sara, who was hard to offend. It was half the reason she liked him so much.

"No way will Jolie do a cheesetastic bouquet toss," I whispered now to Charlie as I searched the kitchen for his leash. "That chick is as antitradition as they come."

Evident by her choice of wedding-cake baker. Despite having her pick of the best bakeries in LA to make her wedding cake (this was a no-expense-spared, unlimited-budget wedding, paid for by Cornelius Jeffries, bajillionaire father), Jolie had asked me. I'd met Jolie back when I was getting my Skinny Bitch Bakes business off the ground, cakes and muffins and cookies and scones and pies for coffee shops all over Santa Monica. That was just six months ago, but my life had completely changed since then. Now, I was baking those cakes and pies only for Clementine's No Crap Café. New note to self:

think about hiring a pastry chef so you can focus on running the kitchen. My other best friend, Ty, the *best* vegan pastry chef, was working in Paris for the year. He'd know someone I could count on.

The other big change? The amazing guy sleeping upstairs. Zach and I had gone from rocky beginning to true love. No one, Zach and I especially, expected a mouthy vegan such as me and a steak-house-owning carnivore such as him to last more than five minutes in the same room together. But seven months later, Zach and I were still going strong.

Not that I'd seen much of him these past two months except for late at night when I'd leave Clementine's No Crap Café feeling exhausted, exhilarated, and covered in tomato sauce and smelling like garlic. He'd pick me up on the Harley (leaving the annoying Mercedes at home), bring me back to this spectacular beach house, make a mess in the kitchen as he whipped us up a late-night snack of spiked fruit smoothies, and then we'd hang out on the couch for a little bit, watching TV and talking until one of us led the other upstairs. Zach was always gone in a suit and tie before I ever woke up. Our hours were as different as we were, but somehow, during the brief time we had together lately, Zach and I had grown even closer.

Zach was a package deal—he came with Charlie, waddling, little beagle, who continued to stare at me, tail wagging. It had taken me a while to win over the ancient, sweet-faced dog, but I'd done it. Which meant I had to take him out for his morning pee and let him get oohed and aahed at by the early-bird joggers on the beach. *If* I could find his leash. Where was it?

I checked all the kitchen drawers. The baskets under the bench at the front entryway and the French doors to the back-yard that led down to the beach. No leash. I poked my head into Zach's office, spotless, unlike my own at the restaurant. No leash on his desk. Charlie followed me, and I swore he was rolling his eyes with a "C'mon, already, Cooper. I gotta goooo." I headed back into the entry hall. Not looped on the coatrack or hanging off the hooks. I checked the pockets of Zach's jackets, including the expensive black leather one he refused to get rid of even for his vegan girlfriend. No leash.

But something else was in the pocket of that leather jacket. Something smallish. Square. Velvet.

Like a jewelry box.

Fabulous earrings for my birthday, which wasn't for another month? I couldn't resist a peek. I took out the little box. Black velvet. I glanced behind me to make sure Zach hadn't myste-riously woken up early for once on a Saturday, but there was only Charlie, still staring at me.

Don't do it, the dog seemed to be saying with those soulful brown eyes. *You put that back, even though it's for you, Clementine Cooper.*

But I couldn't stop myself. I hated surprises. I loved know-ing something was coming—the anticipation of receiving. I opened the lid of the little box—and my eyes bugged out of my head.

Holy hell.

A diamond ring.

Round, glittering diamond. Two carats. Platinum band.

I was about to hyperventilate. *Deep breaths, Clementine,* I told myself.

I stood frozen on the round wool rug in the foyer, barely able to take those breaths. It was as if I had a mini-angel playing a harp on one shoulder as out-of-nowhere wild happiness coursed through my usually cynical, tradition-stomping veins, while on the other shoulder, a mini-devil wielding a tiny pitchfork screamed, *"You can't get engaged! You have a restaurant to run! Staff to manage! Customers to feed! Food critics to impress! The* New York Times *travel section on deck! Wedding plans will derail you!"*

From what I'd seen around me these past couple of months, marriage proposals meant congratulations for weeks on end and multiple engagement parties and wedding plans up the wazoo, and the only plans I wanted in my head were about the restaurant—how to impress the stuffing out of the *New York Times* reporter and ensure Clementine's inclusion in the article. How to keep the joint packed as the months went by so it wasn't just the "awesome new vegan on Montana" anymore.

Then Zach's face popped into my mind. That face I loved, with those intelligent blue eyes that missed nothing. Zach was great. I thought of all he'd done these past seven months— hiring me to create vegan offerings for the Silver Steer, which had led other restaurants that served dead animals to do the same. Hey, it was a start for their blood-dripping menus. And it had been a huge start for *me* when I'd needed to rebuild my name as a chef. I also couldn't forget the time Zach had dropped everything—before we were even dating—to drive me three hours to the hospital to see my dad, who'd been admitted with complications from Stage III cancer. How Zach had calmed me down on the long drive there. How he'd been there for me in every possible way all these months of our relationship. The guy was true-blue and red-hot.

I dropped down on the padded bench lining the foyer wall. I knew that Zach and I were serious, that he loved me, but I had no idea he was thinking about forever *now*.

I loved Zach. I did want to marry Zach. Later, though.

I knew what happened to brides-to-be. Even my sister had got all freaked out because she couldn't find a wedding dress she *liked*, let alone loved. Everything was too bridal, too white or ivory, too traditional, too gowny. In the end, corporate lawyer Elizabeth, the one who wouldn't normally give a flying rat's butt about a dress, drew a pencil sketch of what she envisioned, brought it into every boutique and department store in LA and asked the salesclerks if the shop had something like it. She'd finally found the ecru, kimono-style dress of her dreams off the rack in Nordstrom for two hundred bucks. She'd lost three days of her honeymoon time to her crazed dress shopping.

Then there was my friend Jules, who without warning six months ago went from being a normal, twenty-eight-year-old small-accessories buyer to the biggest, baddest bridezilla you'd never want to meet. No detail was too small, including the push-up bras for the bridal party, which had to be special-ordered for $212 so that we would all have the same-shaped boobs in the $400 pale peach silk dresses she'd made us shill out good money for. No one had seen this crazy Jules coming. I forgave her after the honeymoon, but I did not forget.

Not that there was a chance in hell I'd become some lunatic bridezilla. I knew that. But a big, honking diamond ring on my finger would be a *huge* distraction.

Was he going to propose at his sister's wedding? Or maybe later tonight?

See, I was already distracted by the ring. I had a dog to walk. A cake to bake for 260 guests, many of whom I'd soon be related to by marriage.

Holy shiitake.

I needed Sara. Now. My heart beating like crazy, I ran into the living room to grab my cell phone from the coffee table and was about to text her, but this time I did manage to stop myself. Right now the proposal was supposed to be Zach's secret, unless he'd shared it with anyone. It would be wrong to go blabbing it, even to my best friend.

And guess what was coiled in a basket on the far side of the coffee table, on top of the stack of *Vegan Life* magazines I was always leaving around for Zach never to read. Charlie's leash. I clipped it on him, put a note on the fridge that I was taking Charlie for a walk on the beach, then left in freaked-out wonder.

3

The first time I saw Zach Jeffries I hated his guts. Well, I thought he was gorgeous—tall, lean, muscular, with all that thick, dark, glossy hair and deep blue eyes, impossibly long lashes, and a slight cleft in his chin. But I still hated him. Seven months ago, I'd been in the middle of teaching my first cooking class, in the kitchen of my dumpy little apartment on Montana Avenue, when a loud, booming noise interrupted my scintillating lecture on the wonders of tofu. I'd gone to the living room window to find a giant 3-D sign being erected over the beautiful space where I'd dreamed of one day opening my own vegan restaurant.

What did that sign say? The Silver Steer—complete with a 3-D silver steer's head staring with its dead eyes right into my living room window. I'd marched right into that space and demanded to talk to the owner about taking down the dead-steer head; it had been bad enough he'd stolen my dream location for Clementine's No Crap Café. That owner: Zach Jeffries, thirty-two-year-old entrepreneur millionaire who mysteriously morphed into my boyfriend.

Soon-to-be fiancé.

As Charlie and I sat on the beach, him happily digging, me watching the sun rise over the Santa Monica Pier, I couldn't help but smile as I thought about our early days—a vegan and a carnivore falling in love and trying so hard not to.

"Do you believe this craziness, Charlie?" I asked, scratching behind his floppy ears. He rested his chin on my knee. "Zach is going to ask me to marry him. What do you think of that?"

Charlie snuggled up against me, and for a moment it was so stinking cozy that I put my arm around his furry, little body, thinking that he'd be mine, that Zach would be mine. That Zach, whom I loved, wanted to spend the rest of his life with me.

Wait—now I was about to get all sentimental?

"Charlie, what the hell is happening to me? Now I *want* to get married?"

Because you *can* have it all, I realized. Who said we couldn't get engaged, *not* plan a wedding or talk about it at all, and just elope one day when it felt right to Paris or Barcelona or even Vegas? My restaurant didn't have to suffer. Surely Zach wouldn't be interested in discussing lame cummerbunds and boring centerpieces.

I just wanted to sit there and bask in the amazement of it all, that this would really work, but after the sixth jogger stopped to pet Charlie and remark on his cuteness, we headed back to Zach's house. I had a big-ass wedding cake to bake— for my soon to be sister-in-law.

❧ ◎ ◎ ❧

The five tiers, gradating in size, were cooling on the island counter when Zach came into the kitchen just after nine o'clock. Bare-chested and wearing his Stanford sweatpants, he hugged me from behind, kissing my neck.

"The delicious smell of the cake woke me up," he said.

You're going to propose was all I could think. God, it was mind-blowing.

In four seconds, ocean-blue fondant and the hundreds of tiny, intricate seashells I had to make had been forgotten in the unexpected reality of Zach Jeffries asking me to marry him. An hour ago, I didn't give a gorilla's butt about where my relationship with Zach was headed.

I'd promised myself to focus on the restaurant, on wowing the *New York Times* reporter, reviewers, critics, my customers—even the health inspector. Having my own restaurant had always been my dream—not walking down the aisle in some poufy, white gown.

Seriously, I'd been fantasizing about having my own kitchen since I was five years old, since my dad had handed me a cup of flour and water and taught me how to make pasta from scratch, how to add fresh vegetables from the organic farm he and my mother ran to make a pasta primavera that would rival a five-star Italian restaurant's.

I'd known then, since I was three feet tall, that I would be a chef someday, that I would rule over my own kitchen, but turning that dream into reality had been a long time coming. I'd graduated from the Vegan Culinary Institute and worked at a slew of top vegan restaurants in LA, busting my tush on the way up from trainee to line cook to sauté chef to sous chef. Just weeks before I'd met Zach, a jealous coworker at Fresh had sabotaged me the night a *Los Angeles Times* restaurant critic had come to dine. I'd been blackballed all over the city. So I'd started my own business—and it slowly took off. Personal chef, cooking classes, baked goods. But when I got the money together to open my own restaurant—without a penny from my millionaire boyfriend—and saw my first customers walk through the door on opening night, it was as if fireworks shot off inside me. My fantasy had become hard-won reality.

Wait a minute. *Breathe deeply, Clementine.* I was forgetting again that Zach, who owned his own new restaurant, the Silver Steer (in a different location from the one that had brought us together), understood why I was never around, and best of all, he actually admired me for it. *This* will *work out. You can be engaged and keep Clementine's a success.*

The pitchfork-wielding little devil disappeared off my left shoulder and the smiling angel on my right aimed a mini-remote-control at my brain, reminding me of two weeks ago when Zach had come home exhausted at ten at night from boardroom business negotiations to find me frustrated in his kitchen, my hands coated in tomato guts for a new version of my ratatouille, which was missing something. A producer from *Good Morning, L.A.* was having me on to teach how to make ratatouille in the studio in two days, and my ratatouille was—in my hard-to-impress opinion—a solid meh.

Zonked as he was, Zach had sat down at the kitchen table, kicked off his shoes, Charlie's head resting on his foot, and looked through my three recipes, suggesting what to delete, what to add. He'd tasted all three versions, even though he'd barely been awake by the time I'd finished the third, and declared the third the charm. In the morning, he'd even had the winning ratatouille for breakfast to make double sure on morning brain that it was good enough for the perky hostess, who'd potentially rave on the popular morning show and send hordes to Clementine's to try it in person. It had been, by the way.

The mini-angel switched the channel, this time to my younger brother, Kale, calling me from the freeway a few weeks ago to say he had a flat and could I come pick him up. In the middle of dinner rush at the restaurant. Apparently he'd called everyone he knew in LA and no one was around. So who had left a dinner party with investors to pick up my brother, get his car towed, and loaned him his old Porsche until his ancient Honda was ready?

Yeah: Zach.

The little devil, now on my right shoulder, lunged the pitchfork at the angel and switched the channel to the Ghost of Clementine's Future: Me in some fancy bridal salon in a gorgeous white gown, five seamstresses pinning and hemming for hours. Cut to Zach and I at yet another of his dull business functions, me dressed "appropriately" in a pastel Chanel suit. Eating a cube of *cheese* for some ungodly reason.

Cut to Clementine's No Crap Café with boarded-up windows and a FOR RENT sign across the window.

Beat it, devil. As if any of those situations would ever happen. Cheese? Please. Anyway, Zach was already my partner in life. He knew me. Understood me. Wanted me to succeed on my terms.

"Need any help?" he asked, picking up the wooden spoon from the empty mixing bowl and swiping his finger through the icing.

"Nope," I said, barely able to keep myself from turning around and telling him I'd found the ring, by accident. "I need to get started on the fondant and then I have a million seashells to make, but I've got it."

"Any chance Jolie will come to her senses and call off the wedding?" he said, swiping one more lick of the bowl.

"Seriously doubt that."

"God, I want to object. You'll have to slap your hand over my mouth when the minister brings it up." Sometimes he seemed fine about his baby half sister getting hitched so young, but sometimes, the look that came over his face was like one big, long sigh.

Poor Zach. He wouldn't even get the chance to object.

"Jolie will be fine. Married or not at eighteen, she'll blaze her way through life. You know that."

"You're right. I forget how much like you she is." He kissed me again, told me he loved me, thanked me for walking Charlie, then headed upstairs to change for his run on the beach.

In just hours, we'd be a mile up that beach, attending the wedding, where I'd meet his entire family. Where he'd likely ask me to marry him.

Hell yeah! the little angel perched on my shoulder shouted in my ear.

Clementine's No Crap Café will go to shit, the mini-devil on the other said, jabbing the pitchfork into my neck.

4

I delivered the cake in one piece (with the help of the trusty McMann twins), and it looked f-ing spectacular. Now, at four o'clock, glass of good champagne in hand, I stood barefoot in the sand (my shoes, like all the other wedding guests', were in the boutique hotel's shoe check-in) next to Zach on a private stretch of beach, surrounded by women in brightly colored sheath dresses and men in linen suits, countless of whom were Zach's relatives.

I could relax too. Sous chef Alanna had assured me she was not only fine, but on fire to be in charge for the night, and I'd heard in her voice that she was the same old reliable Alanna McNeal.

The weather gods had been kind for the outdoor wedding—brilliant sunshine, bright blue skies, and low seventies.

The ceremony for Jolie and Rufus, also barefoot, under a white silk canopy held aloft by bamboo poles, had been beautiful, even when the Ice Puppets, the groom's alternative-folk-rock band, sang a nonsensical song-poem they expressly wrote for the ceremony. The bride and groom had gazed at each other with such lovey-dovey, googly eyes that all the preceremony buzz about their age and "rushing into marriage" had changed to "They're so perfect for each other" and proclamations about young love.

Even I, someone who usually reworked recipes in her head during readings of hour-long vows and poetry, was held completely rapt by the Zen Buddhist minister's every word about union and love and forever. The moment Jolie and Rufus leaned toward each other for their first kiss as husband and wife, I started tearing up like everyone else—including Zach. I'd always thought weddings were about frilly, white gowns and an open bar and a zillion-dollar industry that made brides care about crazy stuff. But this wedding was only about one thing: love. As I watched Jolie and Rufus's first dance, to "You're My Best Friend" by Queen, I tightened my hand in Zach's and he squeezed back and smiled at me.

"Uh-oh, tipsy aunt Jocelyn coming toward us," he whispered in my ear. Jocelyn, who Zach had told me was his favorite great-aunt, had been at our table for dinner. She was hilarious and told me funny stories during every course about Zach and his siblings as children.

The tiny, elderly woman, so elegant despite her bare feet,

with white hair coiled atop her head like a crown, ambled over in the sand, trying not to slosh her glass of champagne.

"You two had better be next!" she said to us, her pale blue eyes twinkling. "I'm eighty-six years old and want to see my eldest nephew walk down the aisle before I kick it."

Since we'd arrived an hour ago, Aunt Jocelyn was the third person to use the words *next* and *us* in a sentence. Each time, Zach smiled uncomfortably and changed the subject. If I hadn't seen that ring with my own eyes, I might have thought marriage was the farthest thing from *his* mind.

Workaholic, cookaholic or not, all the mushy-gushy emotion in the air had gotten to me. It had started with the bride and groom's engagement party a few months ago—with a toast Zach had given. Zach was close with his half sister, but when Jolie had first announced she was engaged, right around the time that Zach and I had started seeing each other, Zach and Jolie had argued every minute. His baby sister, marrying at age eighteen? Throwing away her future and a free ride to UCLA to instead become an actress? The double whammy had had Zach apoplectic. I'd gotten to know Jolie pretty well, and she might be young, but she was smart and she knew what she wanted. And what she wanted was to become an actress and marry Rufus. Trying to get Zach to see Jolie's side of things had almost torn us apart before we'd even gotten really started. In the end, it had been Zach who'd convinced their father not to disown Jolie, as Cornelius Jeffries had threatened.

But Zach's toast at their engagement party, held at his beach house, almost made me cry, and I wasn't a crier. He'd clinked on his glass with a dessert spoon, then told the hundred plus guests how much he loved his half sister, fourteen years his junior, that she had a good head on her shoulders and a big heart. That it had been Jolie who'd gotten him through the toughest time of his life, when their dad had had a massive heart attack a few years back. Jolie, just thirteen then, had had utter faith that their dad would be okay, that he'd pull through because he was Cornelius Jeffries and nothing could ever strike him down. Everyone, including the big man himself— a toughened multimillionaire in the brown Stetson he wore everywhere—had started tearing up. But when Zach had said how lucky Jolie was to have found the person she wanted to spend the rest of her life with—that was when *I* almost started crying. Especially when he'd added, "Because, when you find that person, you don't let them go."

I wasn't letting Zach go for anything.

"Now, dear, listen to me," Aunt Jocelyn whispered, wrapping her arm around mine. Her diamond bracelets jangled against my skin as she leaned close. "If you do want to be next, there's only one way to get there. Be yourself. Be amazing. Kick tush," she added with a smile.

I couldn't wait for this awesome woman to be *my* aunt. "Oh, I plan to," I assured her.

"Telling Clementine embarrassing stories about me as a kid?" Zach asked.

"Just giving your date some pointers about life and love," Jocelyn said with another grin. "Your uncle Frederick and I have been married for sixty-four years this summer, testament enough."

"Well, how about a dance to celebrate six decades of marriage, Aunt Jocelyn?" Zach said, handing their glasses of champagne to a passing waiter. He led his great-aunt to the dance floor erected on the sand and twirled her around to the band's playing Frank Sinatra's "Fly Me to the Moon."

As the bandleader announced that it was time for the cutting of the cake—and it had come out as perfectly as I'd hoped—Zach came back over, draping his arm around me.

Cornelius Jeffries's fiancée, soon to be wife number four, clapped her hands three times and trilled, "Family pictures by the cake, please!"

Jolie's mother, ex-wife number two, a hippieish artist in her midforties with white-blond hair to her waist, seemed only too happy to let the outspoken fiancée who'd stolen Cornelius from wife number three, who'd stolen Cornelius from her, take over. No wonder Jolie was so cool—her mother was awesome.

"I'll hold your champagne," I said, reaching for Zach's glass.

Zach put both our glasses on a waiter's tray. "She said family pictures. And where I go, you go." He took my hand and led me over to the cake, under its own canopy.

"Clementine!" the bride said, rushing over to give me a big hug. "I've barely gotten to talk to you all day! We have to catch up when I get back from Europe. Everyone!" Jolie called out.

"Clementine, my brother Zach's girlfriend, made this incredibly gorgeous cake. She owns Clementine's No Crap Café on Montana. You have to check it out."

Jolie rocked. The smiling bride and groom pushed down on the knife and cut the cake. Jolie put a little piece in Rufus's mouth, and he put a little piece in hers, then they kissed, and Rufus dipped her, eliciting claps from the guests.

Those two loved each other and would be just fine.

As Zach and I were surrounded by people, some catching up with him, others asking me about my restaurant, waiters came around and handed out plates of cake, which got me many oohs and aahs and compliments.

"At least a hundred people have asked me how serious you two are," Gareth, Zach's brother, said as he came over and stood beside me. "If one more person asks me anything about you guys, I might have to smush the rest of my cake in their face. Or toss them in the Pacific."

"Clem made the cake, and trust me, you don't want to waste it," Zach told his brother, once again sidestepping the question of how serious we were. How next we were. And we were very next. I could get engaged. I could run Clementine's. *I am woman, hear me roarrr my ass off.*

"Ooh, the woman I've been dying to talk to all afternoon is finally standing alone," Gareth said, staring at a redhead on the other side of the dance floor. He handed one waiter his half-finished cake, took two glasses of champagne from another, and headed over. Gareth Jeffries was five years younger than

Zach, every bit as rich, and every bit the playboy that I'd once thought Zach was. But like Zach, he would do anything for his family, and the more I got to know him, the more I adored him.

"All the singles ladies, please line up!" Jolie's stepmother-to-be called out.

Oh, fuck no. I tried to move behind Zach. I wasn't alone, either. Not one woman stepped forward.

"See, Lydia," the bride called to her stepmother with a shake of her head. "I *told* you. It's not 1982!"

But Lydia rolled her eyes and dragged a few singles front and center. They looked absolutely miserable. "It's tradition, dear," she said, snagging another ringless woman.

"I think the single *men* should line up and catch the bouquet," Jolie called out, and I couldn't help clapping.

Big mistake. "You too, Clementine," Lydia said, taking my hand. "And Avery, get over here, young lady," she shot at Zach's fraternal twin sister. "I see you hiding behind Uncle Desmond."

Avery Jeffries slapped her palm to her forehead. "Someone save me."

Within seconds, the stepmother had a lineup of around twenty sheepish-looking women.

Sara, who'd become friendly with Jolie through me, was hiding behind her mammoth boyfriend—six feet four and at least 250 pounds. Her unadorned left hand was behind her back to avoid Lydia's eagle eyes for lack of ring.

Jolie stood by the water's edge, facing the water. "Sorry," she called out with a shake of her head. "Here goes."

"And somebody had better catch it," Lydia shouted. "It's seriously bad luck for a bouquet to land on the ground."

Jolie flung. The bouquet was headed straight for me. No one moved, including me.

If I didn't put my hands out, the red-and-white monstrosity would land in my face and blind me. I had no choice.

"Yeah! Clementine's caught the bouquet! She's next!" Lydia shouted.

I caught a glimpse of Sara practically doubled over in laughter next to Joe, who was stuffing his face with my cake.

Holy hells bells, this was embarrassing. I glanced over at Zach, but he was deep in conversation with a cousin, thankfully missing the entire thing. As I walked over, I overhead at least ten people joke to Zach that they expected to be invited to his wedding. Again, strained smile.

Ya'll are ruining his surprise, I wanted to shout at them. *Leave the guy alone. Getting married is about two people who love each other, not all this crap.*

Suddenly, I wanted nothing more than for Zach and me to take a long walk down the beach, hand in hand. For him to tell me he loved me, that he wanted to spend the rest of his life with me. I'd run Clementine's just fine with Zach as my partner in crime.

Just as I joined Zach, his father disengaged from a group and came over to us. "Is this some kind of vegetarian cake?" Cornelius Jeffries asked as he approached us, forking a piece of cake in his mouth. He wore a suit and his trademark Stetson. Cornelius looked like a sixtysomething version of his sons—tall and muscular, his thick, dark hair shot through with gray. "It's not half-bad."

A vegetarian cake, ha. *Yes, Cornelius, there's no ground beef in* this *cake.* "Actually, I'm a *vegan,*" I told him. "But the cake isn't. Full of eggs and butter." In the name of friendship, sometimes you had to get your hands dirty.

"Now it makes sense," he said, taking another bite before getting pulled away into conversation with a group of men.

Zach was about to say something to me, but his cousin Griff, whom Zach had introduced to me earlier, pulled him aside with a maniacal look on his face. Seriously, the guy—early thirties, like Zach—looked to be freaking out, but in an excited way. I took a sip of my champagne and watched as Zach and Griff headed over by the huge planters in front of the hotel, as if hiding from view. But through the stalks and leaves of a giant bird of paradise, I saw Zach reach into his pocket and hand Griff the black velvet ring box.

Cute, I thought. He must have confided in Griff about proposing to me, and Griff wanted to see the ring—for some un-guy-like reason.

They shifted a bit farther behind the huge plant. Griff opened the little velvet box, took a deep breath, smiled that maniacal smile again, and then closed it. Next came a cousinly embrace. As they headed out from behind the giant plant, Zach caught up to some relatives heading into the hotel, and I watched Griff go over to a blonde in a short, pink dress. He led her farther down the beach, then got down on one knee—the black velvet box proffered in his hand.

Wait a minute. That was *my* ring. Wasn't it?

A second later, she jumped up and he swung her around.

My ring on her finger.

My hard-won yes coming from her mouth.

5

I wasn't proud of my next move, but after Cornelius Jeffries's third story of roping a buck at a dude ranch out West, and the bajillionth toast to Griffin and his new fiancée, I faked an emergency at the restaurant and got the hell out of the hotel lounge (where the family had migrated once the reception had wound down) with its wall-to-wall Jeffrieses.

Rejoice! the little devil on my shoulder screeched with a jab of his pitchfork. *You just dodged the bridal bullet!*

You didn't want it, then you wanted it, now you're not getting it, the angel said with a strum of her harp. *That's what you get for snooping.*

Zach glanced at his watch. "It's just after eleven, and the place is closed. Can't it wait till tomorrow?"

Nope, I thought, my stomach churning. *It can't.* "I'm really sorry, but I'd better go handle it. I'll see you tomorrow." I gave him a quick kiss on the cheek.

He looked at me quizzically, but handed me the keys to his car and I bolted.

Actually, there *was* an emergency (my feeling like a big, fat fool), so I didn't feel *that* bad about taking off on the after party. And I did go straight to the restaurant, the only place that could set me straight, make me forget what had just happened.

Remind me of what I was supposed to be thinking about, what I was supposed to be focusing on. It *wasn't* getting married. Jeez.

I parked in the tiny alley behind Clementine's No Crap Café and headed in the back door, the place dead quiet and sparkling clean. Just a few hours ago, the noise in the kitchen would have been deafening on a busy Saturday night, but now, at eleven thirty, it was my peaceful sanctuary, where I could shake off feeling like a dumbhead and work on my rustic potpie.

I put a Clementine's No Crap Café apron over my midnight-blue halter dress, took off the four-inch heels, cranked up the *Saturday Night Fever* soundtrack on the iPod dock, and got to work at my stainless steel station, slicing carrots into chunks and chopping onions. Sweet potato for the whole-wheat-biscuit crust or pumpkin? It would take forever to bake a sweet potato right now, so I'd use pumpkin tonight and see how it came out.

I added mushrooms, peppers, peas, corn, some fresh thyme, pepper, and sea salt to the carrots and onions, then brushed the veggies with extra-virgin olive oil and slid them into the oven to roast. Mmms, the smell of caramelizing onions never got old. As I started pressing dry the tofu, I kept thinking about that ring, so of course I started pressing too hard. Slam. Wham. Bam. Shitzam.

Focus, Clementine, I ordered myself. *That's what you're here for.* I put aside the tofu to start the crust when I heard my phone ping with a text.

I'm out back.—Z

I should have known he'd come after me. I went to the back door and let him in.

"The emergency was *cooking*? I smell something good."

The emergency is that I didn't want to marry you ten hours ago. Now I do. What am I supposed to do with that? Think fast, Clem. "One of the McMann twins thought he left a burner on, and then when I got here, I realized I might as well work on my rustic potpie for the *Times* reporter. I only have six weeks, and—"

"Can you bring over the ingredients to my place? There's something I wanted to talk to you about." His expression was dead serious. He looked kind of . . . nervous.

He was dumping me. He was moving to New York. Hong Kong, maybe. He wanted to see other people. "What about?" I asked, trying to keep my voice level.

He took a deep breath. The kind of deep breath you take when you're about to tell someone something he or she won't want to hear. "Let's go. We'll take Charlie for a walk on the beach."

That's what you get for snooping, Charlie seemed to be saying to me when we got back to Zach's house just after midnight.

It was crazy that I felt like a popped balloon. If I'd never found that ring box, I would never have been thinking about marriage. *Just blink yourself back to six o'clock this morning, before you stuck your hand in that pocket. Before you snooped.*

Before Zach wanted to dump you.

Except once again, Charlie's leash was being clipped on him, which brought me back to that morning.

I just wanted to go home and complain to Sara about what an idiot I was, but she was likely at Joe's anyway.

Zach and I headed toward the Pier, still lit up. Not many people were on the beach this late, but we passed a few couples, walking hand in hand, just like us.

"You okay?" Zach asked, Charlie scampering ahead of us on his leash. "You got quiet at the after party, and then you took off. Did someone really leave a burner on or did my family just talk you to death?"

I smiled. "I love your family. I had a great time today."

"I'm glad to hear that. But you haven't met my mother yet," he added with a smile.

Huh. Maybe he wasn't dumping me. "I'm sure I'll love her too."

Zach had told me a little about his mother, Dominique Jeffries Huffington. For the past few years, they'd been on the outs and had only recently repaired their relationship. Zach rarely talked about it. His father and mother had been archenemies for years and were never in same room—or stretch of beach—together, so Dominique hadn't been invited to the wedding.

"My cousin Griff—the guy who got engaged at the wedding," Zach said, throwing a little piece of driftwood for Charlie to fetch, "he was so afraid he'd lose the ring he asked me to hold it for him until it was time to propose."

Heart clench. "Good thing she said yes, then."

He nodded and tightened his grip on my hand, stopping and looking out at the ocean. "Remember when we took that walk on the beach with Charlie last summer and held hands for the first time? I think I fell in love with you that night." As Charlie came running over with a stick, Zach stopped and moved a lock of my hair from my face to behind my ear. His hand lingered on my cheek, caressed my chin, and the expression in his eyes was so . . . tender.

"I remember," I said. That night, we'd laughed over Charlie looking for the sticks Zach kept throwing for him, and I'd felt as if I were in the middle of an incredibly good dream. "It was soon after we met. You were telling me about how much you loved that we're from the same place, that we both grew up on farms."

Zach and I were both from farm country three hours north of Los Angeles, but the fifty-acre organic-vegetable farm I'd grown up on and the thousands-acre cattle ranch where Zach had grown up were night and day.

Sometimes, such as now, I felt so close to Zach, so connected to him. Getting engaged, not getting engaged. Who gave a fuck? We were together, had a good thing going, and that was all that mattered. Unless he *was* about to tell me he was moving to New York or Paris or Sydney.

"Close your eyes," Zach said.

"Why?"

"Just do it."

I closed my eyes, listening to the whoosh of the ocean, the breeze stirring my hair.

"Open," he said.

I slowly opened my eyes and gasped. What?

He held out an open velvet ring box. Nestled inside was an even more beautiful diamond ring than the one I'd seen earlier. Big, perfect, round diamond in an antique setting, the platinum band studded with smaller diamonds.

I stood there, unable to speak, unable to breathe.

"Clementine Cooper, I love you more than anything in the world."

"I love you too," I whispered. Mind blown.

"Will you marry me?" he asked, lifting my chin.

Only the mini-angel was around this time. "I want to marry you more than anything. I love you, Zach. So, so much."

"Me too," he whispered back, and slid the ring on my finger.

6

First the ring wasn't a surprise and freaked me out. Then it was a surprise and freaked me out even more—in a good way. When had Zach Jeffries not kept me on my toes?

We didn't tell anyone last night. Both of us wanted to keep it our hot secret for the evening. We celebrated with Veuve Clicquot on the moonlit balcony outside Zach's bedroom, talking for hours about the past, present, and future, where we wanted to go for a honeymoon (Bali, maybe) and even how many kids each of us wanted someday (Zach wanted four, maybe even five—and he wasn't kidding). Kids and me? Maybe ten years from now. It was close to three before we finally fell asleep.

When the sun streaming through the filmy, white curtains woke me up on Sunday morning, the first thing I saw was my ring, because my face was pressed against my left hand on the fluffy down pillows on the bed. And the diamond was wider than my finger.

I glanced over at Zach, sleeping on his back, watching his chest rise and fall.

I ran a finger down his cheek. How could I love someone so much? What the hell had happened to me? Last year, I was cynical and nowhere over my ex-boyfriend of two years. Then I met the one guy on earth whom I should have had zero chemistry with, and it was like parades in my head every time I looked at him, every time he kissed me. Zach Jeffries had turned out to be everything I never knew I wanted—someone who supported me and challenged me at the same time. Someone who made me melt. Someone who made me laugh and think and feel as if I were both floating on a cloud and standing on solid ground.

"Hey, fiancée," Zach said, pulling me on top of him.

I kissed him, ridiculously happy.

"So what kind of wedding do you want?" he asked, running his fingers through my hair.

The no-wedding wedding. "Maybe we should put off wedding plans for a while. I want to focus on the restaurant, and I know you've never been busier. We can be one of those couples who's engaged for years."

"Only problem with that is that I want to marry you ASAP."

"So we'll go to city hall. Or elope to Paris."

"Clementine Cooper, the antibride." He wrapped me in a hug. "Whatever makes you happy." He headed into the shower.

I called my sister, Elizabeth, with the news that she was gaining a brother-in-law. Despite being an uptight lawyer married to another uptight lawyer, Elizabeth still managed to be one of my favorite people on earth.

"Congrats!" Elizabeth said. "Thank God I know I can count on you to not stick me into some hideous, jewel-toned taffeta dress." Elizabeth's requirements for the maid-of-honor dress I wore to her wedding: something not white. That was it.

"I was actually thinking of pastel chiffon. Bright peach." At her dead silence—as if I could *possibly* be serious—I added, "I kid, I kid."

When we hung up, I called my parents. My dad answered the phone.

"Hi, Dad. How are you feeling?" My father had Stage III cancer and had his good days and bad.

"Feeling fine. I haven't had to use the wheelchair in weeks, and I've been back in the fields, harvesting parsnip. Slower than usual, but at least I'm out there in my favorite place."

I pictured my parents' farm, the beautiful little white house with its window boxes of flowers, the rows and rows of beautiful crops, and trees for as far as you could see. Nothing made me happier than to think of my dad out there with his beloved dogs, pulling up eggplant and stacking them in the wheelbarrow next to the cucumbers and onions and tomatoes.

"I'm dang glad to hear that, Dad. I have good news too. I'm engaged!"

I heard him gasp. Then call out to my mother with "Mayzie, hurry over here. Clementine's engaged!"

"Clem!" my mom said. "I'm so happy for you!"

"You and Zach could come up soon," my dad said. "We have to celebrate. We'll get the whole family together. You don't know how happy this news makes me. If the last thing I do on this earth is see my Clementine walk down the aisle, I'll go a happy man. You know I'm not the sappy, 'my little girl is getting married' type, but I'll tell you, Clem, having your days numbered makes a difference."

Gulp. Forget city hall. Or eloping. We had no idea how much longer he had. If he wanted to see me walk down an aisle, I was walking down an aisle.

"Tell Zach we said welcome to the family," my dad said before we hung up.

Zach came out of the bathroom, his wet hair in peaks, towel wrapped around his waist.

"My parents welcome you to the family."

"I'm honored to be a Cooper," he said, kissing me on the forehead.

"So I've been thinking—how about we get married at my restaurant? It's perfect for the ceremony and reception." I loved the interior of Clementine's No Crap Café so much that sometimes I slept there, in my office.

"Nice idea, but it's not big enough. My parents' guest list alone will be more than two hundred people."

My eyebrows shot up. "What? I thought *we* invite the guests."

"We do. But so do our parents. We can set limits and stomp our feet, but between family friends and business acquaintances, the wedding will be huge."

He reached for his cell phone. "Hey, Dad, I asked Clementine to marry me, and for some crazy reason she said yes." He smiled at something his father said. "I'll tell her. Thanks, Dad." He pressed end call on his phone. "My dad says welcome to the family too. They want to plan a party for us at the ranch."

I pulled the blanket around me, still shocked that all this had happened. A proposal, after all. Calling parents. Parties. An aisle to walk down. Happy as I was, I'd have to guard my time. "Sounds great," I said. "I'm trying to imagine any of the Jeffries at my parents' farm." I laughed, picturing Cornelius Jeffries looking around for the *rest* of the farm.

"My dad would be very impressed that your parents raised three children on that farm and make a decent living. He'd love the place." Zach headed over to the walk-in closet, which was the size of my "bedroom" in the tiny apartment I shared with Sara. "He'd love talking business with your parents."

I leaned up on an elbow. Yeah, right. "Only after I sign a prenup."

He put on a dark gray shirt. "I'm not asking you to."

I raised an eyebrow. "Is this your attempt at reverse psychology?"

He laughed. "Like that would work on you? I'm not asking you to sign anything, Clem."

"Well, I want a prenup. I want it clear to your family that I'm marrying you because I love you, *despite* your money. As you know, your bajillions are the only thing about you I don't love."

He lay back down beside me, wrapping his arms around me. "Let's get you moved in here."

Zach's money was annoying, but his beach house? Less annoying. The kitchen blew my mind every time I cooked for the two of us. Three stories. Floor-to-ceiling windows everywhere. Wraparound decks. Views that calmed me. And it came with Charlie.

But moving in with Zach meant leaving Sara. I didn't know what I'd do without her in the bedroom a foot away, hogging the bathroom, and keeping me up too late every night with hilarious stories about Joe, the boyfriend I loved to hate. If only she could move next door.

⁓ ◎ ◎ ⁓

An hour later, when I opened the door to my apartment, Sara and Joe were sitting at the kitchen table and chowing down on Big Macs, a big box of McNuggets with dipping sauces, two supersize orders of fries, and large drinks.

Hey, I don't judge. Sara could eat whatever she wanted. But she'd been on my Skinny Bitch diet—which basically meant no crap—for months and was feeling and looking amazing. Her skin glowed. Her blue eyes sparkled. Her energy was through the roof. The past few weeks, though, Joe would drive her home from late nights at the studio where they worked with greasy, chemical-laden sludge disguised as dinner from various fast-food joints. The next morning she always woke up with a hangover.

"I thought you weren't going to be home till tonight," she said, pushing the container of fries toward Joe as though they weren't hers, then slid them back over with a smile. "You *did* say it's no big whoop to cheat once in a while," she added as she popped a fry into her mouth.

"Treat yourself to this," Joe said, wiggling his eyebrows and slurping a long fry from the table. He leaned close to Sara with it dangling from his lips. Ew.

They each bit that fry until there were only lips, then they made out.

I hated Joe's guts, but I loved Sara. If he made her happy, then I was happy. And it was sort of thanks to him that I'd been able to open Clementine's No Crap Café at all. Six months ago, I was a contestant on his ridiculous cooking show, *Eat Me*, and I won the live cook-off challenge (Joe "Steak" Johansson vs. the vegan) with my kick-ass eggplant Parmesan. As if the trash-talking slob could have beaten me with his soggy version and slab of cheese.

I won twenty-five thousand bucks, and Sara got herself a great job as a kind of cohost, since she'd dished back to Joe as good as he gave it out when she'd been my assistant at the cook-off. Sara had come home from work on her first day with the moony smile that told me she'd met someone. When she said that someone was Joe, I wanted to throw up, but he was her type. If I didn't hate him so much, I'd admit he was okay about a quarter of the time, in my humble opinion, and Sara did like her men with some edge.

Sara and I had been best friends for five years, ever since we'd met as sweating pretzels in the hot yoga studio we lived above. She'd spent years working annoying temp office jobs while she tried to make it as an actress, but because she used to be forty pounds overweight, she'd rarely gotten callbacks. Now, she'd lost twenty-two pounds, had her dream job on TV every week on a hit cooking show, and had never been happier. A lot of that was thanks to Joe, who seemed crazy about her.

While they got busy on another long fry, I looked around the kitchen where I'd sliced and chopped and baked for the past five years. I'd miss this place. If it weren't for this apartment, I wouldn't have met Zach.

I glanced at my sparkly ring and shoved my hand in my pockets. I wanted to tell Sara my news in private.

Joe got up, shoved a handful of nuggets in his mouth, then bent down to give Sara another slurping kiss. As he headed toward the door, he eyed me and said, "For fuck's sake, Clementine, you're too skinny. Eat a sandwich. I'm making chicken-fried barbecue ribs for tonight's taping. Sara will bring you home a rack."

Ignore him for Sara. Ignore him for Sara. Ignore him for Sara.

And I wasn't "too skinny." I'd been working my ass off since Clementine's opened, maybe literally, but I ate a ton of great food, as always.

I rolled my eyes at him, which made him smile and sock me on the shoulder. Finally, Joe was gone.

"I gained three pounds this week," Sara said, eyeing the two empty containers of large French fries. "*Fourteen* since I met Joe. Being with him is making me gain all my weight back." Her frown turned upside down. "But you know what's amazing? He doesn't even care. I told him he was going to undo all my hard work if he kept encouraging me to pig out with him, and he said, 'Good. I like my women with meat on their bones. More to love.'"

As I said, a quarter of the time, Joe was a pretty good guy. I liked that he liked Sara no matter what.

She gathered up her long, curly, brown hair and twisted it up into a knot at the back of her head, sticking a pencil through to secure it. "But I don't want to undo all my hard work. I kicked my own ass to lose those twenty-two pounds."

Sara used to eat bacon double cheeseburgers and family-size bags of Doritos and drink two liters of liquid Satan, aka Diet Coke, a day.

I wanted her back on the Skinny Bitch plan, but I wasn't going to preach. When she was ready, when she felt like crap daily and started getting zits on her chin, she'd be back.

"It's okay to have McDeath's once in a while, Sara. But a small fries. A single cheeseburger instead of a Big Mac. That's how you'll keeping losing weight, if you want."

"You're not grossed out that I'm eating animals? I try so hard, but I keep cheating."

"You're dating Joe 'Steak' Johansson. I knew it wouldn't be easy for you to stay a vegan."

"You're dating Zach 'the Silver Steer' Jeffries and you don't eat prime rib."

"Yeah, but I've been a vegan my whole life." Which was true. My parents were hard-core vegans, and except for the one summer when I graduated from high school and thought tasting freedom included eating dead animals and gross, chemical-stuffed food, I never veered. Being a vegan was who I was, part of me, like having blond hair and hazel eyes. But newbies struggled, and that was okay. I just had to remind her it didn't have to be all or nothing. Because Sara was an all-or-nothing kind of chick.

She was also my best friend, and I was dying to share my big news with her. We'd been through everything together. Breakups. Getting fired. Insane bosses. Crushing disappointments. And the flip side—amazing, hilarious times.

I went to the kitchen and poured us two mimosas. "Here."

Sara took the glass and held it up. "Oooh, what are we celebrating?"

"This." I held out my left hand.

She grabbed my hand and stared at the ring. "Oh my God. Clem!"

"I know! I can't believe it myself." I'd tell her the whole story later.

Sara hugged me tight. "I'm so happy for you, Clem." Her blue eyes got all misty, and I laughed. "Now I'm sobbing. Can you imagine how I'll be at the wedding? A puddle on the floor."

"Will you be my queen bridesmaid? I have to ask my sister to be my matron of honor. But you can lord over whoever else I ask as a bridesmaid."

She hugged me again. "Of course I will. Me, a bridesmaid at the society wedding of the season," she enunciated in an English accent.

"Ha. I've barely given two thoughts to the actual wedding. I'm just so happy!"

She hugged me again. "My Clem, getting married. I'll never forget that day Zach rang the buzzer after you barged in on his meeting. You could feel the sparks in the air when you opened the door."

I loved remembering that day.

She sipped her mimosa. "So how long do I have you before you move into Zach's house?"

I bit my lip. I didn't know how to tell her I was moving out ASAP. "The rent's paid through the end of the month, and I'll pay next month's also. But I'm kind of dying to move in with Zach right away."

"If I had the choice of living in this dumpy closet with sloping floors or moving to Zach's palace, I'd be out of here in a heartbeat."

I squeezed her hand. "You'll find another roommate fast."

"No one like you, but, yeah, I'm sure I will."

I hugged her again. "I'll miss you, Sar."

"That diamond is bigger than your face," she said, looking at my ring.

Twenty minutes later, as I was getting ready to leave for the restaurant, Zach called.

"My mother's dying to meet her soon-to-be daughter-in-law. She, her stepdaughter, Keira, and my siblings and I will be coming to your restaurant for dinner tonight around seven."

I froze for a split second. Was that the slightest nervous flutter I just felt? Zach's mother had a serious reputation as difficult to please. And I wanted to please her. This was my future mother-in-law we were talking about.

"I'll make their orders myself," I said, going over tonight's specials in my head. I hoped Dominique would order the fettuccine carbonara. I'd worked for months to perfect my sauce. "Can't wait to meet your mom and her stepdaughter."

I knew Zach was a lot happier since he and his mother had started talking again. They'd never been close, not even when Zach had been a kid. His mother had been a flighty jet-setter—still was—and regularly missed birthdays and holidays with a "Now, darling, don't pout. We have right now!" There had been some kind of huge blowout a few years ago, something Zach refused to talk about, but apparently his mother had made amends or had tried to, and now she and Zach met for lunch or dinner every couple of weeks, working on repairing their relationship.

My future mother-in-law. Even when I was imagining all of Zach's relatives as my own, I'd completely overlooked Dominique Jeffries Huffington. Now that she was being all nice and motherly and wanting to meet her future daughter-in-law, we'd get along great. It would be like having a second mom.

I could practically hear Sara laughing in my face at the notion of that too.

7

Clementine's No Crap Café, between a
Pilates studio and a popular new bookstore, gleamed in the
bright California sunshine. The large front window, stretching
across the entire width of the restaurant, was framed by gorgeous burnt-orange curtains pulled back on each side, CLEMEN-
TINE'S NO CRAP CAFÉ stenciled in gold across the glass. Even back
when this space was just that—an empty space with so much
potential, I knew it was special. The shops up on these blocks of
Montana Avenue made for great street traffic. And the cool art
deco office building across the street, which housed a production company, a holistic-health center, and an in-demand acu-
puncturist, had brought me sick business from the beginning.

I was about to pull open the silver front door when a couple, heading toward the bookstore next door, smiled at me.

"This place good?" the guy asked, peering in through Clementine's window.

"It's fabulous, Check out the menu." I pointed at the shadow boxes containing the menus on the side of the door. "Complimentary glass of wine awaits your first visit. Tell the waitress Clementine said so."

I left them eyeballing the menu and headed inside, through the small, inviting waiting area with its cushioned bamboo benches made for me by my brother, Kale, and past the host's station, where I could still smell the lingering fragrance from the beautiful flower arrangement Zach sent every week. The rectangular main dining room was spotless, the wide-planked wood floors gleaming, the polished wood tables, round, square, and rectangular, shining. The pale persimmon walls showcased several local artists' work—large abstract paintings that complemented the Bali-meets-California vibe. Every time I walked through the restaurant, I felt that I was home.

I glanced at table five, on the far side of the window. The large, round table, under a low lit antique chandelier I'd found during a road trip to New Mexico with Sara last year, would be perfect for tonight's special guests—Zach's family. My soon-to-be family.

In the kitchen, which smelled amazing, my staff was prepping on the specials.

"Wait a minute," Alanna said, her hand poised on her knife and an onion. "What is that glittering on your finger?"

They all stopped what they were doing and looked at my finger, which I wanted to hide behind my back. Too late.

"Okay, here's the deal. Yes, I'm engaged, but in this kitchen, I'm a chef, not some bride-to-be. So let's go over tonight's specials and—"

"You wouldn't deny us an excuse to crack open a bottle of champagne, would you?" Alanna asked. For someone who wanted to celebrate, she was eyeing my ring with something like horror in her eyes, as though the ring would turn into an eight-armed monster and attack her. What was up with that?

"One sip for everyone and then back to work," I said. "Drunk cooks mean burned plantains."

Gunnar opened a bottle of champagne, and we clinked our glasses. I was true to my word. One sip and then I got everyone prepping the samples of the specials for the staff meal at three o'clock. Tonight was fettuccine carbonara, Jamaican jerk tofu with baked plantains, which Zach loved, and chickpea curry over basmati rice.

Alanna kept looking at my ring while she cut and peeled plantains. One false move and she'd cut off her finger. "Okay, fine, I'll tell you," she said out of nowhere. "My boyfriend gave me an ultimatum on Friday—right before I came to work. That's why I was such a mess. Either we get engaged or he'll find someone who actually wants to marry him. I'm just *not* ready, though. But I don't want to break up, either."

Ah. Now the glances of horror at my ring made sense too.

"How'd you know you were ready, Clementine?" Alanna asked.

"Good question. I guess I said yes because I know he's it for me, regardless of how busy I am."

Gunnar rinsed basmati rice in a silver colander. "He's probably not it for you, then, Alanna. Dump the poor schlub and move on."

"But I do love him," Alanna said. "I'm just not ready for marriage and all that. What is the big rush to get married? So what if I'm thirty."

"You're just not that into him," Gunnar said, stirring the rice. "If you were, you'd want to marry him. It's like chef said. Her dude is it for her. That's all she needs to know."

"Maybe I'll be ready next year. Or the year after," Alanna said. "Right now, being *here* is the most important thing to me. Working my way up to executive chef one day. My boyfriend hates when I say that. He keeps saying, '*I* should be the most important thing in your life.'"

"What a whiny wuss," Gunnar said.

"You're not ready and *that's* the thing you need to know," I said, sautéing the vegan pancetta for the carbonara sauce with crushed garlic and minced onion. Mmm, it smelled amazing.

Alanna sliced the batch of plantains, brushed them with oil, and laid them on a baking sheet. "I know. I just don't want him to dump me."

"Maybe *you* should dump *him*," Gunnar said. "Put him out of his misery. If you really loved the guy, you'd want to marry him."

Not necessarily true. Though it sometimes was. Who the hell knew? Timing was everything.

"See what you started?" Alanna asked, wrinkling up her face at my ring. "Let's change the subject before I start throwing chickpeas at Gunnar for his annoying honesty."

Gunnar's expression softened. "Sorry. So who's on tofu?"

That got us back to work on the samples, which did double duty as our staff meal and a tasting for the waiters, so they'd be able to answer questions about what was scrumptious and what they liked better, in their humble opinions, and what was spicy or not. With Alanna, Gunnar, and the McCann twins hovering around my sauté pan, I went over the steps for making my new carbonara sauce, which the *LA Times* had said last week was "deliciously indistinguishable from the one-hundred-fat-gram version." My version: ten grams, and worth every one.

The waiters arrived at three, and we sat down to the staff meal, everyone taking a little bit of everything. The three waiters were dressed in their uniforms: black pants and silver T-shirts with the No Crap logo, a tiny platter of vegetables in batik. The kitchen staff wore the same under their chef jackets.

"VIP coming in tonight," I announced, taking the serving bowl of fettuccine from Alanna and adding some to my plate. "My fiancé's mother. Her stepdaughter, Zach, and his siblings are all coming too. I hear his mother is a foodie, so I'll make her order. Who wants the table?" I directed to the waiters. "Zach's a great tipper."

No one raised a hand. I eyed Finn, secretly my favorite of the waitstaff. He was a great waiter—patient, friendly, smart, and fast, and he knew the menu inside out. He was also incredibly good-looking, which got him insane tips.

"Oh, fine, I'll take it," Finn finally said. "But if I trip and spill jerk tofu on your future stepmother's head, you can't fire me."

By 6:55 p.m., the restaurant was so busy that I barely had time to look out into the dining room to see if Zach and his family had arrived. Every table was taken, except for the big, round one by the window, with its special RESERVED placard. The specials were selling like crazy, as was the always-popular harvest pizza.

Even with one eye on the huge silver clock on the wall, one hand stirring the fragrant pot of Jamaican jerk tofu, and the other hand working a *sofrito* of onions and garlic sautéing in olive oil, I couldn't help but close my eyes and breathe in the delicious aromas of the kitchen. The ginger, limes, cayenne, and bit of maple syrup in the jerk sauce wafted up from the pot in front of me. I had to remember to bring home some of the jerk tofu for Sara—she wasn't crazy about tofu but loved jerk seasoning and called it Jerk Joefu.

"They're here," Finn said, coming into the kitchen. "Matteo just sat them."

The infamous mother had arrived. I glanced around for a spare hand and spotted Evan McMann helping Gunnar chop; I waved Evan over to stir my pots and headed over to the *out* door, which had a small window.

I didn't have a perfectly clear view of table five across the restaurant, but I could see Zach pointing at the menu and saying something to his brother, Gareth, who sat beside him. Seated on Zach's other side was a striking woman in her late fifties, tall, regal, and quite beautiful. Dominique Jeffries Huffington. She wore a black, sleeveless dress, a lot of bling, and the kind of small, weird hat you'd spot at a British royal wedding. Sitting next to her must be the stepdaughter, Keira, no older than twenty-one, twenty-two tops, also tall and thin, with long, ombré-brown hair, small, dark eyes, a long, sloping nose, and a wide, glossy mouth. The features combined to make her almost beautiful. Next to Keira was Avery, Zach's fraternal twin.

"I wonder how long you have to be on best behavior," Gunnar said as he slid vegetable chunks on a skewer for blackened kebabs. "Family isn't family until you're arguing over stupid crap at Thanksgiving."

"Hold the fort and wish me luck," I said to the kitchen staff.

I pushed through the swinging door of the kitchen into the main dining room and headed toward table five. A smattering of people waited in the open lounge area on the padded benches. The juice bar was full of those waiting to be seated, ordering from the bar menu of tapas and drinking my energy smoothie. I smiled at my guests as I walked through the room. I asked one table how the fettuccine was, and I welcomed a new table that had just turned over, signaling a waiter to refill lemon-water glasses.

As I approached, Zach stood up and took my hand.

"Mom, Keira, this is Clementine."

"I'm thrilled to finally meet you," Dominique said, grasping my hand in both of hers. "You're as lovely as everyone told me."

I beamed at her. "Thank you. I'm so happy to meet you too."

Zach looked a lot like his mother—the almond-shaped blue eyes, the perfect nose, the dark hair, and something in their expression.

"Me too," Keira said. "Congrats on getting engaged."

They were both much nicer than I expected.

Avery and Gareth stood up and hugged me. As Gareth sat back down, he said, "So what should I order?"

"I'll bet you'd like the Jamaican jerk tofu," Avery told him. "I've had it and it's amazing."

Keira was looking at the back of the menu, where drinks were listed. "I don't see Diet Coke and I'm dying for a cold blast of caffeine."

"The place is called Clementine's No Crap Café for a reason," Avery told her. "No crap."

"Is caffeine crap?" Keira asked, clearly confused.

"Diet Coke is drinkable chemicals," Avery said, saving me the trouble.

"Oh," Keira said. "I'll have a Diet Sprite or whatever, then."

"We don't serve soda," I said. "We have all kinds of great juices and smoothies and wines and beer."

"Avery, order something I'll like," Keira said.

"Well, this is such a darling little place," Dominique said, glancing around, her gaze stopping on the hipster couple at the next table.

If I weren't so focused on her, I might not have noticed the slight edge in her voice, in her expression, but *darling little place* was usually code for "shit shack." *Smile, Clementine,* I told myself. *Say thank you and get back to work.* "Thank you. Well, I'd better get back to the kitchen and let you look at the menu."

Zach squeezed my hand and I headed to the kitchen, looking back to see them all perusing the menu. Just then Dominique glanced up at me and lifted her chin, her smile . . . full of something I couldn't quite pinpoint.

The food would win her over. That I was sure of.

◠◎ ◎◡

Five minutes later, their orders came in. I'd asked Finn to note Dominique's—and was happy to see she'd chosen my fettuccine carbonara. While Gunnar prepared their salads, I helped Alanna with other orders, and when the salads went out, it was time to start on table five's dishes. I gave Alanna and Everett Zach's, Avery's, Gareth's, and Keira's orders, and I went to work on Dominique's dinner. The strips of fresh fettuccine, which I'd made in batches through the afternoon and evening, were hanging over dowels on the back counter, some dry and ready to go, some drying for later orders. I took a just-dried portion and put the pasta in a pot to boil, then started the sauce—almond milk, crushed garlic, onion, and my own months-in-the-perfecting vegan pancetta. I dipped in a spoon to taste—delicious but just slightly too thick. For Dominique, the sauce had to be perfect. I started over, and this time the sauce was just right.

With Finn's tray loaded and ready to go, I gave each plate the once-over. Perfect.

Five minutes later, Finn was back with an untouched plate of fettuccine carbonara. "Um, chef?" He set the plate down at my station. "Zach's mother said the pasta wasn't toothsome enough."

I stared at him. "Wait—what?"

"She said—"

"She took a bite of the fettuccine and said it wasn't *toothsome* enough?"

Finn backed away a bit. "Well, she waved me over and said, 'Darling, the sauce is lovely, but the pasta isn't quite toothsome enough,' and then she pushed it away."

My heart sank. The pasta was perfect. I knew it was.

Was Dominique trying to tell me that some no-name farmer's daughter who owned this "darling little place" wasn't good enough for her son? No. Why did I even go there? When did I become such a drama queen?

"Clem?" Finn said as I stared at the pasta, trying to figure out her game.

"Yeah?"

"What does *toothsome* even mean?"

"It basically means just right. Not too soft or too firm."

"Ah. I told her I would bring her another plate right away, but she didn't say anything. She just sipped her wine and started talking to the person next to her."

"Don't worry about it, Finn. I'll go out."

Never in the history of Clementine's No Crap Café, which had, granted, been open for only two months, had an entrée been sent back to the kitchen. Overcooked, undercooked, underseasoned, overseasoned—not in my restaurant. Not while I was in the kitchen—and I was always in the kitchen.

Hadn't the restaurant been written up for the second time in *LA Magazine* as the hottest new eatery in Santa Monica—for vegans *and* nonvegans? Yes, it had, I reminded myself—confident that the fettuccine was *not* the problem.

Then again, if my fettuccine couldn't wow my future mother-in-law into eating up instead of complaining, how could it be good enough for the *New York Times* reporter?

I closed my eyes and counted slowly to five, as Zenia, my Pilates teacher, had taught me. Pilates had kept me sane during the first weeks of opening the restaurant. *Breathe, Clementine,* I heard her whisper in my ear, Tibetan bowl music pinging in the background.

As I walked over to the table, Zach was looking at me with an expression that said, *Don't take it personally. This is who she is.*

How could I not take it personally, though? Even if the fettuccine sucked, the kind-mother-in-law thing to do would be to say it was delicious. Especially since this was the first time we'd met. If I were invited over to her house and she served something I didn't like, I certainly wouldn't tell her.

She'd sent back her plate.

And everyone at the table was digging in except for Dominique, who sipped her wine and had an untouched piece of focaccia on the little plate in front of her.

"Clementine," she enunciated as I came over, "I hope I didn't cause too much of a fuss. But a pasta really should be *tooth*some."

Okay, first of all, who said *toothsome* with a straight face? And second, well, shit. This wasn't how this was supposed to go.

"Of course I wouldn't have breathed a *word* if you'd made it yourself," Dominique said, barely looking at me. "But I thought you'd want your chef to know," she added in an exaggerated whisper.

"Actually, I'm owner *and* executive chef and I did make your dish myself," I said, my knuckles practically white from gripping the back of Zach's chair.

Zach turned and shot me a look that said, *Did you have to go there?*

Yeah, I did. I could pretty much be counted on to say what needed to be said. Wasn't that why he'd fallen in love with me?

A faux smile spread across Dominique's matte-red lips.

"Well, dear, even the best chefs have something to learn. You're all of what—twenty-five, Clementine? Though I must say, having your own restaurant, even a cute little place like this"—she glanced around—"is quite an accomplishment."

Even. Ha. She was everything Zach said she'd be and more. She'd looked at him pointedly as she'd said that last bit, which meant she thought Zach had funded Clementine's No Crap Café. For the record: I hadn't taken one penny from Zach. Not that he hadn't tried to foist his money on me. But I opened this "cute little place" with my own blood, sweat, and hard-earned cash.

And by the way, I was twenty-six.

"Well, my Jamaican jerk tofu is fabulous," said Zach. "And that's coming from a serious carnivore."

"Agreed," Avery said, taking another bite of her own jerk tofu. "And I know vegan food. This is the best I've had."

Gareth took a swig of his beer. "I have to admit—my burger is pretty damned good for sprout food."

I smiled at them. The Jeffries siblings were keepers, definitely.

Considering that Zach had told me that Dominique preferred caviar to just about anything else, I'd take Mommy Dearest's opinion on my precision-timed, homemade, organic pasta with a few grains of sea salt. Even if it still stung.

Keira, Dominique's twenty-two-year-old stepdaughter, wrinkled her nose at her lasagna, one of tonight's other specials. "Clementine, I wasn't going to say anything, but since we're on the subject . . . Um, I'm really sorry, but I'm not loving this

Parmesan cheese." She leaned in and whispered, "It tastes a little . . . funny."

"It's vegan Parmesan," Avery told her. "It's not supposed to taste like the stuff you sprinkle on pasta."

"Oh," Keira said, poking at her lasagna. Keira was the only child of Dominique's second and current husband. Dominique and Zach's father had divorced when Zach was a teenager. Dominique had been married to her second husband, even wealthier than her first, for sixteen years, and according to Zach, she considered Keira her own flesh and blood. "I keep forgetting what's vegan and what's not."

Avery saved me from schooling her. "Keira, vegans don't eat anything that comes from an animal, and that includes dairy, which includes milk, which is turned into butter or cheese."

I needed to get back into the kitchen before I said something that would get me in trouble. "Well, let me get started on another plate of the fettuccine," I told Dominique.

"Oh, don't trouble yourself," she said. "I had two bites, and that's really all I allow myself of overly rich food. But on the next order, remember that a toothsome pasta is neither too soft nor too firm. And, sweetie," she whispered, "the salmon walls are a bit *too* orange. A more subtle shade would work better. And the silverware could be a hair heavier. Just a hair." She smiled at me.

I had spent hours torturing the paint mixer at Home Depot to create that exact shade of shimmery persimmon. "Perhaps it's a generational thing," I blurted out.

She fixed a death stare on me. "Yes," she drawled out. "It's like I always say. Youth is absolutely wasted on the young."

Zach was staring at me with an expression that implored, *Not. Another. Word.*

I forced myself to smile and headed back into the kitchen. The moment I stepped inside the noisy, bustling space, I felt instantly more at peace.

"I will keep my mouth shut. I will keep my mouth shut," I said to my sous chef, Alanna. "I will slowly count to five."

"I won't even ask," Alanna said, sliding mushrooms into a pinging hot pan.

I counted to five. I breathed. I focused on the next orders, pouring olive oil in a pan to help my vegetable chef keep up with the demand for the roasted vegetable skewers.

"Clem? You okay?" came Zach's voice from behind me.

I closed my eyes for a second. No way would I admit—even to myself—that his mother had gotten to me. I turned around and smiled. "I'm fine. No worries. Go finish your dinner." I gave his hand a squeeze.

"Clem. You're forgetting that I know you."

"The pasta was perfect," I whispered, hating how stung I really felt. "I made sure of it."

"I'm sure it was. She's just . . . difficult. Look, you're my brand-new fiancée. She's my mother. Just ignore her when she gets to you. Don't even bother engaging. Okay?"

For a second, as I looked at Zach, this guy whom I loved

so much, I felt all the anger whoosh out of me. But a moment later, it was back.

I motioned for one of the McMann twins to take over my pan. "Zach, if she insults me, I can't just not say anything."

"You can try. For me. 'Letting it go' is how she and I manage to have a relationship. If I want her in my life—and I do—I need to accept her. When she crosses a line, believe me, I tell her."

His expression changed for a second, and I realized he was talking about the incident that had blown up their relationship a few years ago. She had crossed a line—I had no idea over what. And he'd told her. The result? They hadn't spoken for three years.

"I have to pick my battles, Clem. That means letting go of what's really just nonsense."

Letting it go wasn't in my vocabulary, though. Since Zach and I had been together, I'd listened to his stories about his mother, how difficult she was, how long it had taken him to accept that she was who she was. That meant not jumping on every misstep she made. But my motto was more along the lines of *Start as you mean to go on*.

"I'll try," I said. "But just like you don't expect her to change who she is, don't expect me to change who I am."

"I don't want you to change," he said, pulling me close. "I love you just as you are, Clementine Cooper."

"I love you too," I whispered.

"You basically told her she was old," Zach said with a rueful smile.

"I used the word *generational*," I reminded him. "Completely different."

He rolled his eyes at me, but kissed me on the cheek and headed out of the kitchen into the dining room.

I walked over to my station and took over my pans from Evan.

"Ah, fighting over food and relatives. It's like they're already family," Gunnar said with a firm chop of his knife into an artichoke heart.

8

At just after midnight, Zach and I sat on his couch, Charlie curled up beside me with his warm, little head resting on my leg. I'd taken a long, hot shower so that I no longer smelled like garlic and pancetta and cinnamon churros.

"What's that?" I asked, pointing to a huge, antique-looking book on the coffee table.

He pulled it over to his lap. "It's an old photo album from when I was a kid. I rarely dig it out, but the conversation at dinner got me nostalgic, I guess."

"What was the conversation at dinner? Besides how much your mother hated my restaurant."

"She didn't hate it. In fact, she was quite impressed by it, by you. I could tell."

"Ha."

"I'm serious. I know her, Clementine. In fact, at dinner, she said you reminded her of Aunt Jocelyn. Even though Jocelyn is my father's aunt, my mother was very close with her when she and my dad were married."

"I remind her of an eighty-six-year-old woman?"

Zach smiled. "In her day, Jocelyn was a live wire. The first to try something new, anything daring. Tell her no, and she'd find a way to accomplish it. Her least favorite word has always been *appropriate*."

"I knew I liked Aunt Jocelyn. Are she and your mother still close?"

"They had some big falling out during my parents' divorce and they never recovered."

He opened up the photo album. I usually wasn't into looking at people's old photos of their family, relatives posing in front of cars on dull cross-country trips, endless shots of sunburned kids at beaches, but *this* family was going to be my family.

"Were you and your mother ever close?" I asked, looking at the next photograph, of his mother on a boardwalk in her swimsuit, absolutely stunning, even with her early-eighties, huge hair.

"Not really. I was much closer to my father."

"What was the big fight about?"

He leaned back on the couch and rubbed Charlie's belly. "She came between my sister and her boyfriend—someone Avery really loved. The guy was a starving artist, hipster, and hippie rolled into one, and Avery was about to move with him to New York City and fund his life. My mother did everything she could to break them up."

What? Awful! "Like what?"

"Planting seeds of doubt, making up stories about a friend who had fallen into the same 'trap' of supporting a failed artist—that kind of thing. Manipulation at its worst. Avery became a wreck and all her sudden doubting started huge arguments with her boyfriend. In the end, my mother got her wish, and Avery was left with a broken heart. Three years later, she's never found anyone she loved like she loved that guy. My mother still thinks it's for the best."

Dominique was some piece o' work. "Did Avery pull away from your mother?" From what I could tell during the family dinner at my restaurant, Avery and her mother were chummy. No bad blood there. And Avery seemed very much her own person.

Zach shook his head. "She actually ended up running *to* her for comfort, and my mother was there with open arms, of course. Dominique got exactly what she wanted. The whole thing infuriated me. My mom and I had a huge argument about it, both said a bunch of stuff we regret, though half of what I said I did mean. We didn't speak for years."

Not that family discord and estrangements were a good thing, but I was glad to hear Zach had stood up for his sister, stood up for what was right. "What got you talking again?" I asked, looking at another photo, of Zach as a young boy, so adorable, holding his mother's hand, his twin sister, Avery, on the other side.

"Aunt Jocelyn. She asked me to make peace with her, said life was too short for grudges, just make peace and let live, et cetera. I realized how much it bothered me that my mother and I were on the outs, and for so long, and I decided my aunt was right. We made peace, never discussed the fight, and now we're just having a nice, superficial relationship."

"Same for your brother and sister?"

"My sister's a bit closer to her, but, yeah, same thing."

I thought about Jocelyn, that beautiful, elegant elderly woman, more full of life and energy than some slugs sitting around looking bored at Jolie's wedding while Jocelyn twirled around the dance floor. "So did Aunt Jocelyn take her own advice? Did she make peace with your mother too?"

"She said she tried, but my mother wouldn't budge."

He turned the page and laughed at a photo of his brother, Gareth, no older than five, crying in a mud puddle at a zoo.

I tried to imagine not talking to my mother. I could talk to my mother about anything. I didn't often, but I could. Back when Zach and I were trying to figure out how to have a relationship without killing each other, I'd confided in my mother, and her words of wisdom—that I'd find my way with him, that I'd figure it out—went a long way.

He closed the photo album and slid it back on the coffee table, then pulled me close against him. "So you see why I asked you to just let stuff go? Not important stuff, Clem. The *small* stuff—little zinged comments should roll off, not offend you."

I wasn't so sure I agreed with that. Why did she get to shoot her zingers? Just because she was capable of much worse? "But then doesn't what needs to be said just go unsaid forever? Are the choices really just no relationship or a very superficial one?"

"Dominique and I are both trying. Taking baby steps. She's who she is—but who she is, is my mother. She's the only one I have."

I took his hand and held it. "Okay. I'll hold my tongue. For you."

I could do that. After all, it wasn't as though Dominique would be a huge part of our lives.

My cell phone, on Zach's bedside table, woke me up. I glanced at the time. Just past 9:00 a.m. Zach and I had stayed up talking until two, and how he'd gotten up at seven and headed to his health club for an hour before work was beyond me.

"My mom just called," he said. "She feels terrible for getting off on the wrong foot and wants to make amends by planning the wedding. We don't have to do anything but show up and then take off for Bali for two weeks."

What?

I bolted up in bed, hoping this was a dream. A nightmare. But I was definitely wide-awake.

"Zach, considering that your mother and I don't see eye to eye, I'm not sure handing over the wedding is a good idea."

I couldn't even begin to imagine what a woman who'd dissed the color of the walls of my restaurant—at our first meeting—would try to get me to agree to. And hadn't Zach just shared the extent of her manipulative powers? Not that they'd work on me. But still.

"Clem, didn't you say you wanted to be engaged for years or elope because you were way too busy to plan a wedding? I wouldn't sic my mother on you if I didn't think she was in her element. She has incredible taste. The worst it'll be is too expensive."

"Zach, I—"

"It's an easy way for her to be a big part of the most important event of my life. And a way for you two to get to know each other. It would mean a lot to me, Clem."

Oh, hell.

I wanted to shout, *No fucking way.* Instead I said, "You owe me."

◦ ◎ ◎ ◦

The minute Zach and I hung up, I called Sara.

"Help. Zach's mother insists on planning the wedding. Zach and I just spent hours last night talking about how much it means to him that his mother is back in his life. It's so important to him that we get along, that she's a part of this. But she's a maniac!"

"Can't you tell her you've already hired a wedding planner?"

"She'd tell me to fire whoever it was."

"I'll think of something," Sara said. "Subterfuge is my gift."

The restaurant was closed on Mondays, but despite that *Good Morning, L.A.* was bumping my ratatouille segment until next month, I still had a packed day, starting with an interview with a local magazine, lunch with my sister, who thought the whole thing with Dominique was hilarious and some sort of karmic payback—for what, I had no clue—a trip to the farmers' market for fresh produce for the next few days, and a coffee date with Alanna to plan the specials for the week. I had no time to think up excuses or white lies or even think about my wedding for a minute.

Every time my cell phone rang, I looked in dread at the caller ID, expecting it to be Dominique. But she hadn't called once. Maybe she was off and running without even asking me what I thought. Or maybe she wouldn't be so in my face about her ideas. Maybe I'd been worrying for nothing.

"Okay, here's the plan," Sara said into my iPhone on Tuesday morning as I headed up Montana Avenue to the restaurant. "It's so brilliantly simple I can't believe I didn't think of it yesterday. Just decide what kind of wedding you want, tell Dominique, and she'll plan that, your dream wedding. Done."

"The weight of the silverware at the restaurant wasn't good enough for her. What I'd want and what she'll want are two very different things."

"Just arm yourself. Know what you want and stand firm. You should have no problem with that, Clem."

Sara was right.

Except my relationship with Zach had taught me a word I was never familiar with before: *compromise*. I was used to it now. And I liked it. I felt that I was growing up. Not everything would go my way. Caring about him meant seeing things through his eyes too. I was marrying a man who owned a steak house, for fuck's sake. I was the Queen of Compromise. I'd tell Dominique I wanted vegan food only at the wedding, she'd demand a mix, and I'd compromise. Fine.

As I was about to pass Weddings by Francisco, a bridal boutique I'd never noticed before even though it was next door to Tea Emporium, where I got my morning chai to sip on the way to the restaurant, I stopped in front of the window. My eyes! A rhinestone-studded hanger was suspended by wire from the ceiling, and flowing down was a hideously poufy, white gown with overlays and tiers and puff sleeves and a pale pink bow between the boobs. Gah. Who wore this stuff?

At least I knew what kind of dress I didn't want.

Just decide what kind of wedding you want and she'll plan that, your dream wedding. . . .

So what kind of wedding *did* I want? Eloping to Vegas or Paris was out since it would break my dad's heart.

I thought about the bunch of weddings I'd been to in the past few months. There was my culinary school friend's Disneyland hell, with Mickey and Minnie hanging out at the reception. And the get-married-where-you-met idea, à la my sister's wedding in a bookstore—definitely not big enough for three-hundred-plus guests. Besides the place where Zach and I actually met—the space where he'd almost opened his steak house, across the street from my apartment—was now an expensive hair salon. Forget lotus position in the woods; Zach couldn't even get into lotus position. Jolie's wedding was beautiful, but I'd been to so many beach weddings in the past year that it was getting old.

The only place I wanted to get married—Clementine's No Crap Café—was a no go.

I had no idea what I wanted. Nothing sounded right. Not the beach, not a hotel, not some random space.

Yet I still had a feeling that no matter what Dominique came up with, my answer would have nothing to do with "letting it go."

Maybe I was impossible too.

9

As I walked up Montana Avenue, I had nightmare visions of standing on a little step stool in the fitting room of some horrendous bridal salon with the five seamstresses hemming and pinning my huge, heavy, white princess ball gown, and Dominique Huffington barking instructions at them: "Tighter, tighter, tighter, until she can't draw breath!"

With a half hour to spare before I had to hit my office in the restaurant, I ducked into the Tea Emporium for a chai and to decompress and focus. Not on Zach's mother. Or the wedding. I settled into an overstuffed chair and pulled out my notebook, flipping toward the end where I'd written, *New York Times Travel Section: Ideas for recipes.* I had six weeks to settle on five dishes, in addition to five appetizers and three salads, to serve the reporter, who was bringing three friends. Based on her and their reactions to the food, ambience, service, locale, and me, Clementine's No Crap Café would either make it into the article—or not.

Butternut squash in garlic sage sauce. My kick-ass chipotle chili. Mediterranean lasagna. My award-winning blackened-tofu stir-fry. Maybe the roasted-vegetable napoleon—in phyllo. Perhaps my spaghetti and wheatballs, which Gunnar's little girl liked better than the "real" thing. The bruschetta, which no one could resist.

"Hey, Clem."

I looked up to find one of my favorite people, Alexander Orr, fellow vegan chef, standing in front of my chair with a blueberry muffin in one hand and a take-out cup of something in the other. He looked fresh scrubbed and cute as always with his tousle of sandy-brown hair and dark brown eyes and constantly popping dimples. I stood up to hug him. "Got a sec? You're just the guy I need to see right now. The *New York Times* might include my place in a piece on vegan restaurants and I have to get in. What five dishes would you make?"

He mock-stabbed himself in the heart. "I should have known you'd be my competition."

Of course Fresh got the call too. It was one of the best vegan restaurants in LA. Alexander had replaced me as sous chef after his asshole boss fired me last summer for supposedly adding butter to a food critic's ravioli.

"Wow, congrats. Can I bribe you to take a dive the day the

reporter comes to Fresh?" He raised an eyebrow as though I could possibly be serious. "Kidding. May the best chef win."

"Or both of us." He sat down across from me. "Because guess who'll get promoted to chef if the reporter includes Fresh in her piece? Emil's hardly ever in these days because he and his wife are trying to adopt a baby, so his head's there instead of in the kitchen. My lucky break. I'm still sous chef, but I'm acting chef. If I get Fresh in, Emil promised me the job."

Fuzzballs. That kind of sucked. Figured Emil—my former bosss—would tie Alexander's promotion to publicity for the restaurant. The guy was a classic douchecanoe. I hated Emil's guts for firing me, though he'd ended up doing me a huge favor by forcing me to kick-start my own business. I wanted Alexander to get his totally deserved promotion, but I wanted Clementine's No Crap Café in that article.

"No one, not even me, can come close to your blackened-tofu stir-fry," he said, getting up. "But you didn't hear that from me. Emil would bloody have my head."

I smiled. Alexander was one cool dude.

"I miss hanging out with you, Clem. I haven't seen you in weeks."

"Me too. I'm always at the restaurant."

"Who isn't?" He went completely still for a second. "Whoa. Is that what I think it is?" He was looking at my diamond ring.

"Just got engaged Saturday night."

I caught the slight slumping of his shoulders. "Zach's a lucky bloke," he said in his usual earnest, wistful way that always made me want to hug him. I'd met Zach and Alexander around the same time, had everything in common with Alexander and zippo in common with Zach. But kissing Alexander had had the same noneffect as kissing my own brother on the cheek. And kissing Zach? Firecrackers. Marching bands. Sappy love songs.

"If you want to try out some recipes on me, you can count on me to be honest," he said. "Even if we're competition."

"Same here."

Then he took one last look at my ring, bit his lip, and was gone.

By noon, my ring was covered in pastry dough and lemon zest as I made blueberry pies for tonight's dessert. I was my own pastry chef, so it was just me in the kitchen. ABBA's "Take a Chance on Me" blasted from the iPod dock, six pies were either done or baking, and I was ready to move on to the other dessert specials, the baklava and mini vanilla-chai cupcakes.

For me, baking was as good as yoga and hikes with Zach and Charlie on the trails up in the mountains. The process unwound tight muscles, unclenched overworked brain cells. I always got the hard stuff out of the way first, so I'd attended to the books and inventory and paperwork in my office for the first hour, then I'd put on my apron, turned up the iPod, and forgot all about future mother-in-laws, soulless weddings, and competitions that might get a good friend fired and got baking.

I'd just measured out a cup of agave nectar for the baklava when ABBA's "Fernando" was cut off. Startled, I turned around, and there stood Dominique and her stepdaughter, Keira.

"Sorry to startle you, Clementine," Dominique said, "but that music was so loud you didn't hear us arrive."

What were they doing here? They looked so out of place in the kitchen.

Dominique wore a bright white sundress with the usual pound of bling, her huge pearl-white sunglasses atop her head. "Keira and I were shopping in the neighborhood and took a chance you'd be here. Zach says you practically live here."

"That's true," I said, covering the agave nectar.

Dominique was staring at my ring, coated in dough. She looked horrified. "Of course, we haven't discussed the actual date for the wedding, but if we're to secure the places I've jotted down, I'll need to give my personal assistant the information."

Personal assistant—perfect. I could boss him or her around and wouldn't have to deal with Dominique herself. "We haven't even thought about a date yet. Zach and I are both so busy that—"

"Yes, well, we'll likely choose the date based on availability," she said, whipping out her iPhone, white like her dress. "I'm thinking the Beverly Hills Hotel, Chateau Marmont, or the

Peninsula. I've taken Shutters off the list, since Jolie got married there, and of course you'll want an original venue."

No on all the above.

And I loved how it didn't even occur to her to ask me what I was thinking.

"Dominique, Zach and I haven't even discussed where we want to get married. For all I know, we'll elope to *Vegas* and get hitched by an Elvis impersonator." I said that only to piss her off a little.

She visibly shuddered. "Darling, no one is eloping. I'm so delighted to plan the wedding." She stepped toward me and lowered her voice. "As you may know, Zach and I have had our differences, and we've only started to get closer recently. It means the world to me to help plan the most important day of his life."

Dang. Was she being decent?

Keira, in bright red, skinny jeans and a long, flowy tank top, was making "aww" faces at her.

"Clementine," Dominique said, "I can see you've got your own style. Of course I'll take that into account. I'm having one of my favorite designers sketch some dresses, including, of course, the Kate."

"The Kate?" I repeated.

She rolled her eyes. "Kate Middleton." At my blank stare she said, "Future queen of England."

Hadn't I seen Prince William and Kate Middleton's wedding photos on the cover of a zillion magazines? Kate's dress had sleeves. *Long* sleeves. "I can tell you right now that my wedding dress will not have *sleeves*."

"Open mind, darling. *Both* of us."

I raised an eyebrow and she smiled. Which meant she was trying. I could hear Zach's voice asking me to try too.

"Okay," I finally coughed up, in the name of compromise. "But I get veto power. Everything gets run by me."

She stared me down. "It's usually others running things by me."

I stared right back but couldn't help the smile. "Yeah, me too."

"I like you, Clementine Cooper. You're your own woman. I think we'll get along just fine."

Ha. But maybe.

She and Keira then made small talk about the cooling pies and asked what I was making. I was in the middle of explaining baklava, which neither of them had ever had, when Dominique cut me off.

"Oh, Clementine, you just reminded me of the real reason we dropped in. I have a huge favor to ask."

Okay, what was this? I should've known—buttering me up with that "you're your own woman" stuff?

"Based on the other night," Dominique began, "I could tell you needed some additional help in the kitchen, and Keira is thinking of getting involved in the cooking world. I've tried to tell her that culinary school or, God forbid, catering, is not for her, but you know twentysomethings—they think they know it all and sometimes you have to let them make their own mistakes."

Good God.

"So some real-world experience would really help her come to that quicker. She could chop vegetables or what have you."

Dominique had to be kidding me. "I'm sure she'd get more versatile experience at Zach's restaurant. The steak house serves everything. Clementine's No Crap Café is limited to vegan fare."

Keira was biting her lip. "Well, actually, I tried working in the Silver Steer a few weeks ago and lasted for three hours. It's not like Zach's in the kitchen—or there at all—to help guide me. And the head chef? He's vicious! The whole staff is. They screamed at me within the first five minutes because I chose the wrong size sauté pan. Honestly, they scared me to death. And they knew I was the owner's stepsister too."

"That's the way restaurant kitchens are, though," I reminded Keira. I'd worked for some real assholes along the way. Even the nice executive chefs were assholes with orders coming in on a busy night. Screaming, cursing, name-calling, getting singed literally and figuratively. That was life in a commercial kitchen.

"But, Clementine," Keira said, "when we toured *your* kitchen after dinner last night, everyone was so nice. The kitchen staff was actually having a good time—while they were very busy. They were being so nice to each other. It was so . . . Zen."

It was true that I ran my kitchen the way I'd always wanted kitchens I'd worked in to run—a team that helped each other out, not screamed in each other's face or with a head chef that threatened to fire you every ten minutes.

Keira "Oh, I always forget cheese comes from a cow" Huffington in my kitchen?

"I'll work really hard," Keira said, practically batting her eyes at me.

I was about to say no as nicely as I could when my cousin Harry's face popped into my mind. A month ago, Harry, five minutes out of business school with his MBA, asked if I could put in a good word at Jeffries Enterprises. Twenty-six-year-old Harry Cooper was my favorite cousin and had been living three thousand miles away for the past five years when he belonged in LA so we could hang out. Of course I put in a good word, which meant calling Zach and telling him to give Harry a job or else. Harry was now a junior accountant and took his job so seriously that he worked till eight every night and spent weekends in the office.

What was that annoying cliché? No good deed goes unpunished? It stood before me in the form of Zach's stepsister. How could I tell Keira no when Zach told my cousin yes?

A test. A simple test that even Dominique couldn't talk or pay Keira's way out of. I grabbed a tomato from the wire basket on the counter. "Slice this tomato," I told her.

With deep concentration, Keira stepped up to the counter, took the tomato, and eyed the knives on the board. She chewed on her lower lip for a second, then picked up the wrong knife and sliced way too thick.

Sorry, babe. Cousin Harry has an MBA. You can't slice a tomato. "I'm sorry, but I really don't have the time to train someone right now. A new restaurant needs experienced staff."

Dominique pulled me over. "Please," she whispered. "You'd be doing me a huge favor. She'll see in a few days that working in a hot kitchen isn't for her. And, darling, seriously, if family won't, then who *can* we turn to?"

Oh, please.

"I'm a really fast learner," Keira said. "I'll work my butt off, I swear."

Oh, hell.

I thought of myself right around the time I'd met Zach, when I got fired from Fresh because a jealous wannabe sabotaged me. No one would hire me. No one.

"I won't let you down, Clementine," Keira added. "If you'll just give me a chance."

I felt kind of bad for Keira, being set up to supposedly prove Dominique right.

I thought of Cousin Harry, so happy in his charmless cubicle. Damn. And hadn't I planned to hire another pair of hands anyway?

It took forever for me to spit out my next word. "Okay. Your first day will be Wednesday." I waited for her to complain that it was too soon. But she didn't. "And you'll have to start training yourself today until then—I want you to watch a bunch of videos on how to properly cut vegetables." Still no objections. She was nodding quite seriously. "I'll send you some links. Study them and practice. You'll have to prove yourself in the kitchen. If the staff thinks you got hired because you're related to Zach, it'll create problems. You have to show your stuff."

"Swearsies!"

I almost burst out laughing. Gunnar would never forgive me.

Dominique beamed.

⟨ ◎ ◎ ⟩

While the baklava was baking, I texted Zach.

Me: *Your stepsister is suddenly a kitchen trainee.*

Zach: *She's a sweetheart.*

Me: *She can't slice a tomato.*

Zach: *She might surprise you.*

With what else she couldn't do?

10

When I got back to my apartment around eleven that night, Sara wasn't home, so I went into my bedroom to start packing up. Last night, Zach and I had spent hours in bed talking about how living together would be, how we wanted it to be. I'd never lived with a boyfriend before. I liked the idea of coming home to him every night—obviously, since I was marrying the dude. And his place was huge, so there would be a lot of space. Plus, Charlie the beagle. Always Charlie. God, I loved that little dog.

I was working on packing up my makeshift closet when I heard the door to the apartment open and slam shut. Uh-oh. Sara was pissed about something.

I came around the divider that separated my room from the living room. "What's up?"

"Hey," she said, dropping down on the red velvet couch and resting her feet on the coffee table with a thud. "Joe and I got into a huge fight. We sniped at each other throughout the last half of last night's show, which the producer loved, of course. The audience went wild for it. Assholes. And then the fight continued the second we both opened our eyes this morning. I finally left and went to Greasy Spoon and ate a bacon and American-cheese omelet with home fries and then had a slice of cheesecake. So now I feel like double crap."

I sat down beside her and put my feet up too. "What was the fight about?"

"You know how he abuses contestants on the live cook-off show? Yelling at them, berating them, egging on the audience to make fun of them and shout out insults?"

Yeah, I knew. I had been on the receiving end of his abuse on live TV. I couldn't believe the cable network he was on let him get away with all the crap he pulled. But the show was sickeningly popular. Sara had been hired as his "good" sidekick to speak for the contestants who were too rattled to give it back to him. He called them losers who couldn't cook their way out of an Easy-Bake Oven; she shouted back that he probably couldn't even spell *little*. On and on for an hour, twice a week.

"Well, he went way too far with this poor guy who obviously was falling apart," Sara said, "and then the guy burned his hand and forearm pretty bad on the oven rack and left in the middle of the show to go to the ER. So Joe yells, 'The dork forfeits!' And was saying all this crazy stuff, and I just stood there, looking at him, like, who the hell are you? The guy had to go to the *ER* and it's like he didn't even care. All night, I kept waiting for him to call the hospital and see how he was—even to ask his assistant or the producer how the guy was. But he never even mentioned the contestant again."

"Did he see your side of it at all?"

She rolled her eyes. "He told me I was being too sensitive. That it was about ratings and it was the whole point of his show. It really bothered me. It's one thing to be snarky. It's another to be a total asshole."

"Isn't he always like that?" I blurted out before I could stop myself.

She leaned back against the couch cushions. "I guess. But he's worse on camera. Sometimes, when it's just the two of us, when he's not cracking jokes, he can be a good guy. But he's always making fun of people on the street, you know? Like the jerks who used to make fun of my weight. The other day, he was laughing at some kid with bad hair and a shirt two sizes too small for him. Not to his face, but still. A *kid*."

Just listen. Don't say a word against him. She just needs to vent. She'll figure it out for herself on her terms, on her time.

"Part of me wants to break up with him. But part of me still really likes him. Why do relationships have to be so impossible?"

"I know exactly what you mean."

"Ha. Like you have any clue, Clem. You're tall and blond and thin and gorgeous. Everything's always been easier for you.

I lost twenty-two pounds and everything is still the same. *I'm the same.*"

"Yeah, I hope so. I never want you to change. No matter what you weigh, you're awesome and my best friend."

"But everything was supposed to be perfect. I lost weight. I have a great job in TV. On air, no less. I have an interesting boyfriend. So why does everything still suck?"

I slung my arm around her shoulder. Everything didn't really suck. She just had stuff to figure out. And my life wasn't easy and never was. Before I could say a word, though, her cell phone rang and she lunged for it in her bag. *It's Joe,* she mouthed.

I could hear him talking because he did everything on high volume. He was saying something about having called his assistant to ask if someone had checked on the burned contestant, which of course they had, and the guy was fine and wasn't going to sue.

"Maybe there's hope for you yet," she said into the phone with a smile.

"I wish he *would* sue," I heard Joe say. "That would trend on Twitter and get written up everywhere. Great for publicity."

Sara sighed into the phone.

Then I heard Joe say, "Gotta go, hot stuff."

Sara put the phone back in her bag. "Shitburgers, maybe there isn't hope for him."

The opposite of Joe "Steak" Johansson? My cousin Harry Cooper, who had invited Zach and me to lunch—his treat—this afternoon at the Santa Monica Pier to celebrate our engagement. We were meeting at the Mexico Ole food truck.

"I hope Zach won't think that's cheap of me," Harry had said on the phone twenty minutes ago. "But I won't be making the big bucks until I pay my dues and that'll take a while."

"Mexico Ole has the best burritos in LA and everyone knows it."

"Does Zach know it? He probably never ate food from a truck in his life."

"Oh, trust me, I've introduced Zach to all sorts of new wonders. He thinks it's really nice that you invited us out to lunch. Zach's not a snob."

"There are about twenty layers of bosses above me before you get to him. Tell you the truth, I'm surprised he even agreed to go out to lunch with me."

"Zach is a great guy. Yeah, he's megawealthy and runs Jeffries Enterprises. But he's the best."

"He's gotta be if he's marrying you," Harry had said because he's awesome. "See you at twelve thirty, Clem."

Now, Zach and I sat at a picnic table as Harry, who would always look wrong to me in a suit and tie, carried over our orders. The sight of Harry Cooper always made me smile. Tall and lanky, half-surfer-dude with his slightly long blond hair, and half-corporate with his shiny black shoes and wire-rimmed glasses, Harry would always remind me of *home*.

Zach opened up his steak burrito (meat: ick) and took a bite. "So, Harry, how's life on the second floor?"

Jeffries Enterprises had its own gorgeous art deco building, five stories, on Santa Monica Boulevard. Zach's office, twice the size of my apartment, had the top floor with a wraparound balcony.

"Great," Harry said, opening up his black-bean quesadilla. "I'm learning a lot. Reviewing profit-and-loss statements, writing reports on how to maximize profits. Jeffries Enterprises is having a great quarter."

Zach smiled. "I'm glad to have you on board."

I've always been glad to have Harry on board, ever since we were little kids. Harry, son of my dad's brother, was an only, and since we're practically the same age, we were inseparable growing up. He was too old to play with my brother, Kale, who's five years younger. And my sister, four years older, couldn't be bothered with a tagalong boy. But Harry and I were kindred sprits. His house was two miles up the road, and he'd always walk or bike over and spend a good hour talking shop with my parents from a numbers standpoint, interested at age twelve in the cost of doing business. After he jotted down notes in the little journal he carried everywhere, we'd walk into the fields with the dogs and talk for hours about everything—our parents and their rules, school, the opposite sex (Harry always had girls chasing after him), each other, what we wanted to be and do with our lives. I loved that although Harry came from a family of meat eaters, he'd been so horrified by my stories of what happened to chickens and cows and goats at some farms that he'd become a committed vegan at age ten and had never veered—even though I had that one summer when I graduated from high school. When he'd gone to college in New York and then stayed there for graduate school and his first job, I missed him. Just six weeks ago, he'd finally come home to California and settled in Santa Monica. Zach had agreed to look at his résumé, and only if he had the chops would Zach hire him. Harry had the chops.

While I ate my grilled seitan-and-veggie burrito, Zach and Harry bored me to death talking business. After fifteen minutes, though, Zach crumpled up his wrapper and three-point-shot it into a garbage can.

"I'm sorry to have to cut lunch short, but I have a meeting I couldn't change at one fifteen. Thanks for lunch, Harry." Zach kissed me on the cheek. "I'll call you later, Clem."

"Let's see a movie tonight," I said. "Harry, want to join us?"

"Oh, I can't tonight," Zach said. "But you two go ahead." He nodded at Harry, gave me a brief smile, and walked away.

"Everything okay?" Harry asked, looking at me pointedly.

"Everything's fine. He's just incredibly busy. I've barely seen him the past couple of days."

"You still mad at me for having to hire his stepsister?" Harry asked, taking a bite of his burrito. He knew it was a trade of sorts.

"Yes. I'll be mad at you for that forever."

In just a few hours, Keira Huffington would start at Clementine's No Crap Café as a trainee. I had no doubt her first night would be a total disaster.

⁓ ⊙ ⊙ ⁓

According to the big silver clock on the wall, it was 3:59 p.m., which meant I had exactly one minute left before Keira would arrive like a wrecking ball and destroy my kitchen.

I'd told her to arrive at four, an hour later than normal, and there she was, coming through the swinging door of the kitchen exactly on time, which was a good sign. Her hair was in a low ponytail, she wore the white, skinny jeans and the Clementine's No Crap Café T-shirt I'd told her to wear, and her usual blingfest was gone, except for a delicate silver chain around her neck with a dangling *K*. The necklace would have to go. No one wanted to be eating his or her French onion soup and find a silver initial in a spoonful.

The kitchen staff were eyeballing the newcomer.

"Everyone, this is Keira Huffington, our new trainee. She's going to spend a few days at different stations, learning the ropes. She'll start on vegetables tonight."

Gunnar perked up. He could use an extra pair of hands. Once he saw how she used a knife, though, he might go from his usual seething calm to screaming in her face. How she handled it would determine if she stayed or went. If she could handle Gunnar pissed and didn't quit in twenty minutes, she might work out.

"Hi, everyone!" Keira said. "I'm really, really, really excited to be working with you all!"

Okay, no one liked eagerness. But ten minutes from now, when she'd be racing around the kitchen, grabbing produce from the refrigerator or taking too long to deliver something one of the cooks wanted, sweat pooling on her forehead, she wouldn't have the breath to talk so much.

I went over the specials, detailing the ingredients. Burrito sampler—four-bean, grilled-veggie, and seitan-guacamole with a side of Spanish rice. Harvest pizza. Spicy potato curry. Every Wednesday night was the popular Souptopia, with five soup specials—chipotle split-pea, the French onion, my to-die-for minestrone, Hungarian mushroom, and curried lentil. Alanna and Gunnar and I went to work on samples for the wait staff and quizzed them on the ingredients, which I'd e-mailed to everyone yesterday.

At four thirty it was time to start prep. I told Keira to take off her necklace and stuff it in her pocket, then sent her over to Gunnar, who was about ten feet down the length of stainless steel counter from where I stood.

I could hear her trying to make small talk, something Gunnar hated. I smiled as he held up a hand. "Don't talk. Just watch. This is how I mince garlic. This is how you'll mince garlic."

"Okay!" she said perkily, and took a garlic clove from the basket. "I totally worked on this last night."

I watched her press too hard on it and mangle a clove.

Gunnar glanced at me and raised an eyebrow. He was onto her. There had to be some reason I'd hire a novice, and since everyone knew I'd just gotten engaged, Keira had "I'm related in some way to the owner's fiancé" written all over her face. "No," Gunnar told her. "Just watch me. When you think you can do it like I can, then do your own."

"Um, it's just garlic," she said with a laugh. Hint: never say *um* or that anything was *just* anything to Gunnar Fitch.

He stared at her. "So let me guess. You're the fiancé's sister or something."

"Stepsister, actually."

"What a surprise," he said, rolling his eyes.

She tried another head of garlic and knocked the basket over.

"Jesus!" Gunnar shouted. "I don't care who the hell you're related to. If you don't know how to mince garlic—after I just showed you, after you supposedly practiced all weekend—you shouldn't be here."

"So show me again. *God*," Keira yelled back.

At least she can take it and dish it back, I thought.

Gunnar rolled his eyes and grabbed the knife. "Watch."

Within an hour, Keira had pissed off everyone, including the nicest waiters after I put her on making pitchers of lemon water and the pitchers were full of seeds.

I gave Keira a break in the little alley with a half glass of wine. "I'll totally understand if you want to leave right now,"

I told her. *Please say, "Oh, thank you," and race for the door. Please.* "Tonight's been really rough on you and it's only six o'clock. In a half hour, things are going to get wild in here."

Her eyes widened. "Oh, good! I love a fast pace. So what can I help with next?"

Donkey balls.

By eight thirty, my arm felt as if it were going to fall off from stirring pots of soup. My cell phone rang on the counter. Everyone knew not to call me when I was in the kitchen unless it was an emergency. It wasn't my sister's special ringtone, which I'd set up so I'd never miss one of her calls—the last time I'd ignored a call from Elizabeth, our dad had been rushed to the hospital with complications. The phone kept ringing. Finally, I pulled it out of my pocket. Unfamiliar number. I ignored it. The person called back a second later. I ignored it again. It rang again.

Who the hell was this?

I called over a McMann twin to take over my pots and finally answered.

"Clementine, darling, it's Dominique Huffington. How's my baby girl doing? I would have called her, but I don't want to get Keira in 'trouble' for chatting on her first day."

I wanted to dump the phone in the pot of curried lentils. "Hi, Dominique. Sorry to cut this short, but we're very busy right now. I'll—"

"While I have you, let me tell you your wedding date. It'll be May seventh at the Beverly Hills Hotel. Of course, the date is important so we can plan accordingly for a spring wedding. I would have made you a June bride, darling, but June at the Beverly Hills Hotel has been booked for two years. Tomorrow I'll need you to pop by my house to look at photographs of gowns I've earmarked for the designer to do some preliminary sketches of. You may choose your five favorites."

My five favorites from a preselected group of pictures? Was she kidding? But first things first.

"Dominique, I only have five seconds to talk, and then I have to get back to work or all my soups will boil over. May seventh won't work—it's my father's birthday." My father wasn't expected to live much longer than a year, and I would celebrate his birthday with him and my family. Not at my insane wedding for five hundred strangers.

"Of course it will," she said. "You'll be together anyway."

I stirred the Hungarian mushroom with one hand and the curried lentil with the other. "Dominique, my father is dying of cancer. This is likely the last birthday we'll spend together. The wedding can't be on May seventh. No negotiation on that."

"Oh, darling. I'm so sorry. I had no idea! But, really, once you think about it, you'll see that the very best birthday present you can give your father is to see his little girl marry her prince."

Do not yell into the phone. Do not throw the phone. Take your aggression out on the French bread, which needs tearing up into pieces anyway for the French onion soup.

"May seventh is out of the question. Dominique, I really have to say good-bye now—the chipotle split-pea is about to boil over," I said, even though it wasn't. "Talk soon!" Click.

Keira flew over, holding a knife so carelessly that I motioned to her to put it down. She set it on the counter. "Was that my mom? Checking up on me, huh?" She flashed her too-white smile at me. "Oh, no, the pan I'm babysitting for Alanna is crackling!" Keira rushed back over.

"Jesus Christ, Keira," I heard Alanna yell. "Watch what you're doing!"

But it was too late; Keira had backed right into one of my waitresses, Mia, and the plate she was adding to her tray landed sideways on her uniform.

"What the hell!" Mia shouted, peeling the plate and an order of caramelized eggplant from her silver shirt.

"Sorry!" Keira said, and knelt down to scoop up roasted vegetables that had fallen.

I had to fire her.

And while I was yelling *You're fired!* at people related to my fiancé, I'd include Zach's mother as my wedding planner.

⌒◎ ⑥⌒

"You can't be so hard on people," Zach said into my ear on the phone at almost 1:00 a.m. He was away on business in San Francisco for the next three days and I already missed him like crazy. "Let them be who they are and meet them halfway."

I flipped over onto my stomach in bed, staring out the dark window at the building that had brought us together. "I'm trying. I didn't say a word of what I really wanted to say—to your mother or to your stepsister."

"Good. And you didn't spontaneously combust. You'll get used to them, they'll get used to you, and you'll find a happy medium."

Why did I doubt that?

"And, yeah, Keira screwed up her first day. You have to give her credit for not quitting. She was probably humiliated a hundred times tonight. But she'll be back tomorrow. Give her a chance."

"Can I fire your mother, then?"

He laughed. "She wouldn't let you fire her. She'd just ignore you and keep throwing sketches of twenty-foot-tall wedding cakes at you until you caved and said yes to whatever she wants."

"I miss you. My head hurts."

"I miss you too. And don't worry about either Keira or my mother. Everything will be okay, Clem. Just do what you do and let them do what they do. That's the key to life."

If only they could both do what they did really far away.

11

The next morning, I woke up in a crappy mood and no one was around. Sara had slept at Joe's. Harry was at a seminar on number crunching. My other best friend, Ty, was in Paris working as a pastry chef. I missed him. And Alexander was volunteering at his "little brother's" middle school today.

I had only one place to go when I felt this way and no one was around to tell me bad jokes and drag me out to do some goofy karaoke until I cracked a smile.

Home. My parents' farm.

Three hours in the car, headed north and blasting vintage Bee Gees, helped. So did the turn onto the long dirt driveway that led to my parents' place, their dogs, Willy and Pete, coming to greet me and running along my car until I parked.

The white farmhouse, surrounded by acres of green fields and colorful crops, was better than a double martini. I sucked in a deep, clean breath and looked all around. A few more deep breaths of the country air, a long walk on the property with the dogs, some kitchen time with my dad, and a good talk with my mother, and I'd get my mojo back.

A few hours here always worked. This was the place where I'd been through everything for the first time. The place I'd learned to cook at my father's side when I was five, handing him eggplants and carrots and garlic and watching everything he did. It was the place where I'd had my first kiss as a know-it-all thirteen-year-old. The place where I knew, without a doubt, that I'd fallen in love with Zach whether I liked it or not.

I was about to head into the house when I froze beside the orange trees. This was also the place where I'd have my wedding. Not only did I grow up in this country, so did Zach, just a half hour away. This was home for both of us. And this was where I was getting hitched.

Whether or not the wedding planner I didn't hire liked it.

If it rained, we'd set everything up in the barn, which my parents had built themselves thirty years ago. The barn was gorgeous, seriously. If I could have transported the barn to Santa Monica, I would have opened my restaurant inside it.

"Clem!"

I turned around to see my dad walking—not fast, as he used to, but walking—toward me, in his LA Dodgers baseball cap and short, green wellies, dragging a small, red wheelbarrow behind him as his dogs raced ahead of him toward the crop fields.

"You look great, Dad." I hugged him. Stage III cancer or not, he had good color in his cheeks, his blue eyes sparkled, and he was free of the wheelchair he'd been forced to use when his chemo treatments made him too weak to stand.

"You too," he said, studying me. "Though I know my girl and I can see something's bothering you."

I could never get anything past my father. He knew me better than anyone else. "Actually, something *was* bothering me, but the minute I got up here, I solved it. What do you think of me getting married right here?"

My dad grinned. "You know your mother and I would love that. Come harvest with me; you can check out all the views to see where you want to set up the ceremony and reception." He pulled the wheelbarrow effortlessly.

"Good idea." I followed toward the fields "What are we picking?"

"Mostly eggplant and zucchini. And I think the red peppers are ready. I'm making dinner for our new neighbors tonight—a family of six. When I told them I grow all the food we eat, they were skeptical, so I invited them to come see for themselves. I promised them the kids would eat every morsel of their dinner."

"You must be making harvest pizza, then." I lived on my dad's pizzas when I was a kid.

"Sure am. And blueberry pie for dessert."

"So funny that they don't believe you can actually grow all the food you need."

He nodded. "A lot of my neighbors were like that—until I invited them to dinner, and now they pay me for my wheat and fresh produce. Two families even have a standing order every Friday night for me to bring over two harvest pizzas and dessert."

"Farm to table. That's what I try to stick to at the restaurant. Buying only local ingredients from farmers' markets. Good nutrition and good for the environment."

You know all that gorgeous produce in your supermarket? Yeah, it looks good, but how long were those Maine blueberries in transit? Why buy broccoli stamped with Ecuador when you can buy it fresh a mile up the road? And did you really want to use Georgia peaches for your homemade cobbler when they were sitting on a truck for two thousand miles? Who knew what the hell they were sprayed with?

My dad could pluck some vegetables and legumes from the ground, grab some wheat from his mini-silo, grind it up, and serve the most delicious, healthiest burritos—with his kick-ass salsa—you've ever had. Straight from his farm to your table.

He wouldn't let me pull the wheelbarrow for him, but didn't seem to be short of breath or having trouble. Sometimes, such as now, when he didn't look sick, I could almost forget he had cancer. "Nothing I love more than bringing in a full wheelbarrow and deciding what to make for dinner." He smiled at me, surveying his fields.

I loved nothing more than seeing my dad out among the rows of crops: eggplant, corn, zucchini, peppers, tomatoes, potatoes, at least twenty varieties of lettuce, and every kind of bean imaginable. I plucked a peach from the old tree as we passed the barn and headed toward zucchini rows. I bit into the peach. Hellz yeah, *this* was a peach.

Suddenly, I had the wildest idea.

And maybe not *that* wild, either.

I glanced into the barn. *If I could have transported the barn to Santa Monica, I would have opened my restaurant inside it.*

Clementine's No Crap Outpost, Carlton Cooper, executive chef. Farm to table, vegan.

At thirty by fifty feet, the barn was just the right size to add a kitchen and a small office. In the dining area, I imagined long, wood country tables, where diners would eat communal style, maybe some small tables for more intimate groupings.

My father had always talked of opening a restaurant someday, but he'd never let it go past talk.

This could work. My father's dream could come true. I'd hire a small team for him and drive up a couple times a week.

Clementine's No Crap Outpost. Bloody brilliant, as my British friend Alexander would say.

I had no time in my schedule to open a second restaurant,

but I'd make time. The idea was too good, and it would make my father incredibly happy.

I'd spend some time figuring out the logistics, then get Zach's business expertise, and once I had a real plan, I'd tell my dad.

Clementine's No Crap Outpost. Hellz yeah!

Watching the faces of the Brutman family—a thirtysomething couple and their four children, who were ridiculously well behaved, I got even more juiced about the outpost. Granted, one of the kids pulled every vegetable off his pizza, and another one said the "cheese" tasted weird, but they gobbled up the farm-to-table meal, and the Brutmans couldn't stop talking about how fresh the pizza crust was, how well the soy cheese melted and bubbled, how soft and flavorful the slices of zucchini and peppers and eggplant were.

While my mother was giving Molly Brutman the low-down on the best this and that in the area, and my dad was in the kitchen with Mike Brutman and the kids, showing them how to make their own pizzas, I slipped away outside and texted Zach.

Found the perfect place for our wedding. My parents' farm. What do you think?

No answer. Not an hour later. Not three hours later.

Because he hated the idea? Because he regretted proposing? Changed his mind?

Finally, late that night, as the sound of crickets was lulling me to sleep, Zach texted back.

Agree it's perfect. Let our wedding planner know. Z

⤳ ⊙ ⊙ ⤶

"Darling, you can't be serious," Dominique said the next morning into my iPhone. "The wedding on a country farm? Three hours north of the city? I'm sure it's quaint and all, but just imagine everyone's expensive heels digging into dirt. Surely you understand it's not ideal. I've barely gotten used to losing May seventh at the Beverly Hills Hotel."

"Zach and I both agree that the farm is perfect. This place is really special to me, Dominique. It's more than just where I grew up—it's what made me into who I am. Add in that Zach grew up in the area, and it couldn't be more ideal."

Dead silence. "Well, of course I'll have to come see the venue."

"I'm driving back tonight, so if you want to come up today . . ." *Say no, that's okay, I can't, I'm busy, why don't you just put me in charge of flowers?*

"I'll be there at five o'clock."

She was as relentless as her stepdaughter. I gave her directions and went to tell my parents they were about to meet one of their in-laws. Dominique Jeffries Huffington and the Coopers in the same airspace. I could not imagine.

⤳ ⊙ ⊙ ⤶

The shiny white Lexus SUV pulled in at exactly five o'clock, and naturally, a driver in uniform emerged and opened the passenger door. Dominique, in an outfit she probably wore only to ride horses, stepped onto the dirt driveway in her shiny flat-brown leather boots.

"Oh my," she said, glancing around. "This really *is* a farm, isn't it. I thought it might be more of a farm *look*."

My parents' three big dogs came bounding over to inspect the new arrival, and the look on Dominique's face was priceless.

I laughed. "My parents raised three children on this farm— by planting, harvesting, and selling organic crops. Twenty varieties of lettuce alone."

Dominique stared at me. "That's lovely, darling, really. But you do realize that a wedding here just wouldn't work. It's simply too . . . rustic."

"Think of it as a challenge, then," I said, glancing around. "You have to admit that barn is gorgeous."

She glanced at the old-fashioned, red barn, at the orange cat sitting in an empty wheelbarrow, and tilted her head, as if trying to see what the hell I was talking about.

"Clementine, I tell you this as family." She leaned closer and whispered, "You've known Zach for what—a few months? I've known him his entire life. He doesn't want to get married here. This isn't Zachary. It may be you, but it's not him. I'm sure he agreed to have the wedding here to make you happy, but, darling, don't you want him to be happy too?"

I had to hand it to her; she was good at this. "Zach tells me the truth. If he didn't want the wedding held here, he would have said so."

She slightly shook her head as though I were a half-wit. "Darling, you're so *young*. I'm only trying to help. Think about it and I'm sure you'll come around."

Deep breath, Clementine. In and out, count to five.

Let it go, I told myself, picturing Zach's handsome face, watching his lips say those exact words. *Let it go.*

But a little part of me was busy wondering if she was right about Zach. Maybe he didn't want to get married here. Maybe a fifty-acre organic-vegetable farm wasn't exactly his dream location (if guys had a dream location) for the most important day of his life. Maybe that was why it had taken him so long to respond to my text. Maybe that was why he'd been so scarce lately.

Yeah right. Zach spoke his mind, just as I did. If he didn't want to have the wedding on the farm, he would have said so. I did know Zach. Very well.

"You have to admit, the view is stunning," I said.

She looked at me quizzically. "The view? Where?"

I laughed. "Dominique, do you see that tree line?" I pointed behind her to the far edge of the farm, where majestic evergreens made for a miniforest. "When the sun sets behind them, it lights up the sky in dark pink."

"Trees are a view?"

"They are."

"Well, I think I've seen enough. We'll discuss this once you've had some time to think this through. Talk soon, darling." Then she got back into her car without even meeting my parents.

This had to be good news. When she heard that my mind was made up, she'd fire herself as wedding planner for sure.

12

Via phone, Zach had assured me that, yes, he did want to get married at the farm, and that his mother would not only accept it, but get over it, even if she wouldn't get over herself.

I didn't believe it. I hadn't heard a word from her in days. Which reminded me that I hadn't heard much from Zach in the past few days, either. He'd extended his business trip, but he always called and texted throughout the days and nights when he was away. Even when he wasn't. What was going on? Maybe he was just busy. But he was never too busy for me. Something felt . . . wrong.

On Sunday morning, while I was in the kitchen, drinking green tea and making a list of what supplies I needed for tonight's specials at the restaurant and then a possible menu for the Outpost, my phone rang. I lunged for it, hoping it was Zach.

Dominique.

"Clementine, I've been thinking. You're absolutely right. A wedding at your parents' little farm is a challenge. And one I accept. I'll need pictures of the grounds, from every angle. By tomorrow so that I can get started on my vision."

Zach must have had a few words with her.

"Our vision, right?" I said. "I like beautiful too. But earthy. Natural. Simple."

Silence, but only for a moment. "Of course. Our vision. But you just leave everything to me."

Ha. There was no *our* in *you just leave everything to me.* "Just one thing, Dominique. Less is more."

She let out something of a laugh. "No, darling. Less is always less. Bye now."

With the click, I chucked my phone on my bed, imagining a three-piece classical band hovering by every table. She'd probably figure out a way to block the trees.

The thought of tables got me thinking about the Outpost again, a farm-to-table restaurant right in that beautiful red barn. I envisioned the menu, how the tables would be decorated. I was mentally listing ingredients for a vegetable harvest soup when I heard the front door open.

"Clementine! Tell me you're home!"

I went around the glass-brick divider and found Sara beaming in the kitchen.

"Now it's my turn to make mimosas because guess what?" She was barely able to contain the huge grin on her face.

"What?"

"This!" She held out her left hand. On her finger was a diamond ring. "I'm engaged too!"

What? But she wasn't even sure if she *liked* Joe. "Sara, I'm so surprised!"

"I know! Me too. Joe and I were chowing down on ribs in the insane barbecue sauce he makes—I know, you're grossed out—and he looked at me and said, "Sar, we're so good together. You get me. You know how to deal with me. Let's do it."

Romantic, I thought, trying not to be too judgy.

And didn't she just say a few weeks ago that she didn't want to be "next"? That she'd join a nunnery before she'd ever marry Joe "Steak" Johansson?

"And I said, do what? And he said, 'Duh, get married.' I was so shocked. I mean, the subject of marriage hasn't really ever come up. But the second he asked, I screamed yes without hesitation. So I know I must really want to marry him. How awesome is it that now I don't even have to worry about getting a new roommate. I'll be moving in with Joe."

Okay, I had to tread carefully here. "I'm just surprised because the last time we talked about your relationship, you weren't sure if you—"

"Clem, he asked, I answered, and I'm happy." She turned away for a moment, staring at her ring. She held up her hand, and her smile was back. "I'm engaged!"

"I'm so happy for you." I hugged her.

She disappeared into her bedroom and closed the door. I wondered if she was going for her phone or sucking in a deep breath in the privacy of her bedroom.

Sara made herself scarce all day; she was either on the phone or racing out to meet someone for coffee, and I was in and out all day, shopping at my favorite markets for fresh tofu and interesting breads for tonight's specials. I'd barely had time to talk to her.

Sara. Married to Joe "Steak" Johansson.

Had she ever used the word *love* when she talked about him? I couldn't remember a single instance. She often said they had fun together, that he was so over-the-top all the time that he was like a nonstop comedy routine. Once she told me that he was so intense she often needed a break and was glad she could come home. But who knew how she really felt about him. Sara liked to kid and often kept her truest feelings to herself. Maybe she was deeply in love with Joe. Maybe she was truly happy that he'd proposed.

What I really thought: She was truly happy that he'd proposed. But no way did she actually want to marry him.

"I want to tell him to go screw himself eighty-five percent of the time," she'd said last week. "He's so full of himself and obnoxious—and not in a good way. But the other fifteen percent? Totally great."

Was 15 percent enough?

"He makes me feel pretty. Really pretty," she'd said.

Before she'd met Joe, her last date had been with a jerk who'd made her feel like crap about herself.

But do you love him? I wanted to ask her. She'd throw something at me, but I had to ask her.

Since I had to head out to the restaurant, I knocked on her bedroom door, but she wasn't home. On the kitchen table were at least ten bridal magazines with all sorts of colored stickies poking out of the pages. What the hell? Had some pod-person taken over Sara's body? The old Sara would have drawn mustaches on all the brides and written hysterical dialogue in thought bubbles over their heads. Like "Does this hideous gown make my brain look fat?"

She'd left a note. *Clem, you know you want to look.*

Ugh. I really did not.

In the twenty minutes Keira had been in the kitchen for her third day, she'd dropped a bushel of chickpeas, sending the tiny beans scattering all over the floor, walked through the IN door and bumped one of the waiters, in early to set up, on the forehead, and mistook parsnip for garlic, which was pretty difficult to do.

"At least I don't make the same exact mistakes twice," Keira said with her trademark big smile. "They're always new ones."

I hated that I liked her. She was a walking disaster. But she laughed at herself more than any of us ever could. And she was right. She never did make the same dopey mistake twice, only new ones. Yesterday, she'd left her hair loose, a fuck-no in the kitchen, but today she'd come in with the ombré-brown, loose waves in a secure topknot. She headed over to the produce bins to return the parsnips and get Alanna more heads of garlic for the falafel. On her way back, she bumped into Everett McMann, who was the nicest person in the kitchen and didn't yell at her. "Sorry!" she called after him. I watched her attempt to peel a garlic clove. She'd clearly done her homework the past few nights because she made quick work of the skin and separated the head into cloves. Impressive.

"So what's your story?" Alanna asked, pouring a bowl of chickpeas into the food processor, her own hair twisted into a flaming-red braided coil at the back of her neck.

"I have no story is my story," Keira said. "I graduated from college last year with a degree in communications and no idea what I wanted to do. I've tried temping in all sorts of industries to see if anything interested me, but nothing has. Until now."

"I hope you don't mean working in a kitchen," Gunnar said, one eyebrow raised. He held up a zucchini. "I need twenty-five of these sliced medium thin."

Keira grabbed a basket of zucchini and set it on the chopping block across from Gunnar. "I *do* mean working here— meanie," she added with a smile. "I've been here less than a week, but I feel like I belong here. Even if I don't know what the hell I'm doing." She stared at Gunnar. "Hasn't that ever happened to you?"

"Jesus, Keira, you're about to slice off your finger!" Gunnar yelled, green eyes narrowed at her.

"You don't have to yell," Keira said back quite calmly.

"Obviously, I do," he shot back.

"Gunnar, please demonstrate how thinly to slice the zucchini," I said, and he grumbled, but showed her, and she spent the next fifteen minutes making decent slices for my harvest pizzas.

"Clearly, you don't have a girlfriend," Keira said to him with a smile.

Everyone sobered fast. Gunnar was prickly about being divorced, about being a single father, and as far as I knew, he didn't date. He didn't talk much about his personal life. He worked, he spent time with his daughter, whom he sometimes brought into the kitchen to show her where he worked and how they made pizza, her favorite. Alanna had been trying to fix him up for months, but Gunnar always said he was too busy for a relationship.

"Oh, thanks," he grumbled. No death stare, though.

"So let me guess," Keira said. "Your last girlfriend broke your heart in a million pieces and you've sworn off women forever."

"Actually, no. I broke up with my last girlfriend. Because I'm in love with someone I can't have."

Everyone turned to stare at Gunnar, who never said stuff like that.

And Keira had gotten it out of him. She might not know a parsnip from a head of garlic, but she had some skills, and I liked how oddly brash she could be at the right time. She wasn't such a bad egg.

"So who is this unattainable woman?" Keira asked. "Wannabe model? Actress?"

"Doesn't matter," he said quickly. I couldn't help but notice that Gunnar's usual pale complexion, such a contrast against his blue-black mop of hair, had two reddish circles, as though talking about this caused him serious grief. "I don't have time for a relationship anyway. Any free time I have I want to spend with my daughter." His expression changed and his voice lowered. "And lately things with Violet have been kind of—"

The waiters came in the kitchen with the evening's first orders, so Gunnar was cut off. Usually the moment a waiter entered, I snapped to attention. But even I stared after Gunnar for a bit, wishing he could have gotten out the rest of what he'd been about to say.

Lately things with his daughter had been kind of *what*? The serious nine-year-old, with her long dark hair and huge green eyes, popped into my mind. The last time she'd been at the restaurant, she'd addressed me very seriously as chef, and Gunnar had smiled at me, clearly proud that she'd remembered what to call the kitchen's big cheese. But the two of them seemed a little . . . formal with each other, not that I had any clue about how kids acted with parents. I wondered if Gunnar had friends to talk to. He never talked about anyone except his daughter, and only in the most superficial ways. Until tonight's almost-start.

But talk time was over. Chatty chefs were distracted chefs. We had to forget Gunnar's personal life and get the soups bubbling, the harvest pizzas in the oven, and the lasagnas assembled. Still, I couldn't stop thinking about Alanna and Gunnar and Sara, how confusing their relationships seemed.

Add mine in. Lately, even I didn't know for sure where I stood with Zach. He didn't call at all last night. And when I tried his cell, it didn't go straight to voice mail. Which meant his phone was on and he'd ignored my call.

Why?

"Um, chef?" Alanna said, glancing into the saucepan at my station. "You might want to add the almond meal and herbs and get that stirred fast." I looked down at my pan, chickpea flour for the lasagna's béchamel sauce beginning to burn in the oil.

Bloody hell, as my friend Alexander would say. Now *I* was distracted. Wasn't I supposed to be on hyperfocus, making sure the restaurant ran perfectly?

The stupid mini-devil materialized on my shoulder. *Told you,* he whispered in my ear with a jab of the pitchfork.

13

By the time I walked through the front door of my apartment building, I was exhausted and smelled like a mixture of garlic and one of tonight's special desserts, key lime pie, which had sold even better than I'd expected. The little dog from apartment 1D came bounding over to me on her way out for her late walk, sniffing me like crazy. I wanted to beam myself up the stairs, take a long, hot shower, and crawl under the covers.

And not wonder why Zach hadn't called once today. Not a text. Not a check-in. Nothing.

Was this the old cold feet? Was he just crazed at work? Had he run into the ex-girlfriend he'd proposed to five years ago and fallen madly back in love with her? Had his mother made him see how wrong I was for him?

Okay, I could scratch that last one. Zach might be trying to rebuild his relationship with his mother, but she was hardly a confidante of his. And no way could he be manipulated. He was just busy. I'd call him in the morning and ask him outright what was going on.

Inside the apartment, Sara sat at the kitchen table, staring—glumly—at one of the bridal magazines.

She realized she couldn't marry Joe because she didn't love him?

"What's up?" I asked.

"I've morphed into a bridezilla. I'm making myself sick. Somehow, I love twenty dresses and want them all. I've dog-eared practically every page of every one of these mags. I love everything. Well, except this hideous thing." She pointed at a dress on the next page. "Lots of puff and bows."

"My eyes!" I said, trying to make her smile—and it worked, briefly. "But what's the big whoop about liking so many dresses?"

She slapped the magazine closed. "Turns out Joe wants to elope to Vegas. I used to think that's exactly what I'd want. I used to think big weddings with bands and videographers and five-foot wedding cakes and ten bridesmaids were ridiculous. But suddenly, I don't know. I want a real wedding, the whole thing, you know?"

Okay, I couldn't help but wonder, did she want the wedding more than she wanted the particular groom? If she *was* crazy in love with Joe, wouldn't she want to elope? If I could jet off to Vegas and marry Zach, I'd do it in a heartbeat, tacky wedding chapel, plastic flowers, and all. Not that I had any idea what a Vegas wedding was really like.

Then again, what did I know about what Sara wanted and why? Sometimes you didn't know what you wanted until it was time to make a decision. Maybe underneath all that good snark was a Sara who wanted a traditional wedding now that she was engaged. Nothing wrong with that.

I went to the fridge and took out the leftover chocolate/peanut-butter pie from last night and the pitcher of iced tea I'd made this morning. "Did you tell Joe that?"

She dug into the pie and nodded. "He said we don't need all that crazy bullshit, that we just need him and me and a justice of the peace, maybe an Elvis impersonator for the kitsch factor. I used to love kitsch. Suddenly I want some traditional wedding I would have made fun of last week?"

"Maybe it took really thinking about what you want to know what you want—or don't want."

"But Joe is totally against a big wedding. And that's what I want. Shouldn't the bride rule?"

"I hear you. As you know, my own wedding planner is against what I want."

She smiled. "I'm boring myself. I'm going to eat this pie and forget about anything to do with the 'w' word for the next two minutes at least."

"Ditto." I glanced at the pile of mail on the table, the usual stack of bills—and an oddly shaped, brown-wrapped package. It was addressed to me. "What's this?"

She shrugged. "It was in the mailbox. Who's JJA?"

"No idea." I looked at the return address. JJA, 2061 Dogwood Drive, Woodland Hills. I ripped open the brown wrapping paper to find a card, the front also imprinted with the initials JJA, and a small velvet jewelry box—much like the one I'd found in Zach's jacket, except this one was a dark red fabric. I opened it—gorgeous diamond stud earrings. At least two carats each. "Someone I don't know just sent me these incredible earrings."

Sara glanced at the card. "JJA. Who is that?"

I opened the card. Inside was a folded-up piece of white paper. "It's signed Aunt Jocelyn. Remember her? She was at our table at Jolie's wedding—Zach's great-aunt." Jocelyn Jeffries Ahern. I put the folded paper on the table and read aloud the note written on the card.

My dear Clementine,
At eighty-six-years-old, I don't know how much
longer I have. I hope to dance at your wedding,
but just in case my number is called before then,
I wanted to make sure you had these. Something
borrowed. Something old too. My grandmother gave
me these earrings for my wedding and they brought
me sixty-four years of (mostly) good luck.

I so enjoyed meeting you, Clementine. I think you're wonderful for Zachary. I also adored your friend Sara, who made me hoot with laughter at our table at Jolie's wedding.

I've been going through keepsakes and I found this old list I made right after Frederick proposed to me. All the things I wanted to accomplish and be sure of before I married. I'm embarrassed to say that I never got to check any off. Maybe you'll find the list useful. Nowadays, they call this a bucket list—well, a bucket list for getting married, maybe. I do wish I'd checked off everything on the list. I would have been more sure of myself. Some things got away from me the way things do once your life changes forever.

All my good wishes,
Aunt Jocelyn

"I loved Aunt Jocelyn!" Sara said. "She was so funny at the wedding. Joe kept telling stories about what an ass he is on TV, she didn't bat an eye. Even when he dropped an F-bomb or two. Or three."

"Ha. I remember. She's awesome." I took out my own little enamel cupcake earrings and put in the diamond studs. "Are they me?"

"Well, they do match your big honking ring. I wish I had a fairy god-aunt. Maybe Joe does. So what's on the list?"

I folded open the paper, handwritten in black pen on thin white paper, and read aloud.

1. Be sure you love <u>him</u>.

2. Close all doors to the past by revisiting (mentally or for real) any former beaus you've never been able to forget. Say good-bye once and for all—if you can.

3. Take a weekend adventure with a girlfriend who'll tell you the truth.

4. Make sure that you are the captain of your own ship—even though you and your husband will be steering together. He'll be captain of his too.

5. Make a list of all the things you love about him and all the things you don't. Figure out how you'll deal with what you don't love. (Don't put this off by waiting to cross the bridge when you come to it.)

6. What do you expect married life to really be like? Does it match his expectations?

7. Ask him why he loves you and then jot the reasons down on paper. Reread when you're arguing.

8. Are you expecting him to change once you're married? If so, return the ring or you'll be sorry.

9. Go on an adventure together. A real adventure.

10. Be sure you want to marry him.

"Wow," Sara said. "That's pretty intense."

"Yeah. It kind of makes dresses and ice sculptures seem pretty insignificant."

Sara stabbed a piece of pie. "Well, Jocelyn didn't cross off any of these ten things and she was married for sixty-four years. So I think we'll both be okay if we just focus on which of our old friends don't get to be bridesmaids."

I scanned the list again and wondered what these ten things had meant to Jocelyn. I tried to picture her at twenty years old, dancing with then fiancé Frederick Ahern at some country club and asking herself, *Am I sure I love him? Am I sure I want to marry him?* The *him* underlined, no less. And maybe she hadn't had an honest girlfriend to go away with for a weekend adventure.

What do you expect married life to really be like? Does it match his expectations? Well, shit. I'd kind of rationalized my expectations because I wanted to marry Zach. I could be engaged and deal with distractions of parties and plans and still run my restaurant—and run it well. But a week after getting engaged, Zach was suddenly distant and off on his own. And making me crazy.

I poked at my slice of pie, my appetite gone. "Her letter sounds like it's full of regrets. And according to Zach, Great-Uncle Frederick was a real drag. Obsessed with his work and too serious."

"I can't see that funny, kick-ass woman married to a drag," Sara said. "That's not right."

"Maybe he changed? Or maybe she married him for his good qualities and thought she could overlook the bad—or change him. Maybe that's why she didn't get to check anything off."

I took off the earrings and put them back in the velvet case, snapping it closed. Something borrowed and something old. I felt as if I owed it to Jocelyn to check off everything on the list.

"Be sure you love him," I repeated. "I'm sure I love Zach. Madly, in fact."

"How do you know? Yeah, yeah, you just know, you feel it. But tell me *how*."

I could feel the stupid grin starting on my face. Sometimes, when I thought about Zach Jeffries, the goofiest, mushy-gushy warmth would start in my toes and travel to every spot in my body, the *ba-bump* heartbeat the constant.

"Well, yeah, I just know. But if I had to write down a top ten list, I'd start with how he makes me feel—from crazy happy to on fire to a total gush head sometimes. When I'm with him, I feel even more *me*, if that makes sense. I feel even stronger, maybe because I know he has my back, no matter what. And whenever I go over to his house for dinner, he makes vegan food for us both. He calls my dad every few weeks to ask how he's feeling. He rubs my back after a long night at the restaurant. He tries with his mother, even though she's . . . Dominique. He's smart about people and business. He makes me think and laugh and wonder about things that never crossed my mind before. He's patient when I'd be screaming my head off. He lets me blast the Bee Gees in the car. He gives Charlie bones stuffed with peanut butter. He hired my cousin Harry when there wasn't an opening. And every time we take a walk on the beach and we're holding hands and looking out at the water, I feel *complete*."

"You complete me!" she emoted in her best imitation of the *Jerry Maguire* movie. "And let's not forget the guy eats cheeseburgers and has at least four leather jackets. If Clementine Cooper's marrying a dude who owns a steak house, she's gotta love him bad."

I did. And thanks for making me think about all that, Jocelyn. If Zach didn't call all day, instead of my wondering what was up, I'd think about those walks on the beach or how he stuffed natural peanut butter in Kongs for Charlie. I loved him. He loved me.

Next time I saw him, I'd ask him to tell me how *he* knew he loved me.

"I can skip number two," Sara said, ignoring number one entirely, I noticed. "Revisiting boyfriends past. Luckily for me, I don't *have* any old boyfriends to revisit." She cut another bite of pie, but then set down her fork. "Oh, shitburgers. Do I really love Joe?"

Thank you *again*, Jocelyn's sixty-four-year-old list. "*Do* you?"

She glanced at her ring. "Well, yeah, I do. The guy has a good side—a really good side. And if I thought about it, I could come up with a lot of reasons why I do. But sometimes I wonder if I'm supposed to feel . . . more. Nah. Love is love, right?"

"Well, there's friend love. And then there's romantic love."

She pushed her plate away, her appetite obviously gone too. "Could I romantically love a guy who'd pass a teenager on the street and tell him he had a giant booger dangling from his nose? Joe did that yesterday. The kid turned bright red."

Typical Joe "Steak" Johansson. Off camera, too. "Maybe we should both go over the list. One by one."

"I'm kind of busy," Sara said. "Doing anything else."

"Me too." I chucked the piece of paper on the table. "I guess it's a bad sign that we're both scared of a list."

"Or a good sign. It means we can mentally check *most* things off."

"Or it means we should go over the list very carefully."

"Sometimes, Clem, you're no fun at all. Are you gonna make Zach do it?"

Definitely number one, since who wouldn't want someone to run down the reasons he loved you. But number two: revisiting old girlfriends. Did I really want to have him thinking deeply about a hot French magazine editor named Vivienne?

"I'll show it to him and see what he thinks."

"Maybe I'll do the same with Joe." She pulled out her phone and snapped a picture of the list. "I'm not eloping to Las Vegas and getting married by an Elvis impersonator. I'm the captain of my own ship. Even if we're steering together." She crossed her arms over her chest.

I had no idea where this list would take either of us.

At ten the next morning, Dominique and I sat at a round table at Julia's, one of my favorite coffee shops. She'd called a couple of hours ago to say she had a full plan for the wedding at the farm and would love a "quick meeting" to show me the designs she'd had a graphic artist draw up.

"Now, of course you can make any small changes you like," she said, then took a sip of her iced Americano. "But let's keep changes to a minimum so that we don't upset the overall balance."

I didn't want to see her plans for my wedding. With Jocelyn's list on my mind, I wanted to ask her why she'd married Zach's father. Why she'd married her second husband. What went wrong the first time.

I wanted to ask her what came between her and Aunt Jocelyn.

She pulled out her iPad and put it between us on the table. All I saw was a scanned-in sketch of a huge, white rectangle. "The tent is three thousand square feet and has—"

"The tent?" The point of having the wedding at the farm was to appreciate the backdrop of nature, of the acres of crops. Not white fabric.

And three thousand square feet?

"My assistant has researched the best-quality tents, and—"

"Dominique, I'm not really into the tent idea. A canopy here and there would be fine. But a tent isn't what I had in mind."

She stared at me. "You're not expecting people to sit out in the open and look at a barn and a bunch of dirty carrots coming up out of the ground?"

Fuck yeah, I do. "The *farm* is the backdrop."

She sipped her iced coffee and took a long moment before putting it down on the table. "Clementine, darling, you have a restaurant to run. Staff to manage. Recipes to create. Add in a handsome fiancé and a wedding to fuss over and you'll be stretched so thin you won't know your middle name. You're *so* busy. Just let me handle the wedding plans and you just concentrate on your restaurant."

Talk about manipulation. "I appreciate that, I really do. But my wedding day is more important to me than I realized. My parents' farm isn't just some beautiful piece of country to me, and it's not just where I grew up." I saw the flicker of confusion on her face at the word *beautiful*. How had this woman lived on a ranch, albeit a manicured one, for so many years? "Dominique, I mentioned to you that my father has stage-three cancer. I don't know how long he has left. Do you understand what I mean?"

"Well, honestly, no." She sipped her drink. "My father was a tyrant."

Oh. The personal comment threw me. Until now she'd always kept our conversations so superficial. "Where did you get married?"

"The Beverly Hills Hotel. Both times. God, I love that place. Since the marriage didn't exactly work out the first time,

I figured I'd reclaim the hotel for myself by having my second wedding there. Now I have lunch there at least once a week."

Okay, I had to know. "Can I ask you a personal question?"

"Perhaps."

"Did you like living on the Jeffries ranch?"

She burst out laughing. "What do you think?"

"I think probably not."

"I felt like I was in exile up there. There was absolutely nothing to do but stare out the window and talk on the phone. Nowhere to shop, nowhere to eat. It was awful. But I lived there for fourteen long years. If it wasn't for our weekend place in LA, I might have gone stark raving mad."

I smiled. "I guess compromise is the name of the game."

"I don't know about that. What did compromise get me? Fourteen years of living in a place I hated and a divorce to follow. Maybe if I'd put my foot down after the wedding, insisted we live in LA and spend weekends at the ranch, maybe the marriage would have lasted. Who knows?"

"I wonder what you would have done if Aunt Jocelyn had sent you her marriage list." I sipped my herbal tea.

I was about to explain when she rolled her eyes and shook her head. "Don't tell me she sent you that thing? Do yourself a favor and rip it to shreds."

Interesting. "You know about the list?"

"That meddling old lady sent me a copy when Zach's father and I got engaged. Make sure of this, do that, know this. It's nonsense."

"How is it nonsense? The questions and checklist seem full of wisdom."

Dominique stared at me. "Clementine, do you know what happens when you start digging under rocks? Nice, solid rocks? You find dirt and worms. Why disturb a rock?"

But hadn't she done just that to her own daughter? Disturbed the rock? Made Avery look under it and see all the gook?

She took a sip of her drink and seemed to be thinking about something. "When a relationship is solid, it's solid. You and Zach, for example—solid. I can see that. I knew it before I even met you, just based on what Zach told me about you, the way he spoke about you. You can hear conviction in someone's voice."

I hated the way I leaned in. Maybe Avery had been unsure about her boyfriend, the starving artist, about moving three thousand miles away to New York City to support him. Maybe Dominique had just helped her to see how she really felt?

"But asking questions can't be a bad thing," I said.

"Only if you don't already know the answers. 'Are you sure you love him?' or whatever utter nonsense is on that list? Yes, of course you do. Are you telling me you really need to question that?"

"Well, no, not that." Ugh, how had *Dominique* managed to be right about this? "But there are some good things to think about on that list. A friend of mine is engaged to someone I'm not sure is so right for her, and—"

"Let me save you the trouble of losing your friend. Back off. I assume she's an adult and knows her own mind."

So was Avery, I wanted to shout.

"I'll tell you this, Clementine. Had I spent one minute of time going through that stupid list of hers, I might not have married Zach's father. Sure, things weren't perfect. But a lot was. In the end, I have three amazing children who would not exist had I *not* married Cornelius Jeffries. That's right—there'd be no Zach Jeffries. If it weren't for me, you wouldn't be so happy."

She sort of had me there. What could I say to all that? I held up my tea in a toast and she clinked with her iced coffee. But our solidarity sure felt shaky.

I tossed and turned in my bed in my makeshift bedroom in my apartment, checking my phone to make sure I hadn't shut off the ringer. I hadn't heard from Zach once today. I glanced at the clock: 2:00 a.m. Make that yesterday. Which would be a first since I'd met him.

Cold feet?

Fell in love with some CEO at the boardroom table on his business trip?

Realized he couldn't look into a refrigerator full of tofu and spinach smoothies for the rest of his life?

What the hell is going on with you? I said silently to the ceiling.

And how weird was it that I felt closer to my future mother-in-law-zilla lately than I did to him?

14

In the kitchen the next day, I had so much on my mind that I mistook the sun-dried tomatoes for sweet peppers. Me. The Vegan Culinary Institute graduate and executive chef. Who caught me in the nick of time before I totally messed up the mushroom stew? Keira, of all people. Annoyingly, she wasn't even smug about it. My gaffe got a raised eyebrow from Gunnar and a "Would you like me to make you a double espresso?" from Alanna.

Screw this distracted crap. It was time to corner Zach Jeffries and ask him what was going on with him until I got a straight answer.

So, despite his text to say he was back from his business trip and exhausted and planning to turn in early and he'd "check in" tomorrow, I showed up at his house at midnight.

He wasn't asleep. I could tell by the laptop and papers spread out on the coffee table in his living room that he'd been working. He also looked like hell, as much as Zach Jeffries could look like hell. His hair was mussed, as though he'd been running his hands through it in frustration. His tie was still on, but loosened and crooked.

The look on his face when I arrived freaked me out. Half relief to see me, half "Oh, it's you." Something was obviously wrong.

I slipped the tie from around his neck and tossed it on the coffee table. "Zach, something is clearly bothering you. You've been distant, you didn't call or text much when you were away. And you didn't want me to come over tonight. What's wrong?"

His shoulder stiffened and instead of pulling me into his arms, he dropped down on the sofa and ran a hand through his hair. "Nothing's wrong, Clem. I'm just very busy at work. Busier than usual."

My heart clenched. I crossed my arms over my chest. "Not buying it."

He glanced at me, then closed his laptop and stacked the papers on top of it. "We're acquiring a coffee bar in San Francisco that's been going downhill for a decade, and the logistics and numbers are taking a lot of my time. That's all. It's my new baby aside from the Silver Steer."

"Zach. You can talk to me."

He looked up at me, then stood and walked over and pulled me against him. His arms felt so good. But I knew this guy. He was holding back. I'd been with him through the opening of the Silver Steer, and he'd managed to be very present. Maybe because our relationship had been so new then. "I know I can. It's just a complicated deal. That's all."

His arms tightened around me and I felt him relax. He lifted up my chin and kissed me. "God, I've missed you. You have no idea."

My heart unclenched a bit. "So everything's okay between us? I mistook a sun-dried tomato for a sweet pepper today because of you."

He smiled and kissed me again. "Sorry. Everything is fine between us. Always will be, Clem, no matter how busy I get or distant I seem. I love you." He held my gaze. "More than anything."

"Why?"

"Why?"

"Yeah, tell me why."

He took my hand in his. "I love you because you're you. You're smart as hell, focused, driven, and you fight for what you want, what you believe in. I love you because you're passionate about everything you do, everything you are. I love you because you love your parents and siblings, and your devotion to your dad and what he's going through makes me love you even more. I love what a good friend you are. How kindly you treat your staff. How ethically you run your business. I love how beautiful you are, inside and out. I love your hair." He ran his hand through it. "I love the way you challenge me to care about stuff I don't give two thoughts to. I love how you make me feel. I love everything you are, Clementine Cooper."

"I'm glad I asked." I straddled him and wrapped my arms around his neck. "Because I love you too. So much. Let's go upstairs."

He smiled and took my hand and we headed up to his bedroom. In record time, I had his shirt and pants on the floor and Zach in bed. He slowly undressed me, kissing his way down button by button. Within a half hour, every bit of tension, of worry, of distraction, had left my body. His too.

I lay with my head on his chest, his arm wrapped around me, staring at the moon high above the Pacific. "Oh, hey, want to see what your aunt Jocelyn sent me for our wedding?" I grabbed my bag from the bedside table. I took out the little maroon jewelry box and opened it. "She sent these a couple of days ago with a card that said her grandmother gave them to her for her wedding. Something borrowed, something old. Aren't they beautiful?"

"They are. You made quite an impression on her. She really adores you."

"She totally rocks. She added something else in the package. An old list she made back when she first got engaged. A marriage bucket list. Your mom told me yesterday that I should rip it up, that's it's crap. But you just answered number seven—why you love me—and see all the good it did you?"

Zach smiled and entwined our fingers. "What's number one on the list?"

"To be sure you love your fiancé."

He held up our hands and kissed the knuckles of my left hand. "I think I just covered that. I've never been so sure of anything as I am of that."

Could you hear the relief whooshing out of me? No cold feet. No getting back together with the French magazine editor. No "you can't be serious about that holier-than-thou farm girl" from Momzilla. Just a busy streak I hadn't encountered with him before.

"Me too," I told him. "So maybe we can both cross off number two." I hoped he'd take the bait and talk about the infamous ex-girlfriend—something he never did.

"What's number two?"

"Something about closing all doors to the past by revisiting—mentally or really—any exes you've never been able to forget to say good-bye once and for all."

He nodded, eyes on the moon.

I turned on my side to face him, running my finger down his chest. "I think I mentioned a bunch of months ago that I ran into my ex—Ben. I felt absolutely nothing."

"Glad to hear it."

I waited, but he just kept his eyes on the moon. Well, shit. "So, all your doors closed on that front?"

"I'm marrying you, aren't I?" he said, giving the end of my hair a little tug. As if to say, *Now shut it.*

So just say yes, Zach. "Yes, all the doors are slammed shut. I've easily forgotten the French magazine editor who eloped with someone else after I proposed to her."

Instead he started telling me about the coffee house and its history.

Okay, he wanted off the subject of his ex? Fine. "Speaking of new business ventures, I had a great idea when I was up at my parents' farm. A farm-to-table restaurant in the barn. Clementine's No Crap Outpost. With my dad at the helm as executive chef."

He was silent for a minute. "I've read a lot about farm-to-table, and I know it's trendy, but a restaurant in Bluff Valley? It's not exactly LA, Clem. Which means no traffic, including foot. How into the whole movement are the people in Bluff Valley?"

I turned onto my side, propped up an elbow. "Who doesn't want to eat an entire meal that was grown and harvested two feet from the table? Ever notice how much produce in supermarkets comes from other countries? Do you know how long it takes to transport tomatoes from Peru? What happens to the freshness? How are local businesses and communities supported?"

"A lot of people don't care about that, Clem. And the large groups that do are here in LA. Not the country. I read a study about how often the average suburban and rural family goes out to dinner. Once every two weeks. Here in LA I eat out four nights a week. And my fiancée is a *chef*."

"Well, my father already has a customer base who'll flock to the restaurant. He operates a CSA and has over thirty members. Plus, he sells to supermarkets, health-food stores, and my mom runs his weekly table at the local farmers' market. He has a customer base. Between the buzz Clementine's has been getting in newspapers and morning TV and my dad's reputation, the Outpost has a great shot at success."

"Sorry, Clem, but I disagree. First of all, you'd be spreading yourself too thin. Your place has been open only two months and your focus should be *there*. You're just beginning to learn how to manage a restaurant, manage staff, juggle so many different responsibilities. How are you going to split your time, your focus, between two restaurants. It's a *nice* idea. But it's not a *good* idea."

Okay, I wasn't going all la, la, la, hands over the ears. Zach was a rock star as a business guy and knew what he was talking about. Except everything in me believed the Outpost *was* a good idea.

I dropped down on my back, hands behind my head, staring out at the Pacific through the sliding glass doors to the deck. A good idea, period. But a really great idea for my dad.

Who mistook a pepper for a tomato the other day? the little devil, popping on my left shoulder, asked with a stab of his pitchfork. *You've got to be kidding me. Managing Keira is taking all your time. You're gonna open another restaurant? Ha.*

Shut it, the angel said, strumming her tiny harp. *It is a good idea. Once Clem works out the logistics and presents hard numbers to Zach, he'll see it can work.*

And what if he didn't? I thought about Jocelyn's list, number four. *Make sure that you are the captain of your own ship—even though you and your husband will be steering together. He'll be captain of his too.*

Being captain of my own ship meant doing what *I* thought was right. What felt right to *me*. Even if Zach had the MBA and the business background. On one hand, we were even: we *both* owned restaurants. Yeah, maybe Clementine's had been open only two months, but the place was a success. And the Outpost would be too.

Maybe you couldn't always steer the ship together.

I stared out at the ocean, watching as the waves crashed against the shore. Were you always supposed to steer together? I mean, what if you disagreed on something and one of you went ahead with it anyway without the support of your fiancé/husband. Then what?

No idea.

Sara had an appointment at California Bride and said I had to come or else, so at nine o'clock on a Monday, when I should have been up in Bluff Valley, crunching numbers with the chamber-of-commerce lady who told me over the phone she could provide me with all kinds of interesting data on local restaurants, I was staring at so much white lace and taffeta and satin that my eyes started getting blurry. Sara's plan was to find the dress of her dreams and model it for Joe, who'd be so overtaken by the sight of her, he'd agree to a big, traditional wedding.

I could barely get my mind around the fact that she was going to marry Joe. That she *wanted* to marry Joe. But Sara in a conventional bridal shop with pouf and bows on every gown?

Something was off here that I couldn't figure out. But I would. Eventually.

"I hate that, and that, and that, and that," Sara said, sliding gowns on the rack and restoring my faith. "And this. Although the bow would cover my booty quite well. Still, no. And no. And no." She kept sliding until I heard an "Ooh, now this is gorgeous." She pulled out a white, strapless princess ball gown with beaded lace and tulle. "In a million years, I wouldn't have thought this would be my dress. I thought I'd want something modern or rock-star-ish, and this is so princess for a day I could barf. But I love it!"

I still remembered the day my sister, nine or ten years old, had to go to school dressed as her favorite monster for a *Where the Wild Things Are* celebration, and she borrowed our cousin's Cinderella dress and a tiara and called her costume complete. Half the class moms had been in an uproar.

I smiled. "Try it on."

"Joe will hate it. He'll totally make fun of it. He'd want something vampish."

"It's not *his* dress."

She grinned and brought it over to the saleswoman. They disappeared into the dressing area, complete with settees for friends and relatives and grooms and four private dressing rooms for the bride-to-be to change in. Along one antique sideboard were several veils and headpieces.

The saleswoman picked up a pair of peau de soie heels in Sara's size, and brought her, the dress, and the shoes into one of the rooms. A few minutes later, Sara, absolutely beaming, came out and stood in front of the three-way, floor-to-ceiling mirror.

"This is my dress. Everyone told me you know it when you see it. I know it. I want to sleep in this dress. I'm never taking it off. I'm still twenty pounds overweight and the dress makes my waist look tiny!"

I stared at her reflection in the floor mirror, my best friend of five years with her crazy Botticelli curls in that princess dress and something kind of unexpected happened: I got all verklempt.

"You look amazing in it, Sara. Gorgeous."

"Want to try a veil?" the saleswoman asked.

"That one." Sara pointed to a tulle veil that went perfectly with the dress. "I'll have to do something with my crazy hair."

"I love your crazy hair," I told her. Sara's long, thick, curly brown hair was her trademark. I put the headpiece on and fluffed her hair out.

"Oh my God, I'm going to stand here and bawl like an idiot. But I fucking love this!" She looked at herself in the mirror in every possible direction. She looked so happy. "Oh, wait. I don't even know how much it costs. I'll bet the veil alone costs more than a month's rent."

I found the gown's price tag. "It's three thousand, four hundred."

"Okay, what can I sell to pay for it? My car isn't even worth half that. Maybe I should just go with Joe's idea of eloping. He thinks we should wear regular clothes—our absolute favorites. Like the jeans he wears for a month before washing them. 'The real us,' he keeps saying. I'm not getting married in the gray yoga pants I wear all the time."

"I'll take a pic of you in the dress—send it to your parents. Maybe they'll offer to buy it as your wedding gift."

"Ha. My mother keeps e-mailing me links to dresses with turtlenecks. Strapless ain't her thing." Sara stared at herself in the mirror. "You must think I'm out of my mind. Princess dress. Wanting some big wedding with a cheesy band."

"You're allowed to want what you want. Let's go have lunch. On me."

Twenty minutes later, we were sitting in Turning Japanese with our tofu shuumai and Samurai beer.

"I'm so jealous of you, Clem," Sara said, scanning the menu. "You're going to have the big fancy wedding I want and it's the last thing you want."

"Ha—fancy on the fifty acre vegetable farm. I'm sure Dominique will fight for black tie anyway. I wish Zach and I could elope just to avoid the arguments about three-thousand foot tents. But I do like the idea of getting hitched with friends and family around us."

"My mom is really pushing for us to have the wedding in her marshy, mosquito backyard in Louisiana. Although she did say she'd only host the wedding if Joe promised not to curse during the ceremony."

I laughed, but she looked miserable. "Sara? You okay?"

"My parents can't stand Joe. I hate that. I mean, my parents are . . . my parents are stuck in the early eighties. But I still don't want them to hate my fiancé. Then again, even my best friend hates my fiancé."

"I do not hate Joe. I love that he adores you."

"But you don't like *him*."

"We had a crazy start on his show, that's all." Had I not beat Joe "Steak" Johansson on *Eat Me*'s live cook-off over whose eggplant Parmesan was better, I would not have won the $25,000 that had enabled me to open Clementine's No Crap Café. Then I would have hated him for sure. But a tiny part of me owed the guy.

"I thought about Jocelyn's list all night," she said. "It took me forever to fall asleep. I don't know if I can check off half the stuff on that list."

"Maybe we should skip ahead to the one about listing what we love and don't love about our fiancés. Maybe that'll help clarify something."

"I wish I was as sure as you. Zach is so annoyingly perfect."

"He's not perfect, but he's definitely perfect for me. And like you said, considering that he's a meat-eating, chemical-using environmental disaster, that's saying something."

The waiter came over and took our orders. We picked at the rest of the shuumai.

"Do you think I rushed into saying yes to Joe?" Sara asked.

I wanted to scream, *Yes*. But I wasn't sure. I did believe that part of Sara did truly love Joe "Steak" Johansson. "Can't answer that. Only you can."

She turned over her paper place mat and got a pen from her bag. She wrote *Love* on one side, drew a dividing line vertically down the center, and wrote *Don't Love* on the other side.

"In the Love category: he's six-four, two hundred fifty pounds, and makes me feel petite. He calls me *babe* and *sweet mama* and *hot stuff* all the time. He looks at me like I'm a Victoria's Secret model." She leaned closer and whispered, "When we're in bed, he looks into my eyes and tells me I'm beautiful over and over. I do love that."

"Me too."

"He treats his black Lab, whose name is Meatloaf, by the way, like a prince. He makes me crack up. He's fearless and doesn't care what anyone thinks, even the cable network." She took a sip of her beer. "Although, let's add our first entry into the Don't Love category: he doesn't care what anyone thinks. He can be a real jerk—seventy-five percent of the time. Not necessarily to me, but to everyone else. Sometimes he's a jerk to me but in a clueless way, you know? He just doesn't get it, doesn't see it." She mock pulled out both sides of her hair. "Jocelyn's list is making me crazy. Well, not the list. The stinkin' truth."

"Zach's mother told me I should rip up the list, that it's crapola and asking for trouble. But what could be bad about figuring out how you really feel?"

"Figuring out how I really feel." Sara laughed. "I'm not sure I want to know. I *want* to get married in that freaky ball gown."

Did she just want the wedding and the gown and not this particular husband? Did she just want to get married . . . because her BFF was and her boyfriend asked? I didn't know. "Maybe we should skip ahead to the one about us and not them. Adventure with a girlfriend who tells you the truth— whether you like it or not. That would be you. There are some things I need to think about too. Expectations about married life, for one."

"Ugh, who wants to hear the truth?"

I smiled at her. "It's settled, then. Road trip to the desert. We'll take the pesky list with us but not necessarily go over it unless we feel like it."

Sara clinked my glass with her own. "I won't feel like it. Which is why we should tape it to my forehead."

15

Since we were leaving for the desert on Monday morning for a two-day trip, Zach invited Sara and Joe over for dinner Sunday night at his house—*our* house, he kept reminding me. Not that it felt like *our* house since he kept coming up with excuses about why we couldn't get together, or why I shouldn't come over after I closed up the restaurant.

I wanted to talk to him again, ferret out what was up with him, but with Joe and Sara coming over any minute, I could forget that. He'd issued the invitation, which was something. At first I hadn't wanted to take off a night from the restaurant, but Alanna, who'd been back on track like her usual kick-ass self, was only too happy to take over as chef in my absence.

As Zach cooked—a huge plus on the What I Love about Him side—porcini ravioli, he was quiet.

"Smells good," I said, snaking my arms around him at the stove.

He froze for a split second. What the fuckety-fuck?

How many times was I was supposed to ask what was going on with him without sounding like some shrewish nag? And how many times was he supposed to say the same thing— everything's fine—when it obviously wasn't?

Maybe he was asking himself a bunch of questions too— without even having a list in front of him. Like *Do I really want to do this? Is she it?*

Blast this needy crap. Zach loved me. I knew that.

And just because I loved him didn't mean there weren't some things I didn't love. Jocelyn's sixty-four-year-old list made that timelessly, classically clear. I couldn't remember which number it was, but I did remember what Jocelyn had written: *Make a list of all the things you love about him and all the things you don't. Figure out how you'll deal with what you don't love. (Don't put this off by waiting to cross the bridge when you come to it.)*

What I didn't love: this sudden distance. The pulling away. The not telling me what was wrong. Was this how he was when he got stressed? Was he stressed? No clue. And I had no clue because he wouldn't talk to me about it.

Didn't love: that he didn't open up to me with what was bothering him.

Didn't love: that I asked and asked and asked and he still wouldn't tell me.

Didn't love: how he'd shut down my idea for the Outpost without seeing a business plan. Not that I had one yet. But I would in the next couple of weeks. If he didn't think something was a good idea, he eighty-sixed it without a second thought.

Which brought me back to number seven on Jocelyn's list: *Ask him why he loves you and then jot the reasons down on paper. Reread when you're arguing.*

Hadn't he told me how smart, driven, and passionate I was about what I did? Maybe I had to remind him of that. To trust me. To say, *If you think it could work, I support you.*

What was that one on Jocelyn's list about expectations? About what I expected married life to be like. I *expected* Zach to support me, even if he disagreed with me.

Right, so how was I going to deal with this . . . distance? Zach had never acted like this before. But maybe when he got stressed, he needed space or shut down or something.

Whatever was going on with him had nothing to do with me. Was he not cooking dinner for me and my friend and her train wreck of a fiancé? Did I not just catch him staring at me, in my skinny jeans and flowy top, with the kind of smile that always made me melt, as he walked to the door to let in Sara and Joe?

"Jesus H. Christ, this place is sick," came Joe's booming voice. He wore an *Eat Me* T-shirt, complete with a picture of him chowing down on a huge slab of meat. And I guessed those were the jeans Sara had mentioned he wore a month without washing, since a mustardlike stain was on the thigh.

As Zach gave him the grand tour, I heard him say that same thing: "Jesus H. Christ, this place is sick," or some variation, at least ten times. To his credit, the house *was* sick.

We sat outside on the deck, the wine poured, the salad eaten, the bread broken. "The vegan's influence, I see," Joe said with an exaggerated grimace after a bite of ravioli, upping his chin at me.

"I end up eating vegan most of the time when I'm with Clementine," Zach said. "No complaints. But nothing beats a good steak."

That got a good eye roll from me.

"Damned straight," Joe said. "The other day, on the live cook-off, we had this loser vegetarian on. I'm telling you, this dork's complexion was so pasty I offered him five hundred bucks to eat one meatball just to get some iron into him. Seriously, I thought he was going to pass out from lifting the cast iron pan." Joe let out one of his trademark snort-laughs.

"I'll bet he won, though," I said.

"Yeah right, Vegan Girl. I *crushed* him in the taste-off vote. The dipshit didn't get one vote for his vegetarian chili. I swear he started crying. His own mother was in the audience and started yelling at me for humiliating her son. Like I told him to get up on national TV and make an idiot of himself?"

Sara was covering her face with one hand from sheer embarrassment at the story. "I tried to help the guy out, but the audience had turned on him early on in the show. Once the mother starting yelling, the audience began chanting, 'Mama's

boy! Mama's boy!' It was awful. He ran out after the next commercial break."

Zach's eyebrow went up. "I guess you have to come on
strong, take it from him and dish it back, like Clem and Sara
did when they were on the cook-off."

"Exactly," Joe said. "That's why I'm marrying this fiery chick.
She tells me off all the time. I love it."

As Joe went on and on about another contestant he'd tried
to destroy on TV, a soldier recently back from Afghanistan
who'd been calm and cool while working on the barbecue-
chicken cook-off until he slammed a left hook into Joe's gut
and then walked off set, I watched Sara cringe.

She didn't look like a woman in love. She didn't look like a
glowing bride-to-be. She looked as if she wanted to run off the
set of her life.

But every time I saw her slightly shaking her head, her gaze
would go to her ring, and then she'd try to redirect Joe to normal conversation about a movie they'd seen.

Maybe I would tape Jocelyn's list to Sara's forehead. That
way *I* could see it.

⁓◎ ◎⁓

Sara and I were so sick of talking wedding, guys, and lists that
we banned all mention for the road trip to Palm Springs. We
blasted the Red Hot Chili Peppers, sang at the top of our lungs,
and two hours later pulled into the drive of our swanky hotel,

right on Palm Canyon Drive, which was lined with twenty-foot-tall palm trees, boutiques, art galleries, nightclubs, and restaurants.

We were an hour early to check in, so we left our bags in the car and headed out to the hotel's back deck for their all-day happy hour in the glorious sunshine. Since it was only two o'clock, we practically had the place to ourselves, except for a couple who held hands across the table, leaned across to nuzzle noses, and didn't look away from each other's eyes once.

"Okay, normally that couple would make me stick my finger down my throat," Sara said. "But you know what? Joe and I kinda get like that. I don't mean just staring at each other with googly eyes, but we get caught up in talking so much and laughing our asses off that we never even notice who's around us."

Huh. Zach and I were like that too—usually.

"Hey, I can cross that one off Jocelyn's list," she said. "About what my expectations of marriage are. *That's* what I expect—talking, laughing, hanging out. Like us. But with the bonus of great sex."

My grandmother once said to me and my sister, *Let me tell you something right now, girls. Don't expect a husband to be like a girlfriend. That's how a marriage lasts.* We'd been in the kitchen at my parents' farm, working on a vegetable soup from produce from the back garden, and our grandmother Lucille was shaking her head and muttering every few minutes about her daughter-in-law, my cousin Harry's mother, who'd moved into the finished basement at Lucille's farm because her husband ignored her, even when she busted out the sexy lingerie. Elizabeth and I kept saying, "TMI, Grandma! TMI!" but she'd kept on muttering about how Harry's mom expected to be treated like some kind of a queen.

"Why the hell shouldn't she?" Elizabeth had said as she'd peeled her millionth potato for the soup.

Grandma Lucille seemed to realize suddenly she'd been letting loose to her daughter-in-law's two teenaged nieces, and she'd said, "Well, she should and she shouldn't. But for God's sake, let me tell you something right now. Don't expect a husband to be like a girlfriend. That's why we *have* girlfriends."

"I'm going to expect the f-ing world," Elizabeth had said. And judging from how incredibly satisfied she was with her life and six-week-old marriage, I'd say she'd gotten it.

Every now and then over the years, Harry would mention that his mother had packed a suitcase and moved downstairs. Last I heard, she was back upstairs.

I didn't expect Zach to act like a girlfriend. But I did expect support—especially based on what he knew to be true of me: that I could run a restaurant and make it a success. That I would put 1,000 percent of myself into it—without letting anything slide at Clementine's. Did I not have a strong staff at the restaurant? I could count on Alanna and Gunnar to hold the fort while I was at the Outpost. I *could* make it work.

But did that mean he was supposed to yes me to death even if he disagreed? Hellz no. But shut me down? Also hellz no. Shut me out? *No.*

Just as I was about to tell Sara about Grandma Lucille's pronouncement to see what she thought, a waiter came over with a bowl of edamame, which I always appreciated, and took our orders of two appletinis. Then a group of people, eight or ten of them, suddenly appeared on the grass on the other side of the fence separating the deck from the open space. They all stood with their eyes closed and one hand touching the bark of a tree.

Sara's right eyebrow shot up. "Are they communing with nature? They look like morons."

"Do men in suits commune with nature?" I asked, gesturing at the uptight-looking dude in a striped tie. Next to him, with her arms practically wrapped around the tree, was a woman in three-inch heels.

What the hell were they doing?

A tiny redhead dressed all in white walked up and down the grass. "Don't open your eyes," she said in a loud yet soothing voice. "Just visualize."

As she neared our table, her hands clasped behind her back as she observed her whatevers, Sara said, "Can I ask what you guys are doing?"

The redhead smiled at us. "This is my Visualize Your Future seminar. You see yourself doing what you want most of all and it helps ground you."

"What's the tree about?" Sara asked.

The woman stretched her arms over her head and then brought them down slowly to her sides. "Just helps steady you, something decades old and rooted in the ground. Would you like to try it?"

"Go ahead," I said, shooting Sara an evil smile as our waiter set down our drinks.

Sara, game for anything, stood up, took a bracing sip of her appletini, and headed over to one of the trees. She stood near the woman in the three-inch heels and stuck her hand on the bark, grinning at me.

"Close your eyes and visualize yourself doing what you want most," the redhead said. "What that truly is."

Sara closed her eyes. She kept her hand on the tree, and I saw her shoulders relax.

A minute later, the leader clapped her hands. "All right, everyone open your eyes. You are forever changed. You're a person who knows what he or she wants, and now you're going to list the steps to make it happen. Let's head inside."

Sara called a thank-you over to the group leader and sat back down. "You know what I visualized?" Sara said to me. "Myself with a regular role on a sitcom. The funny sidekick. The hilarious BFF. Maybe even the star. Same thing I've been dreaming about since I moved to LA five years ago. What else is new?"

This was great. She hadn't visualized herself walking down the aisle in a princess ball gown to Joe dropping F-bombs at the other end of her parents' backyard. She saw herself fulfilling her longtime dream.

"What's new is that I haven't heard you talk about that in forever. You've been working on *Eat Me* for six months, and before that, you were focusing on commercials as a way into the business."

"The sitcom just wasn't happening, though. But can't you totally see me as the hilarious, inappropriate best friend next door?"

"Yup. I can also see you as the star."

"Well, at least I'm on TV, right? Even if it's not exactly what I'd planned."

"So do the next part and list the steps."

She took another sip of her drink. "Wasn't it cheesy enough to think deeply while touching a tree?"

I pulled out my little notebook that I used to jot down recipes and shopping lists. "Here. Write down three ways to get yourself on a sitcom."

She took the notebook and pen. "Hmm . . . I could try to get an agent now that I'm actually working. *Eat Me* is pretty popular." She scribbled. "And I could ask my friend who's a production editor to make a fifteen-minute compilation of my best clips, my funniest cohost moments."

"Perfect."

Her eyes lit up. "And I could take an acting class. It's been a couple of years since I even bothered." She popped an edamame in her mouth. "You can skip this little exercise since you already *have* everything you really want. Bitch." She shot me a smile.

"You mean like my fiancé's mother asking if we could 'spray something to ward off bugs' at the farm? And my new unfire-able kitchen trainee who dropped a block of tofu on the floor the other night and also annoyingly saved me from making a big mistake with my mushroom stew? And then there's my fiancé, who's been kind of . . . something."

"Kind of what?"

Kind of un-Zach-like. Last night, I'd stayed over, and instead of hanging out in bed and watching old *Seinfeld* episodes, Zach had disappeared into his home office for over two hours. I'd found him hunched over his laptop, his expression grim.

"Zach?" I'd called from the doorway. But only Charlie glanced up at me from his little dog bed beside Zach's desk. "Zach."

Finally he'd heard me. "I just need about a half hour to go over a few reports. Boring numbers. Go ahead up." His attention was back on the laptop.

He'd finally come upstairs to bed two hours later, kissed me on the cheek, and turned over.

How were you supposed to get your fiancé to open up to you when he wouldn't?

Figure out how you'll deal with what you don't love. (Don't put this off by waiting to cross the bridge when you come to it.)

"Distant," I told Sara, thinking about how exactly I *was* going to deal with it. "Not around. Even last night, when you and Joe were over, he just wasn't himself—and he hasn't been for more than a week. I can't put my finger on it. He keeps telling me everything is fine, but I know him. He's backed off. It's subtle, but I've definitely noticed it."

"He's probably just insanely busy, Clem."

"That's what he says."

This morning, right before Sara and I had taken off for Palm Springs, I'd texted him a quick *Leaving for the desert. Love you.* It had taken him hours to text back a blah *Ditto.*

An hour later, after I'd checked in with Alanna about how things were going at the restaurant, Sara and I, in bikinis, sunglasses, and slathered in sunblock, were lying on chaise lounges by the pool under the hot, sunny sky. As Sara polished her toenails a sparkly blue, I was half reading and half trying to think about wild mushrooms. *Trying* to think because I kept thinking about Zach instead.

Cremini, shiitake, black trumpets, golden chanterelle. Yes, think mushrooms, Clementine. Think work, the restaurant, specials, recipes. Perhaps a mushroom sauce over pappardelle, one of my favorite pastas. I could do a night of pasta specials, offer little plates of five different pastas.

Sara whipped off her sunglasses. "Holy crap, that guy looks exactly like Gil Gilmore."

I put down the hardcover of *Essentials of Restaurant Success* and followed her stare to a good-looking guy in his midtwenties climbing out of the pool, dripping wet. A few other women were ogling him too.

"Oh, wait," she said as he and his P90X abs passed us. "False alarm. This guy's eyes are brown. Gil Gilmore had the bluest eyes I've ever seen, like electric blue."

"Who's Gil Gilmore?"

Sara put her sunglasses back on and lay back down. "I told you about him. The guy I was in love with during college. He lived in my dorm all four years and I tried to be hilarious and make him fall in love with me, but he always looked at me like I was on drugs. I wonder what he's doing from nine to five now. Probably some master of the universe like Zach."

"Google him. Maybe he's a used-car salesman with a beer gut and a comb-over."

"No way. He'll be hotter than ever." She sat back up and slid her glasses on top of her head. "Sometimes, when Joe's being a real jerk, I do find myself wondering what became of Gil, if I should track him down just to get him out of my system. See him so I can finally forget about him. You know what I mean?"

"I know exactly what you mean. As does Aunt Jocelyn." But as I'd told Zach, when I'd run into my ex-boyfriend of two years, out walking his yellow Lab and looking gorgeous as always, instead of the dagger-in-the-gut feeling I used to get when I saw Ben Frasier, who'd dumped me out of nowhere for a wannabe-model barista, I'd felt zippo.

At least I could check *that* one off Jocelyn's list.

"What if seeing him again doesn't get him out of my system, though?" Sara asked, taking a sip of her bottled water. "What if I see him and fall for him all over again?"

"Maybe that's why Jocelyn put it on her list." I pulled the list from my bag. "'Close all doors to the past by revisiting—

mentally or for real—any former beaus you've never been able to forget. Say good-bye once and for all.'"

"Wouldn't I be *opening* a door?"

"Everything is information."

She whipped out her phone. "Googling." She clicked the little keyboard. "Holy butterballs. Gil Gilmore *is* a car salesman! Brentwood BMW. He lives so close to us!"

Maybe she'd take one look at Gil Gilmore and realize an unrequited college crush had been stronger than her feelings were for Joe. Or maybe she'd feel nothing and wonder why she'd been so in love. Either way, Jocelyn was a smart cookie. Sometimes you had to know if you *could* say good-bye. And if you couldn't . . . "Let's go test-drive something on our way back."

Sara grinned.

◦◦◦

In a showroom of many slick-looking salesmen, I picked out Gil Gilmore in two seconds because of the eyes. Sara wasn't kidding about the electric blue. He had almost-black hair, so the eyes stood out.

"Swoon," she whispered. "He looks exactly the same but older."

While I feigned interest in a brand-new, metallic-red Z4 convertible roadster, Sara sidled up to Gil, who was finishing up with a couple. Before she could launch into her "You look so familiar" spiel, he stared at her and called out, "Omigod, it's Sara!"

Her face lit up with surprise. "You remember me?"

"Who wouldn't?" He reached out to shake her hand. "Wow, you are so awesome! Guys, look, it's Sara from *Eat Me*. We love that show. Man, the way you took down Joe the other night when he was killing that guy on the Italian-sandwich throwdown— epic." Three slick-looking sales dudes came over to shake her hand, and one asked her to sign the back of his business card.

"I try," she said, clearly enjoying the attention. "But, you know, you look familiar to me. Hey, wait a minute." Pause. Deep thinking. "Wait a minute. Did you go to Cal State? Baxter Hall dorm?"

"Yeah! You too?"

"Sara Macintosh. I had the sickest crush on you."

He seemed to be trying to remember. "Wait a minute. Were you that girl who used to walk up to me all the time and tell me a joke?"

"Yes!"

"Yup, now I remember. You know what's funny? I had a crush on you back then but I was kind of intimidated by you."

"By me?"

"I never got any of your jokes. I thought you were too smart for me."

"I do have a brilliant sense of humor."

"Too funny. I was kind of shy back then. I remember really liking how brazen you were."

She grinned. "I'm even worse now."

He smiled back. "Well, if I wasn't happily married with a two-year-old, I'd ask you out for old times' sake."

"I'm engaged, Don Juan," she said, holding up her left hand. "So even if you did, I'd have to say no."

"Well, it's good to see you again, Sara. My wife will be so impressed that I not only saw her favorite celebrity but that I actually *know* you. Did you want to test-drive that roadster?" he asked me.

Sara made a show of looking at her watch. "I wish we could, but we just stopped in to look. We're kind of in a rush."

She took one last look at Gil Gilmore and then we left the dealership.

Back in my car Sara said, "How insane is that? All those years, all this time, I thought he thought I was a big fat loser. And he liked me back. Not that I give two figs now, but it's just freaky how you can be so deluded." She stuck her feet up on the dashboard. "Huh. Makes me think."

So she had been able to say good-bye. Did that mean she did love Joe? Or that time had taken care of an old crush? "About what?"

"About what else I'm letting get away. Like my supposed career. I'm getting recognized for being a snarky cohost on a cooking show, but that's not acting. I fell into it by just being myself. That's the opposite of acting."

"Still pretty cool, though."

"Yeah, it is. But it's not what I want. I want to be an actress—it's all I've ever wanted. I want a regular role on TV on a sitcom. I want to make people laugh."

"So let's head home. Look at the list of stuff you wrote up

about what you need to do to get what you want and make it happen. Would you actually quit *Eat Me?*"

"If it interfered with going on auditions, yeah."

"How do you think Joe would take it?"

"I don't know. He can be really supportive. But sometimes he's like a caveman."

"Zach too. He always thinks he's right."

I thought about how he'd spent an hour trying to get me to agree to raise the price of my soups, which were seven bucks for a good-size bowl. Zach charged thirteen at his steak house and thought I should do the same. But if some fool wanted to pay $37 for a piece of bloody meat, of course they'd fork over thirteen bucks for bland French onion with croutons and a slab of thick cheese. Overcharging for lentils and herbs wasn't going to bring back customers. Good soup at a reasonable price was.

He was that adamant about soup? I'd have to make my business plan beyond solid to turn his "not a good idea" into a "do it, Clem."

"Did you hear from him today?"

Stab to the heart. Stab stab. "Just a text. He's thinking of me. He misses me." I shrugged.

"Well, it's not like he *didn't* say those things."

Why didn't that make me feel better?

16

When I arrived at the restaurant on Wednesday, the kitchen was spotless, and Alanna had left the books in perfect order on my desk. But when she came in at three, she looked as if she hadn't slept in days.

"Hey," she said with a sigh as she put on her chef's jacket.

This couldn't be good. Had the boyfriend made good on his ultimatum? "You okay?"

Before she could answer, Keira arrived, as animated as Alanna was lifeless.

"Guess what?" Keira said. "I'm pulling a Clementine! I'm going to be a contestant on *Eat Me!*"

I almost choked on my chai. "How'd that happen?"

"I called the producer, told him I worked for the vegan chef who took down Joe 'Steak' Johansson and that she taught me everything I knew. And that I could whip his ass too."

This was a new, tough-talking Keira. Still, no way would she survive five minutes onstage with Joe. At her core, Keira was a princess. A nice princess, but royal to the core.

Keira glanced at the listing of specials I'd put up on the bulletin board and began setting out mixing bowls and utensils at my and Alanna's stations. "The producer loved the idea of a 'rematch" of sorts with your protégé. Someone chickened out for next week and I got her slot. We're taping next Thursday. Any pointers? Your friend Sara, the cohost, will help me out, right?"

"That's her job. But, Keira, why do you even want to be on *Eat Me?*" I almost added, *It's not like you need the money.* Her wealthy parents lavished her with everything she needed and wanted, including calling in favors from soon-to-be daughters-in-law.

She carried a basket of tomatoes to my station, then went back to the produce bins for the eggplant. "I need to pay for culinary school myself," she said. "I want to become a chef. Being here these past weeks has me convinced this is what I'm meant to do with my life. I know I have a ton to learn and I'm starting at scratch. But I've never felt more . . . me than I have in this kitchen."

Not a peep out of Gunnar, which was saying something. She'd been proving herself lately. Listening. Working hard. Going above and beyond. And when I got home last night, she'd already e-mailed me twice about videos on braising tofu and sauté temperatures.

"That's awesome, Keira," I said. "And I know the feeling. But won't your parents spring for school?"

"My mother said yesterday that my father has already paid for a very expensive private-college education and that they'd both like me to go into philanthropy and sit on boards like Avery. But Avery loves that stuff. I don't. I want to *cook*."

"So just talk to them," Alanna said.

Keira dropped her head back and let out a hard sigh. "My father said, 'Our family cook is a *servant*. That's what you want to do with your life, be a lowly servant, cooking for other people?' Do you believe him? I talked until I was purple in the face and he still told me I was 'talking nonsense.' Then he said he'd consider paying for law school if I could get a decent score on the LSATs. I never even mentioned law school!"

No wonder Dominique was so pushy and controlling. Her husband was a thousand times worse. She probably had to dig her claws in about the simplest things just to get through breakfast. "Why can't they just let you be what you want?" I asked. "What is with all this pushing other people around? I don't get it."

"It's always been that way," Keira said. "My dad's ears are closed, and my stepmother—well, you know Dominique, Clem. She won't help me get through to my dad."

"Well, then I think it's great that you're going to try to win the money to go to cooking school," I said. "But to beat Joe,

you have to (a) know what you're doing, and (b) not get flustered. If you can do those two things, you have a good shot of
winning over the audience and getting the taste testers to vote
for you."

"Will you help me practice?"

"We'll all help you," Gunnar said, surprising me. "What are
you thinking of challenging him with?"

Keira picked up a tomato, tossed it up, and caught it. "The
producer said it has to be vegan, since that will get the audience riled up. I was thinking lasagna."

"No one can touch Clementine's Mediterranean lasagna,"
Alanna said. "Make that and you'll beat Joe."

"Thing is," Keira said, looking at me, "I want it to be my
lasagna. It has to be *mine*. Just so I can prove to myself that
I can do it. Maybe I can take your recipe, Clem, and make it
my own?"

"Definitely. And you can come in early every day and work
on it here, if you want. Just clean up."

"I'll have my daughter this weekend, but I'll come in Monday and show you how to prep the vegetables," Gunnar said.

Monday was everyone's day off. Pretty decent of Gunnar
Fitch.

"Me too," Alanna said.

"Ditto," one McMann twin said, and then the other.

Oh, hell. "I'll see you Monday at noonish."

Keira beamed. "You guys are the best. First you all hated
me and now you love me."

"Well, I don't know about *love*," Gunnar said, throwing a slice of pepper at her with a smile.

I had to admit I unexpectedly liked Keira. She'd grown on me. And she'd need more help than she realized. Lasagna was complicated and she was a newbie. "Okay, tell you what. I need to work on my lasagna for the *New York Times* reporter. People are always amazed when lasagna is so delicious and it turns out to be meat and cheese free. We'll work on ours side by side."

"Clementine, you absolutely rock," Keira said. "So, Gunnar, what do you and your daughter do on your weekends? You probably spend a lot of time in the kitchen, teaching her to cook."

"Yeah, right. The girl eats nothing but hamburgers. I can barely get her to eat a vegetable. I've tried all your recipes, Clem, but she makes a face and spits out whatever she tries. Sorry."

"Hey, that's okay. My brother, Kale, hated veggies as a kid and now he lives on them."

"I'm supposed to teach her how to bake a cake this weekend so she can enter some contest at her school carnival," Gunnar said, frowning. "It's the one thing I suck at. She's already pissed at me for five different reasons, and now she'll end up making a lopsided cake that tastes like a tire."

"I can bake," Alanna said, glancing at Gunnar. "I learned from the best," she added, upping her elbow at me. "I'll help you guys."

His expression changed from defeated hangdog to hopeful.

"You can use the kitchen here," I said. "Just be out by noon."

"Violet would be really using a restaurant kitchen," Gunnar said, giving Alanna one of his rare smiles. "Thanks."

"Hey, can I come for the lesson?" Keira said. "I'm an okay baker, but I made a tart the other day and it caved in."

"The more the whateverier," Gunnar said, flicking a black bean at Keira.

"Oh, hell, I'll come too," I said. "Alanna can teach and then you guys can help me bake five pies for Saturday night's Pietopia."

Pietopia nights brought in crazy business. Three weeks ago, half the bank employees down the street came in just for the pie, then ended up ordering from the main menu. *Ka-ching*. New customers. Because of *pie*. My dad could offer Pietopia every night at the Outpost.

Alanna added chickpeas to the food processor for falafel. "I'm suddenly jealous of everyone who knows what they want. Clem's got this place and she's getting married. Keira's going to be on *Eat Me* so she can go to cooking school on her own dime. Gunnar's got his knives and vegetables and daughter. And I've got a boyfriend who said tonight is the deadline. Either I tell him I want to marry him or he's leaving."

"I don't get that," Gunnar said. "He loves you to the point that he wants to marry you, but he's willing to walk out of your life? I don't buy this ultimatum crap. If you love someone, you don't try to force them to be what you want. Like Keira's mom is doing to her."

"Yeah, but Alanna's boyfriend can't wait around forever, either," Keira said. "Maybe he just wants to face facts—hard as it is—that he's not the one for Alanna. Maybe that's all he's asking—if he's the one."

"And I'm being forced to decide now when I'm not ready. He might be, I don't know. I'm not even ready to think about it." Alanna stared into the food processor, then added the garlic, onion, cumin, and coriander that Keira had set out for her. "Don't worry, Clem. I'll bring it tonight. I'm just talking out loud."

The bigger problem was that she'd gotten me thinking. About Zach. First, I hadn't been ready. Then I was. And now maybe he'd decided he wasn't, after all.

⸺◎ ◎⸺

Text from me to Zach: *Should I bring over a late plate for you?*
Zach: *Crazed right now—no appetite. Maybe tomorrow. xZ.*
Maybe tomorrow.

⸺◎ ◎⸺

Did I have time to think about what the shizz was going on with Zach? Not with paychecks to process, invoices to go through, inventory to count, specials to decide on for the *New York Times* reporter, and a bajillion phone calls to make about the Outpost. I got myself up and out so early Thursday morning that the birds were chirping in my ears as I walked up Montana, and I had to share the sidewalk with all the dog walkers and joggers. It was barely seven o'clock, but who could sleep when her fiancé was acting all weird? The only way to get him off my mind was to hit the office and take care of business.

The chirps reminded me of my parents' farm, which got me thinking about the red barn and how I'd approach the renovations. A small, but decent-size kitchen, with a back door leading directly to the fields. An office just big enough for me and my dad to share. The main dining room and lounge, and of course a juice bar. My mom, gardener extraordinaire, could take care of the landscaping right around the barn and create a simple back patio.

"Woof! Woof woof!"

I was a million miles away in my head, but I knew that bark. Lizzie, one of Alexander Orr's dogs. I glanced up the street and there she was, wagging her tail and pulling on her leash to get to me. And there was Alexander, bigger dog Brit's leash in his other hand, looking fresh-scrubbed and hot at the same time, as usual.

I had to admit that sometimes, such as now, when Zach was pissing me off, I thought of Alexander and wondered what life would be like with him. Alexander didn't play games, not that Zach was playing a game, exactly, but it felt like that. What's wrong? Nothing. Is something bothering you? No. Zach, what's *up*? Just really busy, Clem.

Right.

If something was bothering Alexander, it would show immediately in those earnest brown eyes, and when I asked, he'd spend an hour telling me every detail. The guy talked. Shared. He cared so much about other people's feelings that he wouldn't want to make someone worry about what was wrong in the first place. I wouldn't even have to ask Alexander what the problem was. He'd tell me.

"Hey," he said, as I reached down to give Brit and Lizzie vigorous rubs under their chins and to scratch behind their ears. "Just getting home from last night?"

"Ha. I'm heading to the restaurant early to take care of paperwork. And I'm gonna start deciding on the specials for the night the *Times* reporter comes. Do you know what you're offering?"

"Emil's making it Mediterranean night, so that gives me a lot of leeway. Wish I could steal your falafel recipe. Yours is the best I've ever had."

"Why thank you," I said, always happy when Alexander— who knew his food—complimented my work.

He glanced away, then down at his sneakers, then in the nowhere-distance.

"Alexander?"

He shrugged, moving up the sidewalk a bit to let the dogs sniff a little plot of grass around a tree. "I hate this. I want you to win. But I want my bloody promotion."

Aha, I was right. Something was bugging him? He spilled— immediately. He didn't disappear. Communication was everything. "Same here."

"Well, if I lose, at least you're in. But I really want in."

I laughed. "Me too. Maybe a little competition will be good for us. Up our game."

He nodded and looked at me for a moment, the way he did when he was getting all regretful that we weren't a couple. "I'd better get these guys home for their breakfast. If you need anything, call me. Even though I'm the enemy."

"Ditto." I absolutely loved Alexander Orr.

Ten minutes later, chai in hand, I headed into the restaurant and went straight to my office. I took care of the boring stuff first, then planned to add a few new possibilities to the specials for the *Times* reporter, but at the thought of Alexander forever a sous chef or even fired for not getting Fresh in that article, I decided to forget that for right now and focus on the Outpost. I picked up my cell, my Outpost notebook and pen at the ready. First call: to the loan officer at my bank to talk numbers. Yeah, my eyes bugged a time or two during the convo, but the numbers she talked about let me put a check mark next to *Loan*. Second call: highly recommended contractor for a basic idea of renovation costs on the barn. More eye-bugging, but now that I had an idea of what kind of loan I'd get, I knew my budget, and I could go with the good contractor instead of the crappy one my sister's law firm used to add showers (because sometimes she and her coworkers actually slept at the office— *shiver*). Third call: president of the Bluff Valley chamber of commerce for info on how many restaurants were within a fifteen-mile radius (twenty-three), not including fast-food joints, how many vegans (one), how many farm-to-table restaurants (zero), how many restaurants on a farm (zero).

I heard Zach whispering in my ear: *There are none because it's not sustainable. Because there's no market.*

But I believed there was a market. And once word got out about a farm-to-table vegan restaurant on an established farm, people would flock.

For the next hour, I read five articles on the farm-to-table movement, getting more and more juiced about the Outpost. Hell, yeah, this was going to happen.

◦ ◉ ◉ ◦

"Darling, of course the wedding won't be *vegan*," Dominique said, her expression horrified. "No one besides you and Avery wants to eat beans for the main course."

I'd almost forgotten that Dominique had arranged this breakfast meeting on Thursday morning at her house in the Hills, a beautiful Spanish-style "bungalow" that was at least four thousand square feet.

"You can have a vegan plate. Some interesting pasta." She clicked at her iPhone. Before I could say anything, she'd stood up and clapped her hands, twice. What was that about? "All right. Now, moving along to the fashion show."

"Fashion show?"

Suddenly, the French doors opened and a model wearing a satin wedding gown came sashaying in as though she were on a runway. The dress was white and had a 1920s flapper quality to it with asymmetrical beading and flounced hem. The model stopped, propped a bored hand on her hip, then pivoted and strutted back toward the French doors.

"I thought I was looking at sketches," I said.

"We're way past that, dear," Dominique said. "And besides, this is like live sketches. I liked the lines on this one. Stark, but with a sweet, fierce quality. A bit like you."

Was that a compliment? Of sorts, maybe. Sweet and Fierce headed out and Ethereal entered. There was something angelic meets Roman about the dress. Next was a forties-style lace gown that I loved, something I could imagine actresses like Katharine Hepburn or Lauren Bacall wearing. Something of a ball gown came out next, a bit like Sara's dress, but so intricately beaded it looked heavy. Finally it was the Kate Middleton, with the long sleeves and high neckline.

"Wow, Dominique, I have to admit I liked a few of those very much."

Her look of surprise was priceless, but she tried to hide it. "Of course you did. Which was your favorite? I'll need to book the seamstress immediately."

"I appreciate the fashion show, I really do, but I don't think any of those are really right for the farm. Maybe something like the first one, but without a train."

"Good God, Clementine, you're not planning on wearing something country, are you?"

I smiled. "I don't know. I'm not there yet."

"Darling, why don't you let me worry about the dress. I'll send you over to my seamstress to have your measurements taken."

"Actually, I want to worry about the dress—but not now. When I'm ready, I'll go shopping."

"Well, really, the wedding needs to be cohesive."

"My dress doesn't have to go with the tablecloth and flowers."

"Well, really, it does."

"Dominique, I appreciate all you're doing, but I'll take care of the dress on my own. I think my mother wants to go shopping with me." That wasn't even a lie. My mother did want to go dress hunting with me. She knew my taste and would be a big help.

"Oh," Dominique said, her face falling. "All right then. Of course. I'll need a photograph of it when you get it, to make sure everything else I'm planning follows suit."

Why was so she controlling?

"I have a board meeting in a half hour so I have to zip off, but we'll need to discuss your registry. Of course, you'll register at—"

"Actually, in lieu of wedding gifts, I'd like guests to donate to the SPCA of LA and PETA too."

She stared at me. "You *can't* be serious. I don't even know what those acronyms actually stand for. Something to do with dog shelters and fur protesters?" She mock shivered. "When I was in New York City last winter, some unkempt young woman lunged at me and made growling noises. It took me a minute to realize she was protesting my mink wrap." Dominique rolled her eyes.

Mink wrap. *I* mock shivered. Gross. "As a philanthropist, I'd think they'd be high up on your list. Society for the Prevention of Cruelty to Animals. And PETA is People for the Ethical Treatment of Animals. There's a local shelter I volunteer at whenever I can. The Montana Avenue Rescue. I'd like them added too."

She laughed. "Oh, Clementine. You're darling, really. But there's no need to make a statement at your wedding. Isn't that a little . . . tacky?"

"It's not a statement. Zach and I don't need a Vitamix or someone's five hundred bucks. But the SPCA could use kibble and cat crates and dog beds and money to pay for neutering and vet bills. PETA's awareness campaign—"

"Oh, God, spare me. I have to run, Clementine, but we'll revisit once I discuss with Zach."

Huh. Maybe I should have talked about it with Zach myself.

My face must have given something away because she looked at me for a moment. With concern. "Darling," she said, walking me out to my car, "maybe you *should* go over that list of Jocelyn's—with Zach. You two should make sure you're on board."

"On board with what?"

"Life, dear. The same values. Please don't take offense, but I foresee conflict."

"Zach and I are fine."

She smiled. Smugly. "Oh, you're too sweet. Go over that list with Zach. I forget what's on it, but maybe overturning a rock or two will be helpful, after all."

I wasn't scared of what I might find out, was I?

17

Rustic-vegetable potpie with a biscuit crust. Smoky potato empanadas, falafel with tahini sauce, blackened Cajun seitan stir-fry. The more I heard Dominique's voice in my head, condescendingly calling me sweet (aka fool), the more I cooked. Cooking calmed me as nothing else could.

I stood at my station in the kitchen of the restaurant and drizzled tahini sauce over the three falafel cakes, then slid them inside a warmed garlic-infused pita full of thickly sliced cucumbers, tomatoes, red cabbage, and lettuce. Should I keep my falafel, every bit as *delicioso* as Alexander had said, off the menu just because Fresh was having Mediterranean night for the *Times* visit? Would keeping it be crappy to do to Alexander, considering my falafel had the edge over his?

Wasn't that the point, though? To *win*?

And be the reason Alexander didn't get promoted?

Half the sandwich gobbled up, I put it on the serious-contender list. I'd figure it out later.

I glanced at my watch. Almost noon. Someone else was probably hungry for my falafel. Someone I missed like crazy: Zach. I made another sandwich, wrapped it up, added a piece of my raspberry tort, whipped up one of his favorite juice blends—pomegranate-strawberry—and booked over to his office.

Zach's admin, an officious dude in a sweater vest, said he'd alert Zach that I was here, so I sat down in the reception area. The double doors to his suite opened, and Zach came, a look of surprise on his face.

"I didn't forget we were having lunch, did I?" he asked, looking worried that he had. Which was a good sign that he truly was just crazy busy lately.

I stood up and followed him into his office. I'd only been here once before, and I was still surprised by the size of the place. Bigger than my entire apartment with gorgeous views of the ocean and the Santa Monica Pier. His desk was the size of a king-size bed.

"Just thought I'd surprise you with lunch." I took out the falafel and smoothie and put it on his desk. "I miss you, Zach. And I'm going to say this straight out—your mother is planning every detail of our wedding while I've never felt more discon-nected from you. It's weird."

He took my hands in his and pulled me close. "I'm sorry

I've been so busy, Clem. It's temporary, though. Come sit down with me." He took the falafel and smoothie over to the huge leather (ick) sofa by the floor-to-ceiling window. "Is my mother driving you nuts?"

"I can handle her. She means well—ish." I smiled.

He took a huge bite of the falafel. "God, this is incredible. Thanks for bringing it. I was about to order in again."

"You ready for Sunday?"

"What's Sunday?"

He'd forgotten that my parents were throwing us an engagement party? Was he *this* distracted? "The meeting of the parents. The hippie farmers and the corporate giants."

"My brain is going to explode—if I don't check my calendar every five minutes, I forget what I'm doing next. This acquisition is going to kill me. And I think our parents will get along great."

Talk about brains exploding. The Jeffrieses and Coopers in the same room should be something to see.

"Your mom and I were talking about Jocelyn's list again. Now she thinks we should go over it. Make sure we're on the same page, to use your kind of lingo."

He took a sip of the smoothie. "We *are* on the same page. Despite everything."

"About SPCA and PETA donations in lieu of wedding gifts?" I should probably have asked him if he was okay with that, but I'd figured he would be. Did Zach really want people like my cousin Harry or Sara shelling out 250 bucks to us? Did we want wildly expensive china for sixteen in some ornate pattern? No. We didn't. I understood Zach and he understood me. He'd be fine with the donations.

He smiled. "My mother left a voice mail ranting about that hours ago."

"And?"

"I like cats. And dogs. And vicious minks."

I hugged him. I knew it. "What about your expectations of married life? That's something I haven't even thought much about."

"That's kind of a big question. I guess I expect we'll be partners. In everything."

But what if you disagreed with me on something I wanted to do? Such as the Outpost? I squeezed his hand and said, "Me too," because it was true. And because once I had the logistics of the Outpost figured out and could show Zach real numbers and a business plan, he'd be on my side. If he wasn't, well, guess we'd both find out what happened when we had a stalemate. The Outpost would be mine, and the decision would be mine.

After a knock at the door, a head poked in.

"Oh, sorry, didn't meant to interrupt, but it's urgent."

"No problem," I said to Zach. "See you tonight?"

"Come over after you close." He leaned over and kissed me, his hand cupping my face. He looked at me for a good long moment, then kissed me again.

Finally. My Zach seemed to be back.

"Let me make myself crystal clear, young lady," Dominique screeched into my ear a few hours later. I held my iPhone out a bit so she wouldn't blow a hole in my eardrum.

And hello to you too. I'd barely answered her call before she started screaming.

"Keira will not, under any circumstances, appear on that ridiculous abomination of a television show. She said your friend works for the show, which is how I'm sure she got herself on there. These are not the kinds of connections I'm interested in her making, Clementine. So undo this. Now." *Click.*

Whoa. I was staying out of this one.

When I arrived at the restaurant on Saturday morning, I was just in time to hear Violet, Gunnar's nine-year-old daughter, throw the tantrum of all tantrums. Did nine-year-old's throw tantrums? Guess so.

"No one wants to eat a vegan cake, Dad!" she yelled, tears streaking down her face. "Everyone's gonna think I'm weird. They already think I'm weird. Just forget it!" She slid down the wall to her butt.

Violet Fitch looked so much like Gunnar. Same almost-black hair—except Violet's was past her shoulders in tangles of gorgeous waves—and catlike green eyes, long black lashes, and serious eyebrows. She wore a Fun concert T-shirt, yellow shorts, and flip-flops.

"Violet," Gunnar said, his voice a combination of frustration and weariness. He'd clearly had to drag her here.

"Hey," Alanna said to the girl in a gentle voice I hadn't heard before, probably because I'd never seen her around a kid before. She went over to Violet and slid down the wall beside her. "I'm gonna make you a deal. If you don't love, and I mean *love*, the cake we bake today, I'll invite you and your dad over to my place tomorrow morning and I'll make sure I have all the ingredients for a not-vegan cake. Okay?"

"But why can't we just make a *not*-vegan cake now? Why bother teaching me how to bake a cake I—and everyone in the world—will think is totally gross?"

"Because you're going to be incredibly surprised, that's why," Alanna said. "The cake we'll make today will be *so* good you will want to eat the entire thing. No exaggeration. And I have a recipe for you to take home so you can make it yourself."

Violet stared at her, her expression softening. "I like your hair."

Alanna smiled. "I like yours too."

"So how do we start?" Violet asked, standing up. "Can we make a chocolate cake? My dad said we can."

Alanna stood up too and headed toward my baking station, which was on the other side of the kitchen.

"We're gonna make the best chocolate cake you ever had. And you won't even know it's vegan. Do you know what *vegan* means?"

"That it doesn't have anything in it that comes from ani-mals, right?"

"Right," Alanna said. "So the only things we have to switch out are eggs—which come from what?"

"Chickens."

"Right again. And butter. Do you know why we can't use butter in a vegan cake?"

"Because to get butter you have to start with milk. And milk comes from a cow."

"I see your dad has taught you a lot." Alanna glanced at Gunnar, who was collecting the ingredients from the pantry.

"He taught me how to make spaghetti and meatballs on our last weekend, even though meat makes him gag."

Alanna laughed. "Well, that's love for you."

Violet smiled at her dad. Gunnar smiled at his daughter. Crisis averted, all thanks to Alanna. Who knew she was that good with kids?

As Alanna set out her recipe for Choctastic Cake, and Vio-let started scooping flour with Gunnar, I slipped into my office. I heard Keira arrive with her mega-enthusiastic hello, then a crash, and a "Keira!" from Gunnar's booming voice. Then a lot of laughter.

I closed the door and sat down at my desk and flipped open my notebook for the Outpost. Ten things on my list were checked off. Everything but *Menu*. Over the past few days, I'd sketched out just the basics, the Clementine's favorites that would be no-brainers at the farm. Harvest pizza, of course, made with wheat flour and my father's amazing marinara sauce and layered with the freshest vegetables. Eggplant Parm, veggie and bean quesadillas, pasta primavera. My barbecue-seitan napoleons. The pies my dad taught me to make. I could fill an entire notebook with dishes.

I read over all my notes from the bajillion calls I'd made and the articles I'd read on the farm-to-table movement. There was one more phone call to make.

My sister. The practical lawyer.

She'd either say, "Good idea, but come on, Clem. You've got enough on your plate and it's hard enough to keep one restaurant going."

Or she'd say, "Go for it."

I punched in Elizabeth's number. She didn't say a word as I laid it out for her, how our dad would be executive chef, how I'd hire a small team to work for him, including a part-time manager—a job my mother might want. I gave Elizabeth the details of the loan, the renovation costs, the deets from the chamber of commerce. My menu.

"And Dad, in chef whites," I added. "Can't you see it?"

The hesitation killed me.

Until she said, "I absolutely can. I'll tell you, Clem, it's a lot to take on. But if anyone can make this work, you and Dad can."

Hellz yeah. *Hellz yeah!*

"So how'd the Choctastic Cake come out?" I asked when I finally emerged from my office.

From the smile on Violet Fitch's face, no need to ask. "I can't believe the cake is this good!" Violet said, taking another bite and making a moony face. "Mmmm. The frosting is amazing. Everyone's gonna want to buy slices of it. Will I really be able to make it myself?"

"Definitely," Gunnar said, sliding a thankful smile at Alanna. She smiled back at him, and I couldn't help but notice that they didn't look away in two seconds.

Interesting.

18

My moment of evil, joyous anticipation that Dominique would call back and screech, *And you can forget about my planning your wedding,* was short-lived, since she'd called back in five minutes and had instead screeched that she needed measurements of my head for the veil and a list of all those whom I wanted to speak during the ceremony so that she could apprise them of timing, tone, and theme. That was something I'd conveniently forget to get around to.

On the way to the engagement party at my parents' farm on Sunday afternoon, I didn't want to start an argument by talking about the Outpost, so I filled in Zach on his mother's call Friday night.

"She's going to lose Keira if she doesn't stop meddling," Zach said, turning onto the freeway. He shook his head.

Dominique was headed that way, which was sad. Why was she so controlling? Keira wasn't even her own daughter. "Your mom treats Keira like she's her flesh and blood. I guess that's good and bad. Bad because Keira's probably not attached to your mom the way Avery is."

"Actually, she is. Keira's mother died when she was a teenager, and my mother spent an entire year winning her over. Keira was grief-stricken and railed at Dominique, and Dominique not only took it, she didn't back away once. She fought like hell to get Keira to trust her and think of her like a second mom. Sometimes, when Dominique is driving me nuts, I try to remember that."

"She must really love Keira. Which is why she needs to let go. Even just a little."

"Letting go is a foreign concept to my mother."

Our moms were night and day. I tried to imagine my mother, the most earthy person alive, clinking champagne flutes with Dominique at the engagement party. "Think everyone will get along?"

"My father and Lydia will love your parents and the farm. But Dominique won't be there. She avoids anywhere my father is."

"What about our wedding?"

"The wedding will be so big that she won't mind being in the same airspace as Cornelius. At least when your parents finally meet her, they'll have a good story to tell the grandkids."

Grandkids. The thought made me smile and shiver. I tried to imagine a mini Zach and me, with his dark hair and my hazel eyes. Me, changing diapers and burping a crying little creature? I couldn't see it now, but one day, yeah.

The entertainment at the engagement party? Listening to my sister and Zach's father's fiancée (one of his own divorce lawyers) talk shop with barely contained disdain for each other. The fiancée was sharp, I'd give her that, but Elizabeth seemed to find her ethically questionable, given that Lydia was a divorce attorney marrying one of her own former clients. Finally, my mother commandeered Elizabeth away to help bring out the crudités and my father's amazing five-bean dip.

Zach and his dad were chatting up my dad by the stone fireplace, talking money, land, politics, and cancer. Zach had been right; Cornelius Jeffries, bajillionaire, *was* impressed that this postage-stamp-size farm had kept three kids clothed and fed and still paid the mortgage, year after year. The Jeffrieses seemed truly charmed—and not in a Dominique-style condescending way—by the farm, from my parents crunchy hippie decor to the fields and the dogs running wild. Until I saw the four of them yakking it up about dogs (the Jeffrieses had four themselves), I hadn't realized their getting along—or not—was that important to me. One less thing to think about, distract me. Just as I heard a car going way too fast down the driveway—had to be Joe "Steak" Johansson behind that wheel—I heard my father invite the Jeffrieses over for lunch in a couple of weeks, and the Jeffrieses wholeheartedly accept. I wasn't much of an "aww-er," but that got one out of me.

This party was basically for the parents to meet, but Sara had said there was no way she was missing my first engagement party and had commandeered Joe to make the three-hour drive. He got semi–bonus points for that, at least. And maybe hanging with the families on a Sunday afternoon would make him go a bit easier on Keira at next week's taping of *Eat Me*. Then again, this was Joe we were talking about.

"Clementine, you come sit by me," Zach's aunt Jocelyn said, patting the seat next to her on the couch. Good thing I'd worn the earrings she'd sent me because I hadn't even known Jocelyn was planning to come. I'd given her a big hug and thanked her profusely again and let her know I was making good use of the list. Her husband of sixty-four years, Frederick, had wanted to see the fields and hear about the crops, so my brother, Kale, had volunteered to give him the lowdown. I could see them walking slowly, Frederick pointing and stopping, and Kale clearly enjoying being tour guide. The dogs loped ahead of them.

There was a knock at the door and Sara and Joe came in.

"Let's get this party star-*ted*!" Joe bellowed, nodding as though rap music were blaring. Oh, God, save us all.

"Sara, lovely girl," Jocelyn said. "Come give me a kiss. You look so lovely."

"So where's the Cooper-Jeffries with the weird hair?" Joe asked, glancing around. "The one I'm gonna humiliate in front of all America?"

"Her hair isn't weird—it's *ombré*," I said. The top half of Keira's beach-wavy hair was a gorgeous chestnut brown and the bottom half a graduated shade lighter.

He cackled. "Ombré. I snicker. *Om. Om,*" he chanted as if he were in yoga class, drawing out the syllable with his hands palm up on his thighs. "I'm telling you, people ask all the time if *Eat Me* is staged, and I tell them, you can't make this stuff up. *Ommmm* hair. Vegans. Pure comedy gold."

I glanced at Sara, who was cringing *and* trying to hide her smile.

"What is this about?" Jocelyn asked. "Who is this Cooper-Jeffries?"

"What's her name," Joe said. "The one who works for Vegan Chick."

"Keira," I said through gritted teeth.

"Keira's tougher than she looks," Zach said. "You might be in for a surprise, Joe."

Joe's snort was back. "Yeah, right. I've eaten lasagna noodles tougher than that little thing. Can't wait. She's going down." He pushed one hand to the floor.

"Let's bring my mother to the taping," Zach whispered. "She'll see what Keira's made of."

I tried to imagine Dominique in the audience, listening to the screaming hordes egging Joe on and calling her stepdaughter names. "Your mom will probably give it back to Joe worse than Sara ever could."

"Do you think Keira has a chance?" Jocelyn asked me. "I've only seen the program once and it's not for the fainthearted."

"Got that right," Joe said, double-dipping a pita chip through bean dip. Gross.

"Well, Keira's already proven she's *not* fainthearted," I said. "It's awesome that she wants to earn her own tuition to culinary school. I'm proud of her. She's come a long way in my kitchen. I think she'll make a great chef one day."

Joe snorted. Loudly. "She can't even get her hair to be one color. You think she can layer a lasagna? And make it taste like anything other than dog doo without meat and ricotta cheese?" He rolled his eyes. "This'll be my easiest win yet. Twenty-five big ones to the charity of my choice. Although this Kei-rah-rah chick sounds like a charity case herself." He looked at Jocelyn, nodded his chin toward me, and wrinkled up his face in a *Will you get a load of her?*

I shot him a death stare. "You're talking about Zach's stepsister, so watch it."

My tone got a little sharp, and Sara cut a glance at me. A glance that said, *Don't talk to my fiancé like that.*

This was going to be interesting.

"Anyway, let's change the subject," Sara said. "Where's your cousin Harry? I've been dying to meet him after all your stories."

I glanced around to see if I'd missed him come in, but no Harry. Ten minutes later, another car pulled up, and Harry and a woman walked in. She was almost as tall as he was, rail thin, beautiful in that exotic model way with her wide-set eyes, fine-boned features, and huge mouth, and wearing a tiny, shiny dress and serious bling. New girlfriend? And antitype; Harry had always gone for the typical California girl jogging on the beach. Instead of coming in with a smile, she was checking out her shoes (incredibly cool gladiatorish sandals that went up to her shin) for encrusted farm dirt.

I could see her influence all over Harry. His usually surfer-dude unruly hair was looking more Euro, and so were his long-sleeved, button-down shirt and dark gray pants. And was that a Cartier watch? Harry was more a T-shirt-and-faded-jeans kind of guy, except for the usual work clothes.

"Clem, this is my girlfriend, Nadia. Nadia, my cousin Clementine, the bride-to-be."

She gave me a stiff smile, and I instantly knew he had had to talk her into coming. An engagement party for family in LA was one thing. But a three-hour drive on a Sunday morning? To a farm? She'd probably fought him all night on coming.

"I like your dress," she said, but her eyes were on the crowd, checking out the scene, heavy on the sensible farm shoes.

I looked around for Zach, who actually liked making small talk, to get him to come over, but I saw him slipping out the sliding glass door to the deck and over to the barn. He glanced in, hands on hips, and I had a feeling he was thinking about my idea for the Outpost. I caught the slight shake of his head.

Instead of coming back, he went around the side of the barn, and I thought he was considering expansion or renovation possibilities, but then I saw him emerge on the farm side and head toward the fields. One of my parents' dogs loped over, and Zach just stood there, staring out at the rows of crops, absently petting Pete.

Jeez. Was he torn up about disagreeing with me on the Outpost? Or did this have zippo to do with that? Maybe he'd slipped away from the engagement party because it was a big, honking reminder that he was . . . marrying me. Maybe he'd changed his mind about the whole thing and couldn't deal with telling me. Maybe he'd jumped on axing the Ouptost because it was really me he wanted to ax.

"Where's Zach?" Harry asked as Nadia drifted over to the bar my dad had set up.

"Out there." I upped my chin toward the deck. "I have an idea for a new restaurant and he's not 'on board,' as you corpo types say. It's coming between us a little. I think, anyway." Or something was. Grandkids comment or not.

Harry glanced out the deck doors, and you could just make out Zach in the distance, walking a bit farther away, the dog beside him. Harry put his arm around me. "You'll work it out."

I shrugged. "Forget business today anyway. What's going on with you and the model?"

He smiled, the slow, moony smile of a guy in serious love. "She's *it*. Everything I've ever wanted." He leaned closer to whisper, "I know she might seem a little unfriendly, but she's just kind of serious. She's constantly booked as a model too. She has a go-see to do runway for Dolce and Gabbana tomorrow." He was gazing at her by the bar, slowly sipping what looked like a martini.

"She is beautiful. How long have you been together?"

"Just a few months. Took me forever to get her to go out with me. I think she's more used to Zach types than junior accountants, but I finally won her over with my Cooper charm."

I smiled. "Thanks for coming, by the way. I know it's a big schlep up here."

"Like I'd miss your engagement party? And a chance to see drunk Uncle Bob drop a mini-black-bean empanada on his wife's foot—again?" He nudged his chin by the bar, where Nadia was edging away.

I glanced over to see long-suffering Aunt Lee grit her teeth and wipe her sandaled foot clean of goo.

And out the deck doors, I saw Zach slowly walking back toward the house. Very slowly. As if he couldn't take long enough to get back to me. And our *engagement* party.

"Dear, will you show me the grounds?" Jocelyn asked, wrapping her arm around mine. "I'd just love to see the fields where your parents grow their food. How wonderful that they grow what they eat."

Jocelyn would probably drive up all the way from LA to have dinner at the Outpost.

Arm in arm, we walked past the orange grove and lemon trees, Jocelyn's face lifted up to appreciate the beautiful seventy-degree weather and fresh, clean air, the scent of citrus carried on the breeze. I told her how the farm operated, about my father's CSA, and the farm stand.

"And how are the wedding plans going?" Jocelyn said. "You and Dominique getting along?"

"We don't agree on *anything.*"

Jocelyn laughed. "Well, I think she's met her match in you, Clementine. She's used to intimidating people and having them jump to do her bidding. Now her son's fiancée has a mind of her own and speaks it."

"That gets me a lot of grief. Even with Zach. I know he loves that I don't hold back, that I say what needs to be said, but what are you supposed to do when what needs to be said isn't being said—by *him.*"

"Oh, I have one of those. Frederick keeps it all inside. I can always tell when something's bothering him, but he'll never talk about it. Just huffs off to his den to tinker with who knows what or goes on long walks with the dogs." She stopped to admire the strawberry bushes. "I knew he was like that when I married him, of course. But I didn't work on the things I should have. It's why I sent you the list, of course."

"I wish I knew how to get Zach to start talking."

"You know him best. Just remember that. But more importantly, Clementine, you know yourself best. What you can live with and what you can't. What you need to compromise on and what you can't—or won't. That's how you begin to figure out how to deal with what bothers you but can't be changed."

"You mean by just accepting it?"

She glanced out over the rows of carrots. "Sometimes—the small stuff, as they say. But most times, you've got to fight for what matters. And you should."

How great was she? "Should I confess that one of the reasons I want to marry Zach is so I can call you my aunt?"

She laughed and we headed back to the house, just in time to catch the tail end of Harry's trying to argue-whisper with the model by the buffet table. Nadia shot him a look of pure disgust and crossed her arms over her chest.

"Now there's a couple I don't see lasting," Jocelyn whispered.

When the party started winding down, I was finally able to sneak my dad, who took his host duties seriously, out the back door and over to the barn.

We walked in, and my heart started booming in my chest— that's how *right* this felt, how juiced I was about it. Right now, the building was used for equipment and wheelbarrows and my mother's huge baskets. Six months from now: the Outpost. "Dad, I've been thinking about something. I want to open a second restaurant right here on the farm, in this barn, with you as executive chef. Clementine's No Crap Outpost, farm-to-table. What do you think?"

"Executive chef," he repeated, a smile breaking out on his weathered face. "That's always been my dream."

"I know. You made mine come true by teaching me everything you know. Now I want to pay you back."

He hugged me. "And you really think this is doable? I assume you've done your research?"

"I have. And it's definitely doable, thanks to the work you've already done here over the past thirty years. You've built a base of customers, Dad. Even Elizabeth thinks it'll work." I went over all the details, the logistics, the numbers, the potential menu—and backup for those times when he wouldn't be up to standing on his feet.

"Well, then, sign me on," he said, his voice almost breaking. "I can't wait to tell your mom."

Awesome.

I waited until we were almost back to Santa Monica before I told Zach I was going ahead with my plans for the Outpost. I ran down the list of checkpoints, as I'd done for my dad, but I went more in depth for Zach, since he was in the business.

"You should have seen my dad's face. He's so happy." Just the thought of how my father had looked when I told him made *me* so happy.

"Maybe you shouldn't have told him yet, Clem," Zach said, both hands on the steering wheel, not as usual with one on my thigh. "Why get him excited about something that may not happen?"

"I just told you all the reasons why it will happen."

"Clem. What sounds okay on paper and what works in reality are two different things. You *know* I believe in you. But two restaurants—three hours apart—both needing you on a daily basis, especially a brand-new one? And a month after the novelty wears off a farm-to-table meal, the Outpost will very likely stall."

No, it wouldn't. Not if the food, service, and experience were incredible. Marketing power, publicity, and word of mouth would take care of that. The Outpost would fill a niche. I *knew* it.

Still, I wanted his support. His *hellz, yeah.* Was he just going all conservative on me? Or did he think I couldn't pull it off? If I believed in me, shouldn't he?

I glanced at him, ready to say just that, but I could tell he was dead set against the Outpost.

Shizz.

"We'll have to agree to disagree on this, Zach," I said, using one of his expressions. "I'm going ahead with it."

He put his sunglasses on and didn't say a word until "Bye" when he dropped me off at my apartment.

19

Keira had been doing her homework. When I arrived at the restaurant on Monday at just before noon, she was already hard at work on her red sauce for the lasagna, sautéing onions in coconut oil. In a neat line at her station were the other ingredients: minced garlic, the tomatoes, basil, oregano, fruity red wine, and my secret weapon—a pinch of agave nectar. She picked up the little bowl of garlic.

"Add the garlic only when the onions are tender," I said, glancing into her pan.

She wiped her hands on her apron. "Oh, right. There are so many steps. I practiced making the sauce last night, and it didn't taste right."

"Your sauce will be perfect by the time you get on that *Eat Me* stage. You're gonna bring the panel of judges to their knees with your lasagna. Half of making sure that happens is about confidence."

"Dominique told me I was going to make a fool of myself on national television, that I could forget about any culinary school accepting me afterward. 'You'll make them look bad,' she said." Keira bit her lip and added the garlic to the pan, halfheartedly pushing the bits around.

I put my hand on hers. "First rule of the kitchen—and beating Joe Johansson's ass—don't cook unless you're one hundred percent there. You have to focus every second. On what you're doing, what you have to do next, what you have to do three steps later. Let go of everything else—Dominique, the show, school—and just focus on the red sauce and getting your big pot of water prepared to boil for the noodles."

Kind of like how I had to ignore Zach's reaction to the Outpost and just do my thing.

Something shifted in her expression and light came into her eyes. "Yes, chef!"

"Right now, *you're* the chef, Keira. Go to it."

She shot me her trademark huge smile and stirred in the crushed tomatoes and tomato paste, increasing the heat exactly when she was supposed to.

She just might pull this off.

Alanna and Gunnar arrived together, Alanna sniffing at the air. "That smells amazing. Good thing I didn't eat lunch."

Hmmm. Because she was too busy lip-locked with Gunnar? Had they ever arrived together before? I didn't think so.

They kept shooting little smiles at each other. Something was definitely up with them.

Gunnar eyed the lineup of ingredients that Keira hadn't yet used. "That oregano needs to be more finally chopped." He went over to his station to select the right knife. "This one. And chop it like this."

"Ah, got it. Thanks, Gunnar." She glanced at him. "Didn't sleep much last night?" He looked tired, his hair was more mussed than its usual blue-black mop, and dark shadows were under his eyes. Something in those eyes was different, a glimmer of . . . sadness instead of his usual sparkly grumpiness.

Maybe no hot kitchen romance was going on.

"Are we making lasagna or talking about me?" he asked, turning away.

Huh. Had his daughter's solo attempt at Choctastic Cake for her school fund-raiser come out so meh and she'd gotten all sulky again?

"I'm gonna have to do *both* when I'm cooking on the *Eat Me* stage, though," Keira said. "I watched at least twenty episodes of *Eat Me* on Netflix over the weekend. The chefs get flustered because Joe is up their butt the whole time they're cooking. And the audience gets in on it too. I have to be able to cook and dish it back to him, while endearing myself to the audience."

She *had* done her homework. And she was right. She would have to deal with constant harassment, shouting from the audience, and Joe in her face.

"Did the *Eat Me* producer say you could bring an assistant to help you out?" I asked. I'd planned to ask my friend Alexander, terrific vegan chef, to assist me, but at the time he hadn't been taking my calls (I'd made a huge mistake and almost blew our friendship), so I'd asked Sara. She ended up with a job and a fiancé out of it.

"Yes. And I wish I could ask you, Clementine, but there's no way I'm going to jeopardize your relationship with Dominique. You don't want a war with your future mother-in-law." Keira tasted the sauce, then added the pinch of agave nectar. "The producer said I should choose someone 'mouthy' who could give it back to Joe and the audience."

"How about me?" Gunnar said. "No one's mouthier than me. Except maybe Clementine's friend Sara. And just barely."

Interesting. Gunnar was the most private person I'd ever known. For him to want to go on a TV show was unusual.

"I thought you hated TV. And especially that show," Alanna said. "Didn't you say you saw it once and that it was the bottom of the barrel of cooking shows?"

"It is. But my daughter loves it. It's her favorite show. And I'm . . . kind of in the doghouse again right now. I need to do something, and there's not much I can change. If I can appear on her favorite show, she'll flip."

"Why are you in the doghouse?" Alanna asked. "Don't tell me her cake made everyone sick? Or the kids took one bite and gagged or something?"

Gunnar set down his knife. "No. Actually, the cake was a

hit. And we ended up having such a great time together this past weekend that she got all upset about my having to go to work and leave her with a sitter. I don't even get to see her before she goes to sleep on my weekends with her. Saturday and Sunday, from three to when she goes to bed at eight thirty, she's with a sitter."

"But a lot of working parents use sitters," Keira said. "And it's not like you're going to the movies or something. You're working."

"I know. But it cuts into our time. She wants me to take off weekends so that we're together. But I can't do that. That's not how restaurants work."

Gunnar was the only one of my employees who had a child. I hadn't even considered how his schedule might impact him and his relationship with his kid. Yeah, I needed Gunnar on weekends—the busiest and most profitable nights of the week. But I also needed one of the best vegetable chefs I'd ever worked with to be in a good place when he came to work, not wishing he were back home reading to his daughter on their weekends. "You can," I said. "If you work for a chef who knows how important flexibility in the workplace is. How many weekends a month do you spend with your daughter?"

"Two. And I see her every Monday after school for an overnight since we're off Mondays." He glanced at his watch. "Speaking of which, I need to leave at two thirty to pick her up from school on time."

"So maybe during your weekends with your daughters, you take off Saturday and Sunday. I'll be vegetable chef those nights."

"And I'll pick up any slack, you know that," Alanna said, looking between Gunnar and me.

"Maybe I can apprentice with you so that eventually I can cover for you on those nights," Keira said. "You train me, seriously train me, and you can be my assistant on *Eat Me*."

Gunnar perked up considerably. "Deal."

Keira reached into the canister of organic whole-wheat flour and added two cups to a bowl, then added water, salt, and olive oil. She floured a board and began mixing the dough by hand. Clearly, she'd read up and watched videos on the proper way to knead without overdoing it.

"Think it needs more water?" Keira asked.

"Looks perfect to me," I told her.

She beamed her megawatt smile and set the dough aside, then headed over to the refrigerator for the tofu, which needed to be braised to optimize its flavor for the lasagna.

Keira set down the tofu, sliced it perfectly, and reached for the bottle of sesame oil and soy sauce. "So I dredge the tofu slices in seasoned flour, then sear it, then simmer it on low heat in broth, a little soy sauce, and sesame oil. Covered pan."

"A-plus," I said.

She beamed and got to work.

"So gimme some tips on dealing with Johansson," Gunnar said to me.

I'll never forget how he'd tried to rattle me and how Sara had kept telling him to suck it. The audience had loved her.

"You have to win over the audience by dishing it back to Joe, but making them think you're one of them. Look out at them a lot. Get them on your side. Make exaggerated faces at them every time Joe calls you a skinny turd. And he will."

"I'll prep you tomorrow night during dinner service by berating you and calling you an idiot." Gunnar glanced at me. "If chef approves, that is?"

I'd have to watch Keira like a hawk to make sure she didn't screw up what she was working on.

"Okay by me," I said, "but if it starts affecting the rush too much, turn back to your usual sweet self."

Alanna laughed. "Gunnar, sweet? Ha." She shot him a smile that said she did find him sweet.

"You *have* to beat that dickhead," Gunnar said to Keira. "We lose and my daughter will think I'm a lightweight."

"Oh, we'll win. My entire future depends on it."

Been there, done that.

⌐◉ ◉⌐

That night, Sara and I were watching *Eat Me* so I could give Keira some extra pointers. What I was looking for, and what I didn't tell Sara, was patterns of weakness. Cases when Joe himself got flustered, what was said, what got to him.

Not much. No matter what was thrown at him, he either shrugged it off or zinged it back.

"Ugh," Sara said, her feet up on the coffee table. "See how in the last episode I was looking good, and then in this one I've gained back like ten pounds? You can see it in my face. I liked how I looked before."

She put down her bowl of frozen yogurt (ickeroo), which had as much fat as ice cream and didn't taste as good. I'd tried to get her to eat my homemade strawberry sorbet, but the "chocolate attack" frozen yogurt was Joe's favorite, and apparently they stuck two spoons in the carton and pigged out on it in bed every night.

"How am I supposed to stay motivated to cut the crap out of my life when Joe encourages me to eat all my favorite crap foods? We split a family-size bag of sour-cream-and-onion chips yesterday. I have your recipe for homemade potato chips using vegan yogurt and onions, but it's so easy to just buy a bag in the supermarket."

"You can have your supermarket chips, Sar. Maybe just not every night."

"I'm so bad at moderation." She pushed the bowl of frozen yogurt away from her. "Okay, that's it. I'm back on the no-crap plan. Yeah, I like it that Joe doesn't seem to care what I look like. But I care. I loved how I used to feel. And my skin looks like hell." She dipped her spoon into my sorbet. "Mmm. So good. I'm *back*."

Yeah! I slid the sorbet over to her.

"Oh, hey, did I tell you that Joe and I went over the list together?" Sara asked. "He was totally into number seven."

"Which one was that?"

She grabbed her bag from the coffee table and rummaged through it and pulled out a folded piece of paper. "Number seven: 'Ask him why he loves you and then jot the reasons down on paper. Reread when you're arguing.' Wanna hear what he said?"

I nodded.

"'Because when I'm with you, I feel more like myself, the real me, whoever the hell that is. Because you make me think. Because you make me want to be a better person, not that I probably will be. Because you're smart and funny and speak your mind. Because you have big goals for yourself. Because you're so damned beautiful and I can't stop thinking about you all the time. Because you tell me to screw myself when I deserve it. Because you're the best thing that's ever happened to me.'"

Okay, was that my brain exploding? Did something inside me just shift? I went from hating Joe Johansson to actually kind of . . . liking him for all that. A lot.

"Sara. Holy shit."

"I know." She scanned the list again. "The guy loves me for some pretty good reasons."

"Really good reasons."

"I've asked him before why he loves me, and he's always grabbed me and given me an annoying noogie and said,

'Because you're fucking awesome,' and changed the subject. But something about having Jocelyn's sixty-year-old list made him take it seriously. Plus, I think he likes her."

I smiled. "I'll bet if your mother read what Joe said, she'd change her mind about him."

"You think? Maybe I'll call her later and read it to her. So how do you really think Keira's going to do?" Sara asked. "Can she handle Joe? I'll have her back, but still."

"I honestly don't know. She's still a newbie cook, and he might get to her. Gunnar's planning on berating her tomorrow in the kitchen during prime dinner service to give her full Joe Johansson treatment."

"Think Gunnar will be able to deal with Joe? He seems like a cool guy, but he's the kind of hipster-looking dude in skinny jeans and dyed hair that Joe loves to rip to shreds."

"Gunnar's pretty tough, I think."

"What about Dominique? Has she backed off about Keira being on the show?"

"She texts me like five times a day: 'You're not really going to let her go through with this?' That kind of thing. She texts Zach the same thing, harassing him to talk some sense into me. As if I could stop Keira anyway. Dominique has this crazy notion that people can be controlled."

My iPhone pinged with a text. Of course it was from Dominique. *Darling, still counting on you to talk Keira out of that Godforsaken show. P.S. Veil fashion show Wednesday at ten thirty. My house.—D.*

I was dying to text back a simple *No* on both counts.

My phone pinged again. *Speaking of that awful show, I recommend nixing your friend Sara from the bridal party. Wouldn't want to be upstaged by "celebrity," no matter how faux.*

Grrrr. She was driving me insane. I grabbed my phone and typed back, YOU'RE FIRED, YOU IMPOSSIBLE SHREW. Then, of course, Zach's face popped into my mind, and I deleted it. But it felt danged good for a second.

20

Zach was doing it again. Disappearing. Not responding to texts. Telling me he was working late.

Enough was enough. That mini-devil stabbed me in the shoulder with the pitchfork. *Told you, Cooper. Everything is falling to shit. You'll never impress the* New York Times *reporter now. Not with Zach and his disappearing acts messing with your head.* Clementine's No Crap Café will be history this time next year. You'll be walking into a day spa in this location.

The mini-angel pointed a finger at the devil. *Shut it, you. Whatever Zach is going through, they'll get through it. But right now, go work on your rustic-vegetable potpie. Now,* she screamed in my ear.

Huh. Angel was getting quite the temper.

The next morning I was at my friend Alexander's house, helping him bake the one hundred cupcakes he'd volunteered to make for the fund-raiser for the middle school of his "little brother." If you looked up *good guy* in the dictionary, you'd find a picture and description of Alexander Orr. Every week he hung out with twelve-year-old Jesse, an only child with divorced parents, went to all the kid's school events that his mother (his dad was out of the picture) couldn't attend because of work. And Alexander, who was pretty danged cute, was a great chef.

Baking bored him, so maybe he *did* need my help today. But I was pretty sure he'd just needed an excuse to call me. Before the competition for the *Times* article, we'd call or text a few times a week. Lately: zilch. We both wanted to win, which meant suckish things for the other.

Alexander poured apple-cider vinegar into the bowl of soy milk on his kitchen counter while I got to work on the flour, chocolate, sugar, baking powder, baking soda, and salt.

Forget this tiptoeing around each other crap. Alexander and I were real friends. We could handle competition.

"My rustic-vegetable potpie is missing something," I said. "I'm thinking of offering it as a special for the *Times* reporter, and it'll definitely go on my Outpost menu, but something's wrong with the crust. I made a mistake somewhere in the sauté or in the baking time. I can't figure it out. There's a chewiness that shouldn't be there."

"The Outpost? What's that? And of course I'll help you with potpie."

I dropped my measuring spoon. "I didn't tell you about the Outpost?" How could I not have told Alexander?

He gave the batter a taste and then added a drop of vanilla. "Well, I think you've been keeping your distance from me."

"Actually, it's you who's been keeping your distance from *me*."

"Yeah, it's both of us. I hate that. This can't come between us, Clem. Okay?"

I nodded. "No way." It couldn't and wouldn't. Alexander and I had been through a lot together already. We could deal with this.

As I told him about the Outpost, all my plans for it, how juiced my dad was to be chef, I could hear how right it was, how doable, how passionate I was about it. Why couldn't Zach? Why couldn't he just say, *Of course you'll make it work.*

"Zach doesn't think it's sustainable," I said, mixing my batter. "And that I'll stretch myself so thin everything will fall to crap."

"You're too awesome for that. You're smart, ambitious, efficient, and know how to make things happen. It's a bloody brilliant idea, Clem. Farm-to-table right at the organic farm? In a gorgeous red barn? You'll get a ton of publicity, draw on your great reputation and your dad's, and the place will be packed every night, just like the No Crap Café."

Before I could stop myself my arms were wrapped around him in a fierce hug. I looked up at him, into those warm brown eyes, and for a split second I wanted to kiss him. On the lips, not the cheek. He'd said everything I wanted Zach to say, everything I wanted Zach to believe.

But Alexander *wasn't* Zach. I'd fallen in love with Zach *because* of who he was. His dull concerns about the Outpost weren't off the wall; he was being corporately conservative. He was coming from a business perspective. Alexander was coming from a vegan chef's perspective.

I pulled back. "Thanks for saying all that."

"It's all true." He reached for my hand.

I gave him a smile and slipped away that hand to remove my batter from the mixer. "If Emil finds out you're helping the enemy, he'll have your head," I said to change the subject.

Alexander handed me five cupcake tins and liners and got started lining his own five. "I'm not scared of Emil Jones. You're my friend, Clem. Friends help each other out. Like you're doing for me right now."

As I placed the little colored wrappers in the tins, I wondered what life would be like if I'd gone for Alexander instead of Zach. Alexander and I were a perfect match on paper— both vegans, both giving the finger to unnecessary chemicals and other crap that clogged people's hearts, pores, and brains. We were both chefs, both got seriously excited over new sauté pans and good knives. We understood each other. He was goodness personified too, mentoring a tween, volunteering at the kid's school, bringing homemade soup and dinners to his grandmother, who'd followed him to the United States and was madly in love with Southern California.

Plus, he was incredibly cute with a great body, all tall and lankily muscular, with wavy sandy-brown hair and sharp brown eyes. I knew he was a hot guy. But every time the two of us had kissed? Like kissing my brother.

Still, since Alexander's parents were in England, I wouldn't have the future mother-in-law from KillMeNowVille breathing down my neck.

"Monday, before work?" Alexander asked.

"I don't know what I'd do without you."

He smiled that hangdog smile that said he wished there were an *us*, that I'd chosen him instead of Zach.

The cupcakes cooling and two of them inhaled, we took Alexander's dogs, Lizzie and Brit, for a walk. Alexander filled me in on the woman he was dating, a carnivore like Zach, who was finding Alexander preachy even though he never said a word to anyone about going vegan. It just wasn't his way to get in someone's face the way some other people did . . . such as myself.

"The other night, we were out at a pizza joint, and I ordered a pizza, hold the cheese, and she got all offended. 'It's just *cheese*,' she said. 'It's not like the cow died for it.'"

I rolled my eyes. "What did you say?"

"I tried to explain in a very reasonable and polite way about dairy cows and why they're mysteriously full of milk all the time and how we're the only species who drinks and eats another species' mother's milk, and then I got into some of the environmental issues, and she got up and walked out."

I tried not to smile. "Not a lost cause, though. If I'm marrying Zach Jeffries, there's hope for vegan-and-carnivore love."

"Well, I'll call her later. We'll see."

Brit and Lizzie started barking at a dog walker and his pack of at least ten dogs, so we walked back to Alexander's house and I helped him package up the hundred cupcakes. I'd missed hanging out with Alexander and wanted to just stay and talk, but Keira was having a final test run of her lasagna at the restaurant and I'd promised to be there and watch every step. She'd planned to have *Eat Me* on in the background, turned up loud, so she could get used to Joe's screaming in her face as she cooked.

The minute I walked out the door of Alexander's house, I wanted to be back in there. With all that support. All that Team Clementine. All that . . . tension.

What the hell did that mean?

21

It was so weird being in the audience of *Eat Me*. When I was last in this studio, I was onstage, whipping up my $25,000 eggplant Parmesan. Sara, my trusty assistant, was furiously chopping vegetables and handing me utensils, yelling at Joe to suck it. Now I was in row two, sitting next to Zach, who was texting back and forth with his second-in-command. Did this man ever stop working?

Did I?

Would Alexander Orr be texting at his stepsister's debut on a national TV show? No, he would not.

All night, I'd flopped around my bed so much that Sara had come into my room to ask if I was being attacked by sharks in a dream or something. Every time I'd tried to think about Zach and how I was going to handle our problems, Alexander's cute face would float into my mind.

Romanticizing, I knew. If I were in a relationship with Alexander, we'd have problems of our own. Not Zach-like problems, though.

Note to self: Go back over numbers six and eight of Jocelyn's list. *What do you expect married life to really be like? Are you expecting him to change once you're married?*

Would Zach be texting his second-in-command during our ceremony? Okay, fine, of course he wouldn't. But at the reception? Yeah, probably. Would I be wondering how things were going at the restaurant? Wouldn't my entire staff be at my wedding, anyway? I'd have to close up shop on a Saturday night.

Luckily, the show's taping had been moved to Monday when the restaurant was closed, so we were all here to scream our asses off for Keira and Gunnar. Alanna, the McMann twins, Matteo and his even-more-gorgeous-than-Nadia-the-model girlfriend, and all my waitstaff and busboys.

"Joe Steak, Joe Steak, Joe Steak," a loudmouth in the row behind us started chanting, trying to get the audience riled up with him.

Dominique, on Zach's other side, kept glancing around with a horrified expression, as though she expected someone to jump her any minute. Her husband sat beside her with his arms crossed against his chest, his expression glowering. Keira looked a lot like her dad, Paul Huffington, except Keira was a smiler, and her father hadn't cracked one since Dominique had introduced us.

Sir Paul leaned forward and shot me the stink-eye.

Nice. Did Keira's parents have *any* faith in her?

The producer and her assistant came out from the side door to explain how the show would work and to point out the cue cards they'd use to prompt shout-outs and clapping. When the producer said we shouldn't hold back, we should feel free to shout out whatever we wanted—but no swear words—both Huffingtons leaned forward and shot me the death stare.

"Is *damn* okay?" a guy asked from the row in front of me. "What about *dickhead*?"

"*Damn* is welcome, *dickhead* is not," the producer said. "Just remember, folks, if you wouldn't use the swear word with your aunt Gertrude, don't use it here. Otherwise, don't hold back. Being obnoxious won't get you bleeped!"

"Obnoxious, obnoxious, obnoxious!" chanted the audience.

The Huffingtons both shook their heads in utter disgust and sat ramrod straight.

The lights dimmed and Joe "Steak" Johansson came onstage to thunderous applause. He gave his spiel and spit out the rules: nineteen audience members would be randomly selected as judges to taste-test both dishes without knowing whose was whose. If Keira won, she—and the charity of her choice—would collect twenty-five thousand smackers each. If Joe won, twenty-five thousand would go to the charity of his choice.

"And now," Joe said, "a smokin'-hot woman who needs no introduction!" I thought about his responses to number seven on Jocelyn's list, all the good reasons he loved her. I went from hating the sight of him to . . . liking the dude.

"Sara! Sara! Sara!" the audience chanted.

Sara came out from backstage in a cute sundress and red Chucks, waving and smiling. She scanned the audience and finally found me, giving me a little wave.

"D'oh!" Joe yelled. "Did you catch that, folks? My lovely fiancée is waving at someone in the audience. Her room-mate—a former challenger of mine who narrowly beat me. You might remember the skinny vegan who managed to make the panel of judges vote for her because they felt bad that she eats nothing but plants all day. Well, our challenger is a trainee at her plant restaurant. Learning to cook plants!"

Okay, I might love that he adored Sara, but my intense dis-like of him was back.

Sara put her hands on her hips. "Who ate vegan last night? This guy." she said, jabbing her elbow in Joe's direction. "I made him a primavera pasta with roasted veggies and he gob-bled it up and asked for seconds. All vegan."

"Low blow, Joe!" the audience shouted, the standard chant when he was called on something.

"She tricked me!" Joe called out. "She told me there was steak in it and turned the lights real low. I was *bim*boozled!"

"Bimboozled!" the audience chanted back, hooting with laughter.

I chanced a glance at the Huffingtons, who looked absolutely horrified.

"Would you like to meet my challenger?" Joe said. "This chick with a bad dye job thinks she can make a better lasagna than me. And check this out—her lasagna? No ground beef. No sausage. No ricotta cheese." He snorted. "I even think she'll be using wheat noodles. Ewww!"

"Ewww!" the audience chanted back. "Eww. Eww. Eww!"

"Okay, challenger, come on out. Folks, meet Kei-rah-rah Huffington!"

Keira, in white, skinny jeans, shiny red ballet flats, and a chef's jacket, her hair in a low ponytail, came dashing out, waving her arms above her head. "It's *Keira*," she said, making a comical face at Joe and at the audience. "Keir-a."

"I've already forgotten it," Joe called out. "Now let's meet her assistant, some hipster dude with another bad dye job and skinny jeans." Joe rolled his eyes and snorted. "Here he is, Gunnar GunnaLose Fitch!"

"We're gonna beat your trash-talking ass!" Gunnar shouted, jogging out and throwing his hands up in the air like Rocky Balboa.

"Yeah, we are," Keira shouted, nodding her head at the audience to get them on her side. She wasn't doing a half-bad job so far.

"LOL, guys," Joe bellowed. "This skinny thing with the messed-up hair thinks she can make a lasagna better than I can?"

"The messed-up hair is called ombré," Keira said. "Get with

the times. Oh, and the eighties called. They want back that hideous, loud Hawaiian shirt."

"That's all you got?" Joe shook his head. "Sad, om-head. Very sad."

"Ommmm! Ommmm!" the audience chanted.

"This isn't gonna be pretty," I whispered to Zach.

"Go, Keira," Zach yelled. So sweet, my man.

"Go *home*, you mean," Joe called back to chants from the audience. "Go home. Go home. Go home! And that skinny Gunnar-lose dude with you!"

"Gunnar rules!" Alanna screamed at the top of her lungs, and I had to smile. Those two were definitely involved.

Two screens on either side of the audience allowed us to watch Keira and Joe cook. Gunnar sliced and chopped away, shouting back at Joe whenever Joe tried to frazzle him and Keira. She'd remembered to add the garlic only after the onions were tender. She added the pinch of agave nectar. She didn't overknead the dough for the lasagna noodles.

So far, so good.

The more Joe tried to heckle her, the more she ignored him, focusing on layering the lasagna, letting Gunnar shout back zingers. He was pretty good at it; *quelle surprise.*

Fifty-five minutes later, a bell rang. "Five-minute warning!" Sara called out. "Chefs, begin plating!"

The producer called out a random name from the audience: "Zach Jeffries, please stand up and state five numbers between one and fifty."

Zach picked his numbers, as did four other audience members. Since Zach was selected as one of the people to choose numbers, I knew it wasn't rigged. The people with those nineteen numbers were then called by name to be the judges.

"Okay, time to judge!" Joe shouted. "Who made the better lasagna? Me, who eats lasagna for breakfast half the week? Or the couple with the bad dye jobs and fake meat and cheese?" Joe mock shivered. "Don't those two look like they could use some iron in their blood? Eat a steak, peeps," he said to Keira and Gunnar.

"I could bench-press *you*," Keira shouted back.

"You couldn't bench-press a tomato, vegan trainee!"

"Trainee! Trainee!" the audience chanted.

The voting began and I held my breath and squeezed Zach's hand.

By the second to last vote, it was a tie. Good for ratings, I guess, but we were dying. Whoever got it would win the $25,000.

"What's it gonna be, chickadoodle," he said to the woman, who picked up her fork and tried a bite of both again.

"No contest," she said. "The winner is . . . plate number one!"

"Noooo!" Joe yelped, mock-stabbing himself through the heart. "That's the vegan trainee's lasagna!"

I jumped up. I couldn't help it. "Yeah. Hellz yeah. Oh hellz yeah."

"Joe blow blew it!" the audience shouted. "Vegan, vegan, vegan!"

Keira jumped in Gunnar's arms and he spun her around.

"Oh, God, don't tell me they're dating," her father muttered.

"They're not," Alanna said assuredly. Which meant that she and Gunnar were.

"This is for you, Violet!" Gunnar said into the camera. "This is for my baby girl!" That baby girl would have been in the audience, but no one under eighteen was permitted because of all the trash-talking, not unlike my own, and the occasional bouts of violence that broke out in the audience.

"She's not expected to split the money with that man, is she?" Dominique said. "Though I hope so because she wouldn't have the money she needs for school."

Ha—Dominique was sooo hypocritical! I had no doubt Gunnar was talking about the experience of being on the show, his daughter's favorite. He did it for Violet—and as a favor to Keira. But it just figured Dominique would suddenly give a fig about the money and Keira's plans for it.

"Mom, seriously?" Zach said to her. "Can't you be proud of her? She made something happen for herself for a very good cause."

Dominique gave Zach the most condescending look I'd ever seen. "Oh, Zachary. Just once, please stop rooting for the underdog."

"That'll always hold you back," Keira's dad said to Zach.

That was absurd since Zach was a wunderkind CEO. He smiled at me and shook his head.

Keira came running over and grabbed me into a hug. "I owe everything to you, Clementine. For giving me a chance in the first place. For helping me out. You rock."

Dominique glared at me.

⸻ ◎ ◎ ⸻

In the parking lot, as Zach and I headed to his car, Dominique came storming over.

"You knew how I felt," she said to me through gritted teeth. "You actually influenced her against my wishes."

"Dominique, come on. Keira won! She showed such moxie. She found a way to earn the money to pay for her education, her future. The future *she* wants."

"Oh, please. She's twenty-two years old. She's been everything from one of those perfume sprayers in Nordstrom's cosmetics department to a dog walker. She has no idea what she wants. Culinary school isn't for her. Trust me, she'll drop out in two weeks."

"Mom, she just stood up against Joe 'Steak' Johansson and beat him with a vegan lasagna," Zach said. "I think she'll be fine. And I think she'll do great in cooking school. Obviously."

"Obviously, you don't know Keira as well as I do," Dominique shot back. "She made a fool of herself. She'll never get a decent position in fund-raising or philanthropy with that video out there. Trash-talking or whatever you people call it. It was embarrassing."

"Dominique, you can't control her. She's an adult. A pretty great one. Let her make her own decisions."

"You don't tell me what to do, young lady. And you know what? Plan your own damned wedding. I'm through with you."

Dominique swiveled on her four-inch-high Louboutins and stormed back to Sir Paul, sitting inside their BMW.

So she'd finally quit as wedding planner. Thing was, I wasn't as relieved as I should have been.

<hr />

"Unbelievable," I said to Zach as we drove home.

Silence.

"Zach?"

"I'm sure she'll calm down and be harassing you about gowns and centerpieces tomorrow morning. Don't give it a thought."

"*What?* So she gets away with trying to run Keira's life and taking out her anger on me?" *And she quit! She finally quit! I'm free!*

He let out a harsh sigh. "Clem, she's my mother. She's meddling in Keira's life, yes, but that doesn't have anything to do with you."

"She made it about me!"

He pulled over on the side of the road and took my hand. "Remember how you helped me butt out of Jolie's life when she got engaged and finally see her as adult? Maybe you can help Dominique with Keira. If you got me to see the light about my sister, you can work that magic on my mother."

"I've tried. She's a nightmare."

He didn't blink. "So take it on as a challenge. I know you care about Keira. And my mother respects you. You actually might get through to her." He pulled on the ends of my hair. "Please, Clem? I don't have the time or energy to deal with a war between my fiancée and mother. I'm up to my eyeballs in problems at work. Just fix this, okay?"

"Right now, I'd rather fix *us.*"

He turned away, frustrated as all hell, I knew, but too bad. Enough was enough.

We needed time alone together. Away from LA. We needed the adventure that Jocelyn had written about on her list. "Let's go away together. Can you take off midweek? Even just a couple of days?"

"Now's a really bad time."

"Just two days, Zach. I think we need to go off on some adventure together, somewhere we can get away from everything and not even talk about what's going on with us, with work."

"I don't know, Clem. It's a *really* bad—"

"It's always going to be a bad time. Let's go to the desert."

He took my hand and held it tight, and for a long moment he just looked at me. My heart started booming. *He's going to tell me the wedding's off. That he's changed his mind. That he fell in love with some VP of Finance or something. That he's back with Vivienne. That all my talk of the Outpost made him realize he can't marry me, after all.*

"Fix things with my mother and I'll go wherever you want."

I had no idea how to make that happen, but whatever, I'd do it. "Deal."

⸺◦◎ ◎◦⸺

We tried to figure that out in bed, but all we did was argue. When I turned over because I was sick to death of talking about Dominiquezilla, he must have thought I'd fallen asleep because he tiptoed out of bed and went downstairs, Charlie at his heels. I heard the door to his office close.

What the hell was he doing in there? Sexting some coworker? I didn't believe that for a second. Zach was true-blue. So were things at work really that bad? Was the company about to fold? What, what, what?

Next thing I knew, sunlight was filtering in through the sheer curtains at the window overlooking the Pacific, and I turned over to spoon against Zach. But he wasn't there.

A note on his pillow read, *Went to work early. Love you. Call D, okay?*

I flipped over on my back in utter frustration.

I had to cook. I needed to get my hands full of flour and root vegetables. And I needed help on my rustic potpie if I was going to wow the *New York Times* reporter.

I needed Alexander.

"Charlie, go fetch my phone," I said to the beagle, staring at me from the side of the bed.

He stared at me blankly.

I got out of bed, threw on yoga pants and a tank top, and took Charlie for a long walk in the park, thinking about the situation with Dominique. I couldn't get the woman to see the light about not dousing my parents' small organic farm in bug spray to keep mosquitoes off guests' arms and legs at the wedding. But I was supposed to change her mind about her beloved stepdaughter?

And how had this morphed into my life? Wasn't I supposed to be running my restaurant and thrilling the taste buds of food critics and *New York Times* travel section reporters? Suddenly I was the mediator for a family I hadn't even married into yet?

I pulled out my phone and called Alexander, even though it was barely eight o'clock in the morning.

"Is this a good time to work on my potpie?"

"Always a good time for you, Clem," he said in that gorgeous English accent.

Why the f-balls couldn't Zach say that just once?

On my way to Alexander's, I got a call from the *Times* reporter. "I just wanted you to know your competition has dropped to only one restaurant. It's between you and Fresh."

What? Alexander was my only competition? Getting Fresh in that piece would ensure his promotion to chef and *make* him.

But the piece would also make Clementine's.

Shizz.

22

"I see the problem with the potpie," Alexander said as we stood at the counter in his kitchen. He scanned my recipe, typed on white paper. "The shiitake mushrooms. They don't soften the right way. I'd leave those out—or use button mushrooms—and I'll bet it'll be perfect."

Almost brought down by shiitake mushrooms? Zach loved those. Maybe that was why I used them in so many dishes.

I stared out the window, trying to focus on button mushrooms. White. Cremini. I couldn't even think straight. Fuckburgers.

"Clem, you okay?"

I dropped down on a chair at his kitchen table. "No. Everything sucks. My potpie. My relationship with Zach is off-kilter.

His mother hates my guts and quit as our wedding planner and Zach wants me to fix things. My entire life is a mess right now."

Alexander flashed me a smile, his dimple popping. "Everything's cool between us."

"Actually, it's not. The *Times* reporter called. The competition for inclusion in the article is between my place and Fresh."

"I know. Emil got the same call and screamed into my ear five minutes ago that I'd better 'obliterate No Crap or else.'"

Ass. "You still want to help me make my potpie irresistible?"

"You still my friend?"

"Of course."

"Then yes."

We spent the morning working on the potpie, peeling potatoes, dicing carrots, and springing peas from the pod, making the broth and adding marjoram, cumin, and basil to the sautéed onions and garlic. I made a simple crust of flour and water and olive oil, rolling out the top and bottom. Shredded, braised tofu went into the simmering pot, the broth thickening and the vegetables softening, the aromas so delicious and comforting. An hour later, one taste told me Alexander had been absolutely right about the shiitake mushrooms.

The potpie was orgasm-inducing. Best I'd ever made.

"I wish there was a way we could both make it in the article," I told him, taking another bite of my masterpiece.

"Me too. Especially you, though. Clementine's No Crap Café is all yours. It's different when you own the place. You're an inspiration."

He was always so supportive and generous. "Aww. You'll have your own restaurant. I know you will." I hugged him, and he wrapped his arms around me, lingering a few seconds longer than he should have.

Thankfully, his dogs interrupted us at exactly that moment, begging for a bite of the potpie, so we gave them dog biscuits and took them out for a walk. Alexander told me hilarious stories about what was going on at Fresh these days: A trainee Emil had fired in a humiliating way had tried to get back at him by sneaking in before hours and replacing the soy milk in the refrigerator with cow's milk. Much the way my own saboteur, Rain Welch, had done to me last year. Another trainee with a sharp nose had sniffed out the grossness right away and alerted Alexander before anyone could use it.

When we got back to his house, he whipped us up some frozen pomegranate and strawberry smoothies, and we sat in his little backyard, his dogs playing fetch with the squeaky toy Alexander kept throwing.

"So you and Zach," he said. "You're getting married and that's it? I need to forget you, right? Why can't I seem to do that?"

He was looking at me so intently, his incredible dark brown eyes drawing me closer, closer . . .

For a split second, I forgot everything—the mother-in-law from the black lagoon, Zach's disappearing acts and distance, my all-consuming thoughts about the restaurant and publicity and receipts and codes and bills.

I was inches away from his face, from his lips. From a kiss that would be wrong on a million levels. "I really love Zach. I'm madly, truly, deeply in love with him. We're going through a rough patch right now, but getting through those shitty periods is part of having a real relationship, right?" I had to remember that.

He nodded. "I'll work on getting over what might have been," he said dramatically.

Once again, Alexander Orr had helped me in a big way. I knew, without a doubt, that I wanted to marry Zach. That I loved him. No matter what.

No matter what.

❧ ◎ ◎ ❧

Back at my apartment, I tried to call Dominique twice, but she was clearly refusing my calls, since her cell phone rang five times before going to voice mail. Fine. Whatever. The longer I could put off dealing with her, the better. When my phone rang a few minutes after I'd hung up the last time, I thought it was her, but it was Jocelyn, my favorite aunt-to-be.

She was in my neighborhood and wondered if I was free for a walk around the Pier. Perfect. If anyone could help me with Dominique Huffington, it was Jocelyn.

A half hour later, we met by the Jo Mama Juice truck.

She wore white, flowing pants and a long tunic with a cool necklace, her white hair coiled in a bun. She was so elegant. She linked arms with me, and we walked, people watching and stopping to watch a teenager play some serious violin. Jocelyn put a $10 bill in his open case.

"So how are you doing with the list?" she asked, stopping again to admire a pair of black pugs that were sniffing something by a tree.

"I feel like I can't get anywhere because Zach is putting so much distance between us. He keeps saying he's busy with work, that it's not you, blah, blah, blah. But something is bothering him. I know it. We're going away in a few days, just the two of us, but I want to make things right between us before we go."

"Oh, that's easy. You go to his office, shut the door, and tell him you're not leaving until he's honest with you. If he still doesn't open up, you tell him it's over, that you can't live like this. Trust me, it'll work."

"Been there, done that?"

She smiled. "Frederick finally told me he'd been acting so distant and making excuses about getting together because he was positive he had only months to live. Self-diagnosed hypochondriac! He thought he had five different kinds of cancer. Turns out he had a hernia."

I smiled. "If you could go back to before you married Frederick, would you still have said yes?"

"Without a doubt. But it's better to know that up front than wonder about it later. That's why I sent you the list. Go talk to Zach. Remember—he balks, you tell him it's over. He'll spill it."

I hugged her tight. "One more piece of advice? This time about Dominique?"

"Of course."

"She's furious at me because she thinks I influenced Keira to appear on *Eat Me*. And now that Keira won, she's even more angry that Keira can now finance her own dream of culinary school. Dominique quit as my wedding planner."

"You're not unhappy about that, are you?" Jocelyn asked with a devilish smile

"No. But Zach is. He wants harmony and peace. I'm supposed to smooth things over with Dominique."

"Well, I'll tell you this: the way to do that is to go see her and make her feel important. That's all she really wants. To feel part of things. Keira's defection from Dominique's plan is about loss of control, not holding the reins of her life. She thinks of Keira as her baby, and it's time to let go."

"Zach thinks if anyone can help her see that, it's me. But I feel like she hates my guts. Why would she listen to a word I say?"

"She doesn't hate you at all. She respects that you're your own woman. You'll see. Go pay her a visit—after your fiancé, that is."

"I owe you so much."

Jocelyn patted my hand. "Maybe I'll drag Frederick out to your restaurant one night. He'll kick and scream about 'that crazy food,' but I'll bet he'll love what I order for him."

"On the house," I told her, then put her in her car and watched her drive away, thankful that I had someone so wise and wonderful in my life—and soon-to-be family.

Then I got in my own car and drove straight to Zach's office.

I didn't even have to deal with the sweater-wearing admin. When I got out of the elevator onto his floor, Zach was standing right there, a stack of files in his hands.

He looked surprised to see me. And not particularly glad.

He led the way into his office and closed the door behind him. "Clem, if you're here to rant about my mother, now isn't a—"

Sometimes I wanted to take my hands and wring his neck. I meant that nicely. "This has nothing do with her. And when *will* be a good time? I'm here because I want to know what's going on."

He shifted the file in his hand. "I told you. I'm just crazed."

I didn't want to say the words. But I had to. "Look, Zach. I've had it. Unless you're honest with me, we're over."

He looked at me and closed his eyes.

I could see how weary he was, and I felt like hell about it. But enough was enough.

He squeezed my hand. "I'll call you when I get home. We'll talk, okay?"

"You'll tell me the truth?"

He nodded.

⌒◯◯⌒

Except by midnight, he didn't call. I sat by the window in my apartment, looking out onto Montana and Fourteenth, at the building in which we'd met. So much had happened since that day—he'd changed, I'd changed, we'd changed together so that we could *be* together. But now he was shutting me out. It was one thing to give a guy some space to do what he had to do—whatever that was. It was another to be a fool, to ask and ask and ask for an explanation, to be let in, and to be constantly given excuses.

He said he'd call and he hadn't.

So I called him.

"I guess we're over," I said, my voice barely above a whisper. Angry and hurt were duking it out, and hurt won. I could barely breathe.

"Clementine, I'm not even home yet. I said I'd call when I got home."

"I can't do this anymore. You're not being straight with me, and I can't live like this. I can't marry someone who won't be honest with me. Good-bye, Zach."

I put my phone down and slid down the wall onto the floor and did something I hadn't in a long, long time. I cried.

23

Sara was at Joe's, it was too late to call Ty in Paris, and I could do only one thing to pick myself up. As in old times, I stood in the kitchen of my apartment, cranked up ABBA as high as I could for just past midnight, and dug my hands into a bowl of flour and agave nectar and vanilla and vegan margarine, forcing myself to think about chocolate chips. Yes, I'd add chocolate chips.

Except Zach loved chocolate-chip anything, and my stomach flip-flopped.

Just bake. Forget everything and bake. I could serve the cookies as a special dessert tomorrow with my strawberry sorbet or—

The downstairs buzzer buzzed.

Sara forgot her key? I pressed TALK. "Sar?"

"Clem, it's Zach."

My pulse sped up. Was he here to tell me it *was* over?

Maybe he was here to finally come clean. Which could still mean we were over. He'd fallen in love with a coworker. With Vivienne, his ex. Or he'd come to realize he couldn't live with a mouthy vegan, after all.

I opened the door, listening to his feet as he came up the five flights. He walked slowly and heavily, which meant trouble.

When he appeared at the landing, he looked absolutely miserable.

What the hell was going on?

He came in and shut the door. I backed away without even meaning to.

"Okay, I'm just going to say this straight out, Clem. From everything I can tell, someone is embezzling from Jeffries Enterprises."

Relief came flooding over me, though it still sucked for Zach. It *was* just business.

"But why couldn't you tell me that weeks ago? If you'd just explained that—"

"I couldn't, Clem." He stared down at the floor, toward the living room, back at the kitchen wall.

"Okay, I'm not computing. Why the hell not? *What* is the big deal?"

"Because the embezzler is your cousin Harry."

Sucker punch to the stomach. I stared at him, waiting for the *Just kidding, it's some slime in the cubicle across from Har-*

ry's. Or some wheeler-dealer in a corner office. But Zach let his head drop back with a weary sigh.

This had to be a mistake. Harry Cooper? *Embezzler?* No fucking way.

"Everything points to him. Leads back to him. I've tried a hundred ways to prove to myself that he's not guilty, but he is."

I shook my head. "Well, you're wrong. Harry is the most ethical person I know. He'd never steal from you. You're *wrong*."

A memory flitted through my mind, of Harry, age ten, defending my honor to a bunch of moronic boys from our school who were making fun of the farm and my family for being vegans. He'd told them to shut their stupid yaps, and they'd set upon him, beating the crap out of him. I'd jumped in and had ended up with a black eye and a broken arm. Harry had a matching black eye and a bruised rib. But we'd pummeled those jerks worse and they'd never bothered us again.

Harry, who stood up for vegan cousins and got his butt kicked, who flew across the country for my cooking school graduation, did *not* do this.

"I know you care about Harry. I know you two were very close growing up. But facts are facts. My team is launching an internal investigation to document everything."

"Document everything for what?"

"I'll have to involve the police, Clem. We're talking about millions of dollars that have vanished. Which indicates an offshore account."

I stepped back. This had to be a mistake. "If Harry is guilty, I'll eat a bloody steak at the Silver Steer. You've got be kidding me, Zach."

He turned away. "I don't know how we're supposed to combine our families with something this," Zach said, his voice strained. "This thing with Harry, you can barely tolerate my mother . . . her relationship with Keira is falling apart. Clem"— Zach turned away from me—"I think we should postpone the wedding."

The sound you hear? My heart cracking in pieces. "You know what?" I said, my voice breaking. "I think so too. I can't believe you think he really did something like this."

Zach disappeared into the bathroom. Because he had tears in his eyes, no doubt. What the hell had happened? How could any of this be real?

He came out of the bathroom, holding something. "Oh my God, Clem."

"What? What is that?"

He held out what looked like a pregnancy test. I stepped closer and saw a faint pink line. Holy gobsmackers. Sara was pregnant?

"I found this on the windowsill. Do you have something to tell me?"

I stared at him as though he had three heads. *Oh, yes, I'm pregnant, but thought I'd keep it to myself and just let you tear us apart anyway. What the hell?* "I have a *roommate*, remember? But it's your way to jump to conclusions, isn't it?"

He looked very, very relieved. "So it's not yours?"

I shook my head, wanting him to go, not wanting him to go. Wanting to find Sara.

"I'm very, very sorry, Clementine. I love you, but I think we'd better take a break." He held out the stick, then set it on a side table. "I'm not sure we're ready for any of this."

A second later, he was gone.

Sara wasn't answering her texts. Or phone. I sat in the living room, staring out the window, wondering what the fuzz had happened to my life. How had everything gotten so messed up? How could I fix things that were so out of my control?

I sat there, my mind about to explode, and eventually I must have fallen asleep because I woke up on the couch in a sitting position, the sun streaming in through the windows.

Go find Sara, I told myself. Was she pregnant? Was that why she'd said yes to Joe? The pregnancy test confirmed it? Or had it been negative and now she was thinking of breaking the engagement?

And why hadn't she shared any of this with me? *We're best friends.*

Because all you think about is the restaurant and Zach. Because you practically live there. Because you're so committed to not being distracted that your own best friend didn't tell you she's pregnant. Or isn't.

I took a quick shower, grabbed my bag, and headed over to Joe's house in Venice Beach. His house was gated to keep out his rabid fans—and the challengers he'd humiliated in front of all America. I pressed the buzzer.

"Who goes there?" came Joe's booming voice.

"Joe? It's me, Clementine Cooper."

"The skinny vegan?"

I rolled my eyes. "Yeah. Is Sara there?"

The gate swung open. Joe's house was a lot nicer than I expected. Manicured lawn and all. It was bizarre, of course, tall and white with weird angles and narrow windows.

Sara opened the front door. "Hey, Clem, what's up?"

"Take a walk with me? I have something important to talk to you about."

We headed down the stone path and stood by the gate.

"I found a pregnancy test in the bathroom garbage. Well, Zach did. He thought it was mine."

"Oh, shit, did I leave that lying around? I was so freaked out that I must have forgotten about the test."

So . . . you are? You're not?"

"My period was almost three weeks late. It's never late. So yesterday, I told Joe I was sure I was pregnant. And you know what? He was thrilled. He spun me around, sent his assistant out for cigars, and wouldn't let me do a thing for myself. I tried telling him I hadn't taken the test yet, that I wasn't sure, but he said he could feel it. We were having a baby and he couldn't wait for there to be a mini us crawling around." Sara took a deep breath.

I waited for her to continue.

"So then I took the pregnancy test. And it was negative. So I took another one. Negative. And then I got my period. But for an entire day, I thought I was pregnant and Joe was so happy because he hoped I *was*."

"And you told him you weren't?"

She nodded, watching two huge Rhodesian ridgebacks walk by. "Those few hours when he thought I was pregnant, when he ordered a special bed for a zillion dollars that you can remote-control so I could raise my feet up, you know what I realized?"

"What?"

"That I love the guy. Really, really love him. I was so focused on the fact that he loves me, that he wants to marry me, that I kind of blew off whether or not I loved him."

"And you're sad because you're not pregnant?"

"Nah, I'm not really ready to be anyone's mother. I'm sad because my best friend hates him. Because my mother hates him. Because half of America hates him. I love the guy so danged much, Clem."

I smiled. "I don't hate him. I love that he loves you. You're my best friend, Sara. All I want is for you to be happy. And I know Joe makes you happy. Happier than I've ever seen you."

"Shut up, you're gonna make me cry." She pulled me into a hug.

"Why didn't you tell me you thought you were pregnant?"

"I don't know. I guess because I know Joe's not your favorite person, and I was worried that he'd humiliate your soon-to-be stepsister-in-law and lose, and then you'd hate him even more. And, well, you're kind of busy all the time. It's not that easy to find you just hanging out these days."

"I would drop anything for you, Sara. You know that, right?"

"Yeah, I guess. I just know the restaurant is everything to you and—"

"Sar, you're my best friend. You come first."

"Hey, so maybe we can have a double wedding." She laughed. "Can you imagine?"

For a half hour, I had actually forgot about my messed-up love life. "There's not going to be a wedding—well, on my end, anyway. Zach thinks my cousin Harry is embezzling from his company. He's about to involve the police. We got into a huge fight and he said we should postpone the wedding."

"Ugh, I'm really sorry, Clem. Have you talked to Harry?"

"He's not answering his phone. I don't know what that means."

"Go to his condo. Go."

"Going. Harry? Some sharklike embezzler? Zero sense."

But a lot made zero sense these days.

If I could turn back the clock, go all Superman on time so that Zach hadn't accused Harry of embezzling, hadn't "postponed" the wedding, which had turned into "taking a break,"

I'd be so flipping grateful I'd happily take back Dominique as wedding planner. Well, maybe.

Another buzzer. I pressed apartment 3B at Harry's building. No answer. I pressed again.

"Clem?" Harry sounded weary. And because I knew him so well—scared.

He'd clearly been hiding by the window, peering out. He must be freaking out that the cops were going to bust down his door any minute.

He buzzed me in and I headed up the stairs. I'd barely knocked when the door flew open and he pulled me inside, then locked it up tight again.

Harry looked like a wreck. He had serious bedhead and looked as if he hadn't slept in weeks.

His apartment was in even worse shape. He had a nice place, modern and high-tech, but his clothes were strewn all over his bedroom floor, and various sections of the *LA Times* and the *Wall Street Journal* were on every surface.

Under serious pressure right now, Harry had turned into a freaked-out slob.

"Nadia dumped me when she found out I'm in trouble." He grabbed his hair with both hands. "She's not even standing by me."

Jocelyn had called that one. "Harry, you'll get through this.

Once Zach and the internal whoevers go through the paper trail or whatever you call it, they'll find out it's just a big mistake, some number-crunching error. It'll be okay."

He started pacing, then headed over to the window and looked out. "Clem, I need to get some air, go for a long walk on the beach or something. I'll call you later, okay?"

The guy was a wreck. "I'll come with you."

He shook his head. "I just need to think, okay? Figure out where the screwup happened. If I could just retrace my steps in my head . . ."

"Gotcha. Everything will be fine. Don't worry so much, okay? You're innocent and that's that."

He walked me out, slid on his sunglasses, and bolted in the opposite direction I started walking. Not toward the beach, either.

Not until I was halfway to the restaurant did I realize he'd never said he *was* innocent. But, duh—of course he was.

24

At close to midnight, my buzzer rang. I'd just gotten home from the restaurant and had taken a long hot shower and no longer reeked of garlic and tomato sauce.

Zach.

For a second, I felt huge relief. He was probably coming over to tell me he found the real bad guy or a typo or a mathematical error. But my stomach was flip-flopping and my neck was stiff and every muscle in my body was clenching.

I buzzed him in and heard him taking the stairs two at a time. That had to be a good sign. He wouldn't rush to give me bad news; he'd walk slowly, like to his death or something.

I opened the door and waited.

At the look on his face—pained, regretful, and weary—I took a step back. What the hell?

He closed his eyes for a second, then reached for my hand, but I wouldn't take it. "I had to tell you this in person. Harry will be arrested in the morning. His guilt is beyond a shadow of a doubt as far as my investigators are concerned. I'm so sorry, Clem."

My stomach dropped and I felt as if I might throw up. I shook my head. This made no sense. "Harry's not guilty. He's my *cousin Harry.* This can't be right, Zach."

I just need to think . . . figure out where the screwup happened. If I could just retrace my steps in my head . . .

Had he meant the screwup that led to his *getting caught?*

Oh, Harry. I flashbacked to memory after memory of Harry and me as kids, as teens. Harry had been my first best friend.

"I wish he wasn't guilty, Clem. Because I love you more than anything, and I know what this is doing to you."

Half of me wanted to fling myself into his arms and just let him hold me until the shock wore off. The other half wanted him gone. Now.

"I think you should go."

He looked at me, his expression so full of regrets, then nodded and headed back downstairs.

⁓ ◎ ⊙ ⁓

Between midnight and when I fell asleep on the couch at 3:00 a.m. again, I called Harry's cell at least twenty times. Went straight to voice mail. I had to see him, had to hear him tell me it wasn't true. That this was just a big, stupid mistake, that Zach and his investigators were wrong. That some megamind thug had framed him or something.

When I woke up in the morning, my first thought was that I knew where Harry was. I took a fast shower, grabbed one of my scones and a thermos of strong black tea and hit the road, going as fast as I could without making the cops chase me down.

Three hours later, I walked into my parents' barn and climbed the loft stairs and there he was, sitting against the wall, his knees up. He looked worse than he had the day before—his hair was a wreck, he had dark circles under his eyes, the ole five o'clock shadow, and his pants were stained. Next to him was a pretty full bottle of Jack Daniel's, so at least he wasn't drunk. Unless this was the second or third bottle he had with him.

"I'm turning myself in, in a little while," he said, not looking up.

Turning himself in? What? "Harry, I—"

He leaned his head back against the wall. "I really messed things up, Clem." He seemed about to say more, but then clamped his mouth shut.

"Harry, what are you saying?"

"I'm saying I'm in bad trouble."

He *was* guilty. Holy hellzburgers, no.

I couldn't get this to compute in my brain. "Why, though? I mean, why'd you do it?"

He closed his eyes and sucked in a deep breath. "I had some gambling debts and then they snowballed. And Nadia—when she *was* my girlfriend—likes nice things. One thing led to another and another and another." He dropped his head into his hands.

"Harry, you could have come to me."

"Because you have a half million lying around? Because your fiancé, who happens to be my boss five times removed, would give it to me?"

"So you stole it from that fiancé instead?"

He picked up the bottle of Jack Daniel's but didn't take a swig. "I didn't intend to outright steal it. At first, I moved a little money around here and there, and I always planned to pay it back. But then that snowballed too. And I couldn't stop."

Oh, Harry.

"I'm sorry, Clem. Just know that, okay?"

That sound you hear again? Heart cracking even more. "Me too."

Then he pulled out his cell phone and called the LAPD and said he was turning himself in at noon.

"I'm opening a second restaurant in here," I said numbly. "This loft won't even be here in a few months. That seems weird, doesn't it? Like this whole conversation couldn't have happened—none of it could have happened—because the loft will be gone."

He looked at me. "Good. Like you need to be reminded every time you walk in here?"

Like I'd forget anyway.

I spent the next few hours with my parents, and when my sister arrived to meet with them and Harry's parents—who were sitting in the living room with ashen faces, wringing hands—I finally drove back home.

I stalked around my apartment, then dropped down on the window seat, staring out at the stupid hair salon that used to be the space I wanted for my restaurant, the space where I'd met Zach.

My phone rang: Jocelyn.

"What's this I hear about the wedding being postponed? Avery mentioned it to me. She said she didn't know the details, but that Zach was beside himself."

I told Jocelyn the whole crappy story.

"Clementine, that's terrible and I'm very sorry. I know it seems like a very, very big deal, and it is, but it's not the only bad thing—or the worst—that will happen during your relationship with Zach. In sixty-four years with Frederick, we've been through incidents and events that would bring you to your knees. That's what life is."

"Zach thinks we should take a break."

"Take a break from what? Don't you need each other most right now?"

I did need the jerk. Right now, there wasn't anyone I wanted more. I wished we could just disappear somewhere together and not even talk, not say a word.

I thought about Jocelyn's list. About expectations. Were we going to take breaks every time something crappy happened?

I loved Zach, and he loved me, and, yeah, this whole thing with Harry sucked, but it wasn't Zach's fault for catching him, and it wasn't mine for asking Zach to hire him.

I grabbed my phone and texted him, *Coming over now.*

He immediately texted back, *Okay.*

In Zach's kitchen, Charlie sat between us, staring from Zach to me. It was as if he knew something was up.

"I think we should go away together like we'd planned. *Now.* I'll leave the restaurant in Alanna and Gunnar's very capable hands. At first I was thinking we just needed to disappear together. But now I know we need to talk through some stuff."

What do you expect married life to really be like? Does it match his expectations?

"Let's go," he said.

We found a gorgeous inn that looked like a minicastle (where dogs were kindly welcome) in Carmel-by-the-Sea, and almost five hours later we were walking along the pure white beach, Charlie scampering ahead of us.

"How's your family doing?" Zach asked, throwing a stick for Charlie. We'd barely spoken on the drive up; just being together seemed to be enough for both of us.

"Not great. My dad was so upset he almost collapsed. Harry's his only nephew. And Harry's parents can't even process it. It makes no sense to any of us."

"Did you talk to Harry before . . ."

"Before he was arrested? Yeah. I hadn't been able to get ahold of him and then realized I'd find him in the loft of my parents' barn. It's where we always used to meet when something bad happened to one of us and we needed to talk or just think without being bugged by anyone."

"Did he admit it to you?"

"Yeah. Gambling debts and a gold-digger girlfriend who dumped him." I shook my head, still unable to imagine Harry Cooper as an embezzler and a liar.

Zach threw another stick, shaking his head. "I'm sorry, Clem. I wish this hadn't happened."

Me too. "You gave him a chance and he screwed you. If anyone should be apologizing, it's Harry. And me for asking you to hire him in the first place."

"He blindsided everyone, Clem."

Yeah. Especially me. The whole thing with Harry made me realize that I didn't know everything, even if I thought I did.

I stopped walking and looked out at the ocean, then at Zach. "So, are we taking a break?"

He tucked a breeze-blown strand of my hair behind my ear. "It's hard to take a break when you're on vacation together. Especially here in one of the most gorgeous places in the world."

"I've missed you. Not just the past few days. For weeks. This whole thing sucked. I thought you'd changed your mind about getting married."

"Never." He put his arm around me. "I just had my suspicions about Harry but couldn't say anything until I was sure. And how could I act like everything was fine while I was having an internal investigation of your favorite cousin? Bad situation."

"I understand why you didn't just tell me." He must have felt like hell about the whole thing.

He squeezed my hand and we walked up the beach, not saying a word.

Then he stopped and pulled me close against him, and we stood there for a good long time, Charlie sitting at our feet.

⁓ ◎ ◎ ⁓

In our four-poster bed, wearing our complimentary inn robes on what felt like thousand-thread-count sheets, Zach and I were finishing up our late-night room-service snack—incredible espresso chip gelato—when I told him about Jocelyn's call the other day and how she set me straight.

"I'm not surprised. My aunt Jocelyn is very wise. It's why Dominique can't get along with her. My mother hates to be wrong, and Jocelyn would call her out on how wrong she was all the time. Like you do."

That made me smile—for a second, anyway. "Well, what if your mother's done with me? You okay with having a wife and mother who don't speak?"

"Are you going to let it get to that?" he asked, taking a spoonful of my soup, which wasn't half-bad.

"I don't *want* to. I like Dominique. I actually really do. Not everything about her, but there are pieces of her I really do like. She's blunt and honest and is who she is, and she cares about her kids, even if she's her own worst enemy about getting them to stay in her life."

"She's on her way to losing Keira."

"Well, only your mother can fix that. I know you want me to fix things with her myself, but I don't know if I can. She's wrong about Keira and wrong to be mad at me for encouraging Keira to go after her dream, end of story."

"So maybe just sit her down and tell her that. She respects you, Clem. She'll listen."

I wasn't so sure about that. "But I'll need you to have my back. She respects you too. And she doesn't want to lose you all over again."

"I'll talk to her too. I'll let her know how much it sucks that my fiancée and I are stuck arguing about her on a romantic trip to Carmel."

"Hey. I just realized this counts as our adventure. On Jocelyn's list of things we check off before we get married. Carmel isn't exactly the wildness or anything, but we left home not knowing how things would end up between us. That's going on an adventure."

He leaned over and kissed me. "And everything ended up fine."

"Well, not yet, because you haven't gone over the list with me."

"Bring it."

I laughed. I reached into my bag for the folded-up piece of paper. "I'll substitute the word *her* for *him*. 'Number one: Be sure you love her.'"

"We already did this one, and I've never been more sure of anything in my life."

That got him a smile and a smooch on the lips. "Check. 'Number two: Close all doors to the past by revisiting (mentally or for real) any former beaus you've never been able to forget. Say good-bye once and for all—if you can.'"

I waited for him to change the subject, as usual. Or suddenly want to finish his pasta.

"I actually ran into my ex a couple of weeks ago." He took both our trays and put them on the table. He slid back into bed next to me, his hands behind his head.

"The famous Vivienne."

"You're way more famous than she is," he said, which made me smile again. "I felt the same way about seeing her as you said you did when you ran into your ex. Absolutely *nothing*. She could have been anyone."

"Why don't men just say these things the first time?" I asked, socking him with one of the little throw pillows. "Guys say nothing when saying exactly what you just said is all we want to hear."

He shrugged. "We can't help it. Why say something when there's nothing to say?"

He had me there.

"So what's the next one?" he asked, then sipped his wine.

"'Take a weekend adventure with a girlfriend who'll tell you the truth.'"

"Does a very long golf game with my brother count? The guy never stops talking or sharing his opinion."

"I'd say that counts."

"Want to know what he thinks about you?"

"Is it good?" I asked.

"He thinks you're the best thing that ever happened to me. That before you, no one ever challenged me on anything, but that you're one big challenge. And pretty, to boot."

"I've always liked Gareth."

"Next?" he asked.

"'Number four: Make sure that you are the captain of your own ship—even though you and your wife will be steering together. She'll be captain of hers too.'"

"I'm definitely the captain of my own ship, but I like to steer yours myself sometimes, huh?"

"Not even just sometimes," I said with an evil smile.

"I read over the info you e-mailed about the Outpost. I'll admit, you have a good, solid business plan, Clem. But I'm still worried about you splitting your time, spreading yourself too thin. And ever seeing you."

"I can make it work. I know I can." I wanted him to know that too.

He took my hand and held it. "Of course I know you can, Clem. I just don't *want* you to because I think it's going to be way too much on your plate. But I know you'll make it work, no matter what. You can do anything, Clem."

I couldn't stop my grin. "Did I actually just get Zach Jeffries's blessing?"

"At least all the work you did to get that blessing will now get you the loan. Your business plan is solid and then some."

"You'll have to send your dad and the new wife-to-be to the Outpost."

"He'll have everyone he knows packing the place. My father likes trends. And farm-to-table is a good trend."

"It's more than just a trend, though. It's a lifestyle. It may be all trendy to the general public, but people like my parents, like my entire family, have always eaten this way." I took a sip of my wine. "Ready for number five? 'Make a list of all the things you love about her and all the things you don't. Figure out how you'll deal with what you don't love. In parens: Don't put this off by waiting to cross the bridge when you come to it."

"Hand me the inn stationery and that pen," he said, upping his chin at the bedside table. He spent the next fifteen minutes scribbling, thinking, scribbling, thinking, scribbling. "Should I read it aloud?"

I nodded.

"On the Love side: 'Smart, driven, passionate, vegan.'"

"Wait—you love that I'm a vegan?" Ha.

"It's who you are, isn't it?" He took another sip of wine. "More on the Love side: 'Devoted to family and friends and me. Drop-dead gorgeous and amazing body.' Don't Love: 'Works too hard. Thinks up recipes when she might be massaging my neck. And I've been getting the feeling that Charlie's beginning to like her more than me.'"

I smiled. "So how are you going to deal with that?"

"I guess I'll have to stop thinking of him as only *my* dog."

I slid on top of him and kissed him. "'Number six: What do you expect married life to really be like? Does it match your expectations?'"

"I expect it to be a lot like it's been," he said. "Highs and lows and everything in between."

"Yeah, me too. I wasn't really sure what I expected before I started thinking about it, before I started going through the list. But that's exactly it. Marriage will be like life."

He nodded. "We're whipping through this list. Very good sign, I'd say."

"A lot of the hard work was done for us. We can thank your mother for that. And Harry." I sipped my wine. "'Number seven: Ask her why she loves you and then jot the reasons down on paper. Reread when you're arguing.'" I took the paper he'd written the Loves and Don't Loves on and slipped it into my bag. "I'll hang on to that for when I need to be reminded.

And you." I'd already written up my own list for Zach. I gave it to him, and when he finished reading it, he pulled me into a hug.

"So what's number eight?" he asked.

"'Are you expecting her to change once you're married? If so, return the ring or you'll be sorry.'"

"I never want you to change, Clementine Cooper."

"There is one thing I want *you* to change."

He raised an eyebrow.

"When something's wrong or bothering you, you have to tell me. Right away. Even if it's something like the Harry thing. Bring me in, okay?"

"Deal. And you too. Though you already do that."

I smiled. "Hey, we can check off number nine: 'Go on an adventure together. A real adventure.' Doing it!"

"What's the last one? Jocelyn's probably saved the most important for last."

"'Be sure you want to marry her,'" I read.

He pulled me close to him and looked into my eyes. "I'm very, very sure. You?"

I kissed him on the lips. "A thousand percent."

"Guess the wedding's back on then."

25

My cell phone woke me up at eight o'clock the next morning. Zach and I had stayed up so late talking and having amazing makeup sex that it had been close to three by the time we both drifted off to sleep.

"Clementine, this is Martina Jones from the *New York Times*. I've had a change of plans and will be in Santa Monica for the next two days only. I'll be dining at Clementine's No Crap Café tonight at seven with a party of four."

Holy crapola. I bolted up.

Talk about bad timing.

Then again, Zach and I had accomplished what we'd come here for. Our little adventure had done its job.

Zach turned over and opened on eye.

"It's the *Times* reporter," I whispered. "She's coming *tonight*."

"Let's pack, then," he said, squeezing my hand.

"See you at seven," I managed to spit out to the reporter.

Half of me wanted to call in my staff early, but I had to treat tonight like any other night. Sometimes, the more you went nuts over something, the more you tried to show your stuff, the more things went wrong. We were a great team, we made great food, and we had great service. No matter what Martina Jones and her party ordered, they'd love the food.

Damned straight, they would.

I began prepping for the specials—Moroccan vegetable couscous, mushroom risotto, blackened Cajun seitan stir-fry, and pumpkin ravioli. At three o'clock, Alanna and Gunnar arrived together, which wasn't so unusual lately, but they kept looking at each other with what I could only describe as moony faces.

I headed to the pantry to grab canisters of the flours I needed for the pumpkin ravioli's wonton wrappers—quinoa, coconut, and almond—and on the way back I stopped dead in my tracks. Gunnar was humming. Humming. He never hummed. And Alanna was smiling as she oiled a pan, shimmying a bit to the *Saturday Night Fever* sound track on the iPod.

Okay. Time to get nosy. "Do you guys have something to share?"

Alanna eyed Gunnar, and he shrugged. "Okay, I'll tell! After the taping of *Eat Me*, Gunnar and I went out to celebrate. I was so freaked out about my ex-boyfriend having dumped me the night before because I wouldn't commit in the end, that I poured out my heart to Gunnar in some dive bar. We ended up talking for hours about everything—relationships, what's it like to be a single dad, working here, cooking . . . and then we moved on to a coffee shop and just sat there talking and talking. When we left, we were holding hands."

Alanna was beaming in a way I'd never before seen her, and Gunnar was actually looking up from his station for once—and smiling.

Good for them. I adored them both and I adored them as a couple. "I love it," I said, heading to the pantry for the cinnamon, nutmeg, and ginger.

Alanna followed me, reaching for the arborio rice and couscous. She leaned close. "Remember when Gunnar said he was in love with someone he couldn't have?" she whispered to me.

I nodded.

She glanced back at Gunnar, who was busy at his station, setting out his knives. "Turns out that someone was *me*. He told me he's had an insane crush on me for months. We're going to take it slow—very slow. Gunnar knows I just got out of a long and intense relationship. And I know he has a daughter who needs him and we won't have much time together outside of work. But there's something here."

I smiled. "Awesome. I love you guys together."

She grinned and carried the rice and couscous to her station, and Evan McMann came over to help with prep.

"I have awesome news of my own," I said, turning down the iPod. "The *Times* reporter is coming tonight with three other people in her party. We've got to bring it. I want this and I want it bad."

"We're on it," Alanna said.

We started prep, the McMann twins washing vegetables, Alanna soaking rice, and Gunnar slicing zucchini. I glanced at the clock wondering where the hell Keira was. She picked this night to be late for the first time? Now that she was a big celeb with twenty-five big ones in the bank, maybe she'd quit on me without telling me.

Nah. Keira wasn't like that.

She slogged in twenty minutes late, looking like hell. Her eyes were red-rimmed as though she'd been crying.

"Keira? What's going on?"

She set her bag under her station. "I'm fine." Tears streamed down her face. "I'll just wash my hands and then get started on prep."

I walked over to her. "Come on out back with me."

She followed me out and wiped under her eyes. "Dominique told me she's through with me, that after all she's done for me, I embarrassed her and the family, and from now on our relationship won't be the same."

"*What?* Just because you want to go to culinary school?

That's insane." What the hell was wrong with Dominique? I didn't get this at all.

Keira let out a deep breath. "She went on and on about how she's groomed me to be her protégé, a mini her, that I've been like a daughter to her, and now I've just slammed a door in her face as though her opinion means nothing to me. It's crazy, Clem. Why does she give two figs what I want to do with my life? It's not like I told her I want to rob banks. What the hell?"

"I don't know. She's mad at me too. She quit as my wedding planner." Not that there *was* a wedding to plan anymore. "So how did you leave things?"

"I told her I loved her very much, that she's been like a mother to me since my mother died, and I wished I could make her happy, I wished I could make her proud of who I am, but I guess I can't. Then I said good-bye and walked out."

Good for you, Keira. That's all you could have done.

"My dream is to go to cooking school and be a chef like you. And I have the means to pay for that myself now. Why can't she and my father be proud of that? Be supportive?"

"I wish I knew. But you've got friends who support you a million percent. No matter what you need, Keira, I've got your back, okay?"

She hugged me.

"So get to work, will you? The *New York Times* reporter is coming tonight and bringing friends. We've got to seriously wow her so that she includes the restaurant in her piece in the Sunday travel section."

"Oh, we will." Keira dashed inside.

My phone pinged with a text: *You'll be brilliant as always.—Alexander.*

You'll be too, I sent out into the universe.

⁓ ◎ ◎ ⁓

Martina Jones and her party ordered two appetizers, four soups, four entrées, and two desserts.

I worked on the entrées so that if anything went wrong with the main course, I'd take the blame. The bruschetta and hummus and garlic pita chips were down to crumbs when the waiter cleared the plates. Shit yeah. The soups—my minestrone, split-pea, potato-leek, and chilled cucumber—also came back with bowls practically licked clean. This had to be a good sign. The pumpkin ravioli in my garlic-sage sauce was plated and ready to go. With Alanna's help, I stacked a perfect roasted vegetable napoleon, then put together the blackened Cajun seitan stir-fry and a portobello burger with avocado and red-pepper sauce. Finn brought out the tray to table six, and I peered through the peephole, watching their eyes light up at the presentation, oohing and aahing. I crossed my fingers. *Please, universe, let them love every bit!*

During each course, one of Jones's dinner companions got up and began shooting the food and the interior of the restaurant. For a moment, I stood there envisioning opening the travel section of an upcoming Sunday *New York Times*, and seeing photos of my food, of my restaurant, in the article on "veganmania" across America.

Then I envisioned Alexander a sous chef forever. Getting sacked by my old boss because I'd beat him.

Don't be a ding-dong, the little shoulder devil yelled in my ear. *You're finally almost in and you're worrying about hurting Alexander's wittle feelings? Look at you! Standing here like a wishy-washy piece of cheese when you should be working on the sopaipillas and lava cake!*

The angel hopped shoulders and punched the mini-devil out cold. *It's about balance, Clem,* she said, dusting off her hands and playing her tiny harp. *It's always about balance.*

Balance. I took a deep Pilates breath and headed back to my station, thinking about Alexander as I drizzled Vermont maple syrup on the warm, little sopaipillas. He'd put his all in; I'd put in mine. Whoever won would win fair.

So let's go do it.

I brought out the two desserts myself and four forks, plus complimentary samples of my favorite frozen smoothies.

The reporter bit into a sopaipilla and sighed. "Oh, God, this is intensely good. I can't imagine anything being better than how these taste right now. But we'll have to see what Fresh has in store for me tomorrow night."

I wanted to win this competition. I wanted Alexander to win too.

But no matter *what* happened, we'd still be friends. We'd been through some bad BS before and could withstand being pitted against each other, only one of us getting our restaurant in the *Times*.

As Jocelyn said, as *I* said last night, that was life. Up and down. Down and up. And not walking away when the going got crappy.

Now that I had Zach's go-for-it on the Outpost, it was even more fun to drive up to my parents' place. Would I have gone ahead with my plans for the second restaurant even if he'd still said it was a bad idea? Yeah. But having his green light made it all the more exciting. I got an early start, hitting the road before seven, and made the turn onto the long dirt driveway with its low, brown wooden fence by ten.

I had a good, long talk with my dad about Harry; my sister had recommended a good attorney, and his parents had sold their getaway condo in San Francisco to pay the sick retainer. I could see the stress of talking about Harry was getting to my dad. Like father, like daughter, he led the way into the kitchen and started cooking: banana-walnut pancakes with maple syrup and soy bacon. While we ate, I went over the business plan for the Outpost, and when I asked him to spend the next couple of weeks sketching out a menu of appetizers and main courses and desserts, his eyes lit up.

I spent the next few hours in a pair of old jeans and borrowed wellies, helping my mom clean out the harvesting wagons and getting her truck loaded up with this week's offerings for the farmers' market in town.

Finally, it was just me and the barn. But as I stood in there, instead of remembering how Harry had looked up in the loft, I found myself concentrating on shabby-chic-style tables with vases of yellow and white roses, a zinc juice bar, the sisal rugs, and my father living his dream in the kitchen. I knew right then I'd pull this off. If I could focus on the wall colors and the rug and the type of flatware that would complement the barn setting instead of getting a stomachache over Harry and our last conversation, I could handle anything. Running two restaurants. Getting married. Hanging with Sara. And whatever came next.

It was the Skinny Bitch way.

26

When I got home that night, the first thing I did was text Alexander: *Knock 'em dead, chef (not literally)*.

Then I called Dominique. At the sound of my voice, there was dead silence.

"I'm coming over," I said.

"I might not be home."

"Well, then I'll write what I have to say on your front door. In my dark red lipstain."

"You would, wouldn't you," she said.

"Shit yeah."

I could see the eye roll from here. "I'll be here for another half hour, so you'd better hurry if you want to catch me."

God, she was transparent. She wanted to talk this out as much as I did. Somehow, along the way, I'd gotten to know Dominique Jeffries Huffington.

⁓ ◎ ◎ ⁓

"If you're here to grovel to get me back as your wedding planner, you'll have to do better than this," she said, her expression flat. "Tea?" She gestured at the pot on the ornate tray on the coffee table. Gold bangles clanged on her tanned, toned arm. "The tea is herbal since I know you don't do caffeine. And the croissants are dairy-free, by the way."

She was trying, at least.

"The wedding's been postponed."

The look of alarm on her face surprised me. "Postponed? Why? Is it my fault?"

"Why do you think so?" I knew full well why. I wanted to see if she did. If she had a clue.

"Well, I did raise a bit of a fuss. Perhaps it caused problems between you and Zach."

"I will have that tea," I said, reaching for half of an almond croissant. "Do you want that to be the case?"

"Of course not."

"Then why *did* you raise such a fuss? Why do something that would potentially come between us?"

She stared at me for a moment, then stirred fake sugar into her tea and took a sip. "Well, I was mad as hell, for one."

"You worked so hard to repair your relationship with Zach, though."

"I'm who I am."

"Same here."

"I'm sorry I caused problems with you and Zach. That wasn't my intention at all. I like you, Clementine. To be honest, I like you so much that it made me even more furious that you meddled in Keira's life."

"But that's the thing. I didn't meddle at all. She got on *Eat Me* on her own. She made that happen. She decided she wanted to be a chef and apply to cooking schools on her own. And lest you forget, *you* were the one who asked me to hire her."

"To make her see how awful working a restaurant is. I thought Zach's steak house would knock some sense into her, but one walk through your kitchen and she thought it was all puppies and rainbows because of the vegan influence. I was sure she'd be disabused of that in a day."

"But instead, she found her passion."

Dominique turned away with her teacup, pretending to have great interest in a depressing oil painting of someone's great-grandfather.

"What the hell is so awful about being a chef?"

"My father was a chef," she finally said, getting up and moving over to the window. "He lived and breathed his job and he brought it home with him. Do you know that he made us— my sister and I—respond with 'Yes, chef' and 'No, chef'? He was a tyrant, I think I mentioned that. The thought of Keira entering that world . . ."

Ah. "I'm sorry your father was a tyrant. I've worked for some tyrants and know exactly what you're talking about. But not all restaurant kitchens are run by pricks."

"Even walking into a restaurant kitchen makes me shudder. It's not even something I want to get over. I just don't want to do it."

"I can understand that." I envisioned a six-, eight-, twelve-year-old Dominique hoping for a crumb of good attention and being dismissed or hit with a wooden spoon. "But it's not fair to Keira, is it?"

She was silent for a moment. "I *never* talk about this. Except occasionally to my husband. He takes my side, of course."

"I'm on your side, Dominique. But I'm on Keira's side too. She deserves to follow her bliss. Even if it makes you uncomfortable."

"I think you should go now."

But there was no anger in her dark blue eyes. She was thinking. A good thing.

Around midnight, my phone pinged. Alexander? Finally reporting in on how the visit from the *Times* reporter had gone?

Nope. Not Alexander.

Keira.

It's a miracle. Dominique apologized. Said she'd turned into a tyrant. I'm applying to culinary schools with her blessing! She's going to talk to my dad too. Yay!

I texted back a *yay.*

⁓◦◎ ◎◦⁓

For the first time in the history of Clementine's No Crap Café, I was a customer, sitting in the dining room with Zach and Dominique. I had a great team in the kitchen. I had balance. I had a much-needed night off.

Dominique took a bite of her butternut-squash ravioli. "This pasta is so toothsome," Dominique said without a shred of irony. "Excellent. Even if you didn't make it this time. Since you're sitting right here."

"I trained my staff well," I said, shooting her a smile. "Oh, and, Dominique, I was wondering. I've got a ton on my plate with this place and working on the plans to open the Outpost in my parents' barn. Would you like to handle the wedding plans again?"

She tried hard to hide her smile. "Well, I'll have to think about it. You were a bit of a tough customer, you know."

Ha.

"Okay, I've thought about it. I accept. There goes a pair of my Louboutins sinking in dirt and smelling like rabbit shit."

I had a feeling Dominique and I would get along just fine.

From: Martina Jones
MJones@NewYorkTimes.com
To: Clementine Cooper; Alexander Orr

Hey, Clementine and Alexander,

I couldn't decide between Clementine's No Crap
Café's exceptional pumpkin ravioli, and blackened
Cajun seitan stir-fry, and sopaipillas, and Fresh's
melt-in-your-mouth spanakoptia and vegetable
moussaka, so I decided to include *both* restaurants in
my travel piece on the best vegans across America.
Congrats! And thanks for dinner.

—Martina

Congratulations, chef, I e-mailed to Alexander. Shit, yeah!

A week later, I had another Saturday night off, for a wedding.
Guess whose? Sara and Joe's.

The ceremony was at Joe's house, and the reception in the
backyard.

They turned their master bedroom into a bridal suite, and
when I helped Sara on with her dream gown, which our friend
Ty and I had chipped in to buy as a wedding gift, she looked so
beautiful I almost cried. Until I sat down on the water bed—
that's right, water bed—and the moment was ruined. I did her

makeup and arranged her hair around her veil, long and wild and curly.

In a half hour, Sara Macintosh would walk down the white-rose-petal-strewn aisle to Joe "Steak" Johansson, who cleaned up danged well, I had to admit. Sara's parents had come around a bit, since Joe promised to revert from now on to the altar boy he'd once been in front of them. They in turn vowed not to watch the show.

As I put the veil on and fluffed it around Sara, she said, "You know what I was thinking about last night? That Joe and I didn't get around to number nine on Jocelyn's list. The adventure together."

"You totally did. Same with me and Zach. Your relationship, the engagement. Today. The honeymoon. Your entire future. There's your adventure. Together."

"I love you, Clementine Cooper."

"I love you too."

"How do I look?" She spun around for me.

"Absolutely beautiful."

"Turns out that crazy guy I'm marrying likes me skinny *and* fat. I'm back down the fourteen pounds I gained, and he tells me I look smokin' hot both ways."

"So go marry him."

And she did. An hour later, as I watched her dance with her husband at the reception, she looked so, so happy. Not only had she just married the guy she loved, but she'd gotten her first role on a sitcom and would be quitting *Eat Me* next week.

Joe was planning a special send-off, and then the next week she'd start shooting her new role as the funny best friend and next-door neighbor on a new half-hour sitcom starring someone famous. She'd done it.

Shit, yeah, Sara!

As maid of honor, I'd had to walk down the aisle with Joe's best friend, a guy more vulgar than Joe, which was saying something. But soon, I'd be walking down the aisle to Zach. And I was ready.

EPILOGUE

The weather gods cooperated for my wedding. Sunny, breezy, seventy-one perfect Southern California degrees. The barn, where Clementine's No Crap Outpost would open in three months with my father at the helm, had been decorated with at least a hundred paper lanterns. I had to admit, my wedding planner had done a hell of a job. The farm looked like a farm. Even old my parents' dogs were running around, just as they should have been.

My matron of honor, my sister, Elizabeth, bridesmaid Sara, and bridesguy Ty, who'd flown back from Paris for my wedding, were making a fuss over me in my old bedroom, making moony "awww" faces at my reflection in the mirror. I fluffed my veil, which had been my mother's, and made sure Jocelyn's good-luck diamond earrings were in tight, then took a last look at myself in my dress, which I'd finally found after months of saying no to everything Dominique forced me to look at in her own fashion shows and bridal salons and wedding magazines.

I'd found it in her own closet, which was a spare bedroom in her house. She'd sent me in there to pick out "my favorite of her gowns" for her to wear for the engagement party she threw me and Zach last summer. In the back, in a see-through garment bag, was the most beautiful dress I'd ever seen. For her first wedding, Dominique had fallen madly in love with a gorgeous 1920s, flapper-style gown from a vintage shop, something Katharine Hepburn would have worn, with clean lines and a lace overlay. Dominique's mother-in-law had told her it wasn't Jeffries material and foisted a "suitable" $10,000 monstrosity with such heaving beading that Dominique had almost fainted during the reception. She'd never had the chance to wear the 1920s gown and had forgotten all about it—a dress that had symbolized who she'd once been, who she felt she wasn't anymore.

"This is my wedding dress," I'd told her. You should have seen her trying to hold back tears. Priceless.

"And you're still that woman who loved this gown," I'd added when I'd tried it on. It had barely needed altering.

Dominique Jeffries Huffington, even less a crier than I was, burst into tears and hugged me.

As I stepped out of the house, holding on to my father's arm on one side and my mother's on the other, I glanced out at the meadow, where a stage was set up, covered by a filmy, white canopy that swayed a bit in the breeze. Rows and rows of white chairs, linked by ivy, were arranged behind it, and they were filled with friends and family and business acquaintances, even some of my own.

Alanna and Gunnar, newly engaged, were in one of the middle rows, Gunnar's daughter, Violet, sitting between them. Keira, a California Institute of Culinary Arts graduate, was heading to Le Cordon Blue in Paris in the fall. The trusty McMann twins, Evan and Everett, long promoted to sauté and grill, each brought a date, one of whom was my new trainee, a serious twenty-one-year-old named Juliet. Alexander and his own carnivore, with whom he'd gotten quite serious, waved at me, and I shot him a smile. In the first row with her husband, a handkerchief at the ready, was my wonderful Jocelyn.

Not that I needed to say so, but there'd be no bouquet tossing at this shindig.

As I walked down the aisle to Zach, my once-zipped-up heart about to burst with total happiness, I saw Dominique and Cornelius embrace, stunning everyone. With the first of their children to marry, it was time to let bygones be crappy bygones. Shit, yeah, it was.

And then there I was, walking up the two steps to Zach, with an expression on his face I'd never before seen. A combination of pure love, joy, hope, happiness, wonder. Charlie was sitting by the side of the stage, wearing a little black bow tie around his neck.

This Skinny Bitch was getting hitched.

ACKNOWLEDGMENTS

There are many people to thank who helped in the making of this book. For those I didn't name who had a hand in it, thank you! First and foremost, a huge thank you to Melissa Senate, you are so talented and easygoing. I'm so grateful to have worked with you. Laura Dail, thank you for all you do for me. A big thanks to everyone at Simon and Schuster for making this book possible, especially Karen Kosztolnyik, Louise Burke, Jen Bergstrom, Alexandra Lewis, Liz Psaltis, Ellen Chan, Kristin Dwyer, Stephanie DeLuca, Natalie Ebel, Sarah Lieberman, and Diana Peng. I am beyond grateful to be working with such an amazing team.

Thank you, as always, to my family for their love and support. And thank you to my friends who are always there for me. And thank you Jack for being such a great kid.